By Andrea Semple

The Ex-Factor
The Make-Up Girl
The Man From Perfect

Acknowledgements

Huge thanks to Emma, Gillian, Judy, Jana, Paola and everyone at Piatkus for their hard work and enthusiasm. Equally large thank yous to Paul, Caroline, Camilla, Chris and all at the Marsh Agency. Oh, and the usual love and appreciation to all my family and friends: Mum, Dad, Mary, Richard, Dave, Kath, Phee, Clive, Harvey, Alex and Lucy. And lastly thanks to all my readers and everyone who's been in touch via my site for all their support – I hope you enjoy this one!

To Matt

Rob the Slob

I pick up the phone.

'Hi Ella, it's me.'

It's Rob. The Slob. 'Oh hi.'

'Hi.'

I can hear noise in the background. He's watching football. 'Are you OK?' I ask him, knowing that his head normally has to be on fire before he gets off the sofa if sport's on the telly.

'Yeah,' he says. 'I mean, er, no.'

'Oh?' I say.

'I've just been thinking. About, you know, us. About why you left.'

'Uh-huh.'

'And I reckon I could ... you know ... like, change.'

'Right,' I say, as if I'd just been told they'd found a spotless leopard.

'No, I could ... I really could. I could start being more considerate. I could buy you flowers and ... things.'

'I never wanted you to buy me flowers.'

'I could maybe start alternating Fridays. You

know, only go to the pub every other Friday.'

'And what about Wednesdays and Saturdays and Sundays?'

Thoughtful pause. 'Well, I was kind of thinking maybe one step at a time.'

'Rob, you don't have to change. You just need to find someone who loves you for who you are. We ... didn't fit, that's all.'

His breath crackles through the receiver. 'It's just, sometimes, I miss having you around.'

My heart tugs, for a moment, then I remember who I am talking to and picture him sitting amid his usual daytime apocalypse of lad mags and dirty socks. 'You mean you've got no one to do your washing,' I correct him.

'No. Course not. That's not it at all ...' His voice starts to sound distracted and I can hear the faint roar of the football crowd in the background. Then Rob starts to shout: 'COME ON ENGLAND! COME ON ENGLAND! YES! YES! GO ON ROONEY ... SHOOT ... YEEEEEEEEEES!!! GET IN!'

He's shouting so loud I have to place the phone about a metre away from my ear.

'Er, I'll have to call you back,' he says eventually. 'It's going to go to penalties.'

'Right,' I say. 'Of course. Penalties. That's far more important than trying to sort your life –'

The dial-tone hums its indifference.

Of course, Rob the Slob hasn't always been Rob the Slob.

Only two months ago he was Rob Davis, recruitment consultant and potential husband material. Since I broke up with him I just have to keep on calling him

2

Rob the Slob in case I accidentally suffer from relationship amnesia and forget exactly why I left him in the first place.

So why did I leave him?

Well, there are different reasons, official and unofficial.

Official reasons:

1) He forgot my birthday.
2) He wouldn't cancel one Friday night in the pub for a quiet night in.
3) He made me play Grand Theft Auto on PlayStation for three hours on Valentine's night.
4) He taped *Match of the Day* over my cherished fifteen-year-old copy of *Pretty in Pink*.
5) He forgot my birthday. (Have I already said that?)
6) On Saturday 15 March at 1.30 pm he was in the Cart and Horse with his mates having totally forgotten he was supposed to be sitting in Angelo's Italian restaurant with me and my mum and dad. Even though I'd already met *his* dad about 100 times.

Unofficial reasons:
1) His secret wanking under the duvet when he thought I was asleep.
2) His sex face. (Like a constipated gorilla, only uglier.)
3) His not-getting-any-sex face. (Like an endangered gorilla about to be shot in the head.)
4) His nose-picking.
5) His crotch scratching.
6) His idea of a holiday. Which normally involves 20

days on a coach because he is too scared to fly in a plane.

7) His log files. (I checked on his computer. All porn.)

8) His hygiene problem. Which turned into my hygiene problem when he would give an optimistic nod towards his groin during foreplay.

9) His hatred of most pop stars, most film stars, most writers and most people in general who make him feel bad for being a lazy drunken slob who spends his life playing computer games and eating Pringles and dreaming of owning his own business but never actually doing anything about it.

10) He. Forgot. My. Birthday.

So yeah, Rob was a real catch. One in a million. The kind of man who makes you feel like the only girl in the room, just so long as you've got a bag of Doritos and a four pack of Stella Artois in your hands.

And, as a result of his many crimes against romance, I dumped him.

It was harsh, I admit, but it had become the only option. I was not ready to believe that a lifetime with a sack of potatoes thinly disguised as a human being was the future intended for me. I always hoped he was going to one day turn into his dad (the kindest and warmest former taxi driver you could ever hope to meet). Maybe I'd watched one too many Gillette ads, but I was convinced Rob was not the best a man can get. My perfect partner was still out there, waiting to be found.

And two months on, I still believe the ideal man is out there. I have the same faith in him that I once held

4

in Father Christmas, my first Mr Perfect.

But I don't know if that faith can last one more night of disappointment. If tonight doesn't work out, I am worried that I will wake up tomorrow morning with the sinking feeling you get when you discover the horrible gap between reality and your imagination.

Like when I was seven years old and I pulled Santa's elastic beard slightly too hard, only to discover it was my sherry-sozzled Uncle Eric in a cheap red suit with a pillow strapped to his belly.

Twenty-five reasons

This is all Maddie's stupid idea.

'Twenty-five men in one night,' she said. 'The biggest speed dating event in London.'

She said it would do me good. Help me get over Rob the Slob. And I said I'd go with her, like an idiot, even though I've always hated the idea of these sort of things. Sitting there, with your name badge on behind a table, preened like a showdog, having a stream of three-minute dates.

It always made me think of this place I went to once in Soho. This sushi bar where the food moves by you on a conveyor belt and by the time you've seen something that looks tasty it's passed you, and you're nearly falling off your chair trying to get it. Then by the time it's come back round it's disappeared and you see it being gobbled by some woman with ninja reflexes on the other side of the room.

I'm sitting here, smiling and sticking my chest out, feeling pretty stupid. And there's Maddie on the next table rubbing her hands, sucking on her Tequila Mockingbird and bouncing in her chair as if she's a toddler at a birthday party, waiting to play pass the parcel.

A bell goes *Ding!* and the men start to make their way over.

Seconds out, round one.

1. Steve

Oh, this might be promising. He's half-decent looking. Well, if you cancel out the cheap suit and ignore the fact his forehead is equivalent to the land-mass of Estonia.

'Hello,' I say.

'Hello,' he says. 'I'm Steve.'

'Hello,' I say again, like I'm some Lionel Richie tribute act.

'So,' he says, as if it's an interview or something. 'Tell me a bit about yourself.'

'OK,' I say. 'Well, I'm Ella, as you can see from my badge. Ella Holt. And I'm single, obviously, and I live with my best friend, Maddie, Maddie Hatfield, who's on the next table and is a complete nutcase but is also the kindest and most wonderful person in the world according to the International Best Person Index. Ha!' Oh God, I must be nervous, I'm trying to be funny. 'We're teachers. At a secondary school, Thistlemead Comp. Which isn't as horrible as people say, really, if you ignore the smell ... and the teachers. And most of the pupils. And the graffiti on the front gate which says YOU ARE NOW ENTERING THE SEVENTH CIRCLE OF HELL, which was actually written by the IT teacher five days before his nervous break-down. I teach English. Shakespeare and stuff. I've only been doing it two years so I'm still finding my feet.'

7

There's an awkward silence. So I look under the table and point to my feet and say 'Oh there they are' and try to ignore the fact that I've just made the worst joke in the history of comedy.

I look at his face, fishing for a smile. Or anything. But there's not so much as a flicker.

'Anyway,' I say. 'Your turn.'

'Well, I work in computing. I'm a systems analyst at Microtech which works for various business clients to ensure their security and back-end systems are all fully functioning. This basically means we look at their firewalls, their intranets and their extranets and . . .

Zzzzzzzzzz.

He's still talking, but I have no idea what the words droning out of his mouth actually mean. I just nod and smile and pray for the bell to ring.

Even as he sits across the table from me I'm starting to forget what he looks like. I tell you, if ever Einstein needed to help his fellow physicists appreciate that time is a relative concept he should have arranged an evening of speed-dating and invited Steve.

Three minutes in his company starts to feel like three hours. I've had entire relationships that have felt shorter.

Ding!

Ah, the bell.

I smile and try not to look too relieved as he makes way for the next Romantic Possibility. The smile quickly evaporates as the seat is filled by a pipe-cleaner with a crew cut and army camouflage and eyes so close together he very nearly qualifies as a Cyclops.

2. Brendan.

'Hello Brendan,' I say, reading his name badge.

'Hello Ella,' he says, reading mine and checking out my cleavage at the same time.

'So what do you do?'

'Army,' he says. Then, after a brief and inconsequential conversation, he decides to let me in on a secret. 'I can kill someone with these two fingers.' He moves his thumb and index finger towards my neck.

'Oh,' I say. 'That's, erm, really useful.'

'Hold down on the pressure points. Five seconds later, heart stops completely. Dead.'

'Right.' I look over at Maddie who's on the next table and who has just suffered the Brendan experience three minutes before me. She winks and places her thumb and index finger on her throat, miming a Brendan-induced suicide. I laugh out loud.

'What's so funny?' Brendan asks.

'Nothing,' I say, keeping a careful eye on his hands. 'Nothing at all. I'm a bit nervous, that's all. This is the first time I've done this. Are you nervous?'

He laughs nervously. 'Nervous? When you've had an AK-47 pointed at your skull, the sight of twenty-five women desperate for a shag is nothing.'

'Hey! Who said anything about! –'

Ding!

9

3. Philip.

Philip is a mild-mannered guy wearing a faded X-Files T-shirt who works in Blockbuster. He seems half-normal until he tries to convince me that the world is run by a global elite who are genetically descended from an extra-terrestrial race of reptiles that arrived on earth centuries ago in the form of humans and who practice rituals such as blood-drinking and child sacrifice.

Ding!

4. Nicholas.

Nicholas is smoking a roll-up cigarette and has long curly hair that covers three quarters of his face. Judging by the quarter that remains visible, this is probably a good thing.

'Hello Nicholas.'

A thirty second silence. Then: 'What you into?'

'Sorry?'

'Music. What's your scene?'

'Oh, um –'

'I have to know what music a girl is into before I make the effort man. You know, just in case, she turns out to be, like, into fucking Shitney Spears or something.'

'Oh, right. Well, I really like the new Alicia Keys album,' I say, deciding it might be best not to tell him that my all-time favourite records include the *Dirty Dancing* soundtrack and Kylie's greatest hits.

'Corporate soul, man. It's fake music.'

'Oh,' I say. 'So what music do you like then?'

'Joy Division, The Jesus and Mary Chain, Echo and the Bunnymen. The good stuff. Before all this corporate shit. You know, all this commercial music-

10

by-numbers, this bling-bling shiny happy hip-hop consumer crap.'

'You feel quite strongly, then.'

The voice continues, somewhere behind the smoke and hair: 'Yeah, music died with Kurt, man,' he says, tugging out his Nirvana T-shirt. 'You gotta fight the power and escape all this false noise. It's like no one cares any more, no one gives a shit about the way the commercial mainstream has taken over everything, it's like no escape.'

'Maybe sometimes life is depressing enough without having to be reminded of it all the time,' I tell him, to my own surprise. 'I like shiny and happy stuff because it makes you feel life can give you what you want, even when you know it can't really.'

He looks at me in a kind of stoned anger.

The anger is contagious. I am about to get out of my chair and whack the patronising tosser around the face, when I am saved by the bell.

Ding!

As the night 'progresses' twenty-five Romantic Possibilities starts to feel like twenty-five reasons to switch my sexual orientation.

There is Rav, the investment banker, who spends the whole time telling me how rich he is, bombarding me with six-figure sums as if I am something on auction. There is Dave, who tries to sell me a wrap of cocaine. There is Brian, the farmer, who is looking for a housewife. Peter, the car mechanic, who already has a housewife and is looking for a bit on the side. After Peter, there is Eugene, who is, well, called Eugene.

11

And after that, the names become a blur. There is the guy with the eye-patch. And the one with breath so bad I spend the whole three minutes with my nose in a wine glass, scuba-diving in Chardonnay. And then there's the clinically depressed dwarf, who hasn't had a job since the Snow White pantomime three Christmases ago.

There's the stripper, who asks if I want to see his pierced willy. (Of course, Maddie had already accepted the offer and had laughed herself under the table.)

Oh, and there's the total dickhead who can't keep his eyes off the airbag-breasted blonde in the corner of the room.

There is the bloke with the stutter who gets halfway through his first sentence by the time the bell goes, the guy with the video camera who wants me to say something dirty, the exceptionally ugly man, the naturist, the hypochondriac, the hunchback, the fascist, the sexist, the one who wanted a threesome with me and Maddie (Maddie had agreed on my behalf) and the lanky PhD student who describes speed dating as 'the post-modern equivalent of the high society balls found in Jane Austen's era' before sneezing snot all over the table.

And last and definitely least, there is number twenty-five.

I try and read his name badge, but am far too drunk.

He looks at me for a very long time.

'How much you cost?' he asks me, eventually, with an accent I can't quite place.

'I'm sorry?'

'For fucky-fuck. How much? Fucky-fuck and

12

maybe suck my cock too? How much you say?'

'Erm, I think you are in the wrong place.'

'I sorry. No understand.'

'This is not a brothel. This is *speed dating.*'

'You nice titties. How much for feel?'

I'm furious. 'My body is not on sale,' realising too late that the music has cut out.

'Why you here? Why you sit behind table selling yourself to the men? Why you do that if no on sale.'

'I'm here to meet men I might have something in common with. And maybe form a friendship or a romance.'

'Men no want romance. Men want fucky-fuck. How much?'

Ding!

I sit in the back of the cab travelling back to Tooting and stare out of the window while Maddie gropes around with Boring Steve the systems analyst, whom she has decided to pull for no other reason than he was the last man she spoke to and she fancies a shag.

If the fucky-fuck man had been her number twenty-five she'd probably be groping around with him right now, and making a bit of profit while she was at it.

I've let her down. She probably wanted me to have done the same, pulled anything I could for the sake of a quick cuddle and a meaningless shag. And tomorrow she will no doubt go on about my high standards.

But, I don't think my standards are too high. I honestly don't. Hey, any girl who can spend a year dating Rob the Slob can not be accused of standards in excess of the legal limit.

OK, so my standards aren't as, erm, *democratic* as

Maddie's. Hell, you couldn't even limbo under her standards. But then, Maddie doesn't want a relationship, or at least, not one that lasts more than one night.

I keep staring, out of the window, out at a world of men. Vomiting in doorways, crawling on curbs, starting fights. And I wonder, foolishly, if among that chaos of masculinity, there could really be a Romeo or a Heathcliffe or a Mr Darcy.

Because that's the trouble. No matter how much reality tells you otherwise, romance is a hard dream to squash. And no matter how much I know the perfect man does not and cannot exist, he stays there, in my mind, as a future possibility.

When we get home, I follow them into the house and observe the bizarre sight they make. Maddie, dressed like a technicolour whirlwind, is only five foot. Steve, dressed like a systems analyst, is as high as a lamp-post. Not that Maddie will be bothered. Her attitude to men is the same as other people's attitude towards a healthy diet. The more variety, the better. One night she'll have a breadstick, the next she'll have a pickled gherkin.

'Sssh,' I say, when they clatter through the door and fall over the bike propped up in the hallway. 'Pip's asleep.'

'Oh yes,' says Maddie, with a mischievous giggle. 'Serious faces.'

I sigh, and leave her and Boring Steve to whatever drunken half-delights lie beyond Maddie's bedroom door.

The yellow envelope

Pip, my other flatmate, is a total psycho.

Look at her.

It's Thursday morning. It's a quarter to seven. And she's in the middle of our dingy living room punching and side-kicking to her favourite workout DVD, *Tae Bo Extreme: Get Ripped*.

'*Jab, jab, uppercut, uppercut,*' she pants. '*Jab, jab, uppercut, uppercut...*'

She does this every morning, before having her breakfast (half a pink grapefruit) and preparing her packed lunch (carrot salad, no dressing).

'Morning,' I say.

'*Jab, jab,* morning, *uppercut ...*'

I love her workout face. It's so funny. So intense and angry with that little vertical crease in her forehead.

In fact, it's only a slightly exaggerated version of her normal face. The face indicative of moderate psychopathic tendencies that she wears when she's tidying or preparing her geography lessons or checking the calorie content on one of Maddie's many chocolate indulgences or looking at the scales or

15

magazines or the mirror or anything at all in fact.

Of course, she's not a real psycho. To the best of my knowledge there are no bodies she has hidden under the floorboards after delivering a fatal Tae Bo uppercut to the chin. It's just that she's pretty intense. It's as though life's this big equation she could solve if only she took a little bit more control over it. And she's been like this ever since she was dumped by a media sales dickhead called Greg who said she had a flabby arse. Which she totally hasn't. *'Jab, jab, hook, side kick ... mother ... fucker ...'*

I leave her to it and go and check the post.

The electric bill.

A menu from a new Pizza takeaway.

And a yellow envelope addressed to me, in type.

There's a logo on it, next to the stamp. A weird sort of upside down triangle, with the word PERFECT underneath it. I look closer and see that the upside down triangle is meant to be a heart.

Curiouser and curiouser ...

Inside, there is a small white card that looks like a wedding invitation, with the heart logo embossed onto it.

Then I look at the words and find myself reading aloud to absorb their meaning.

Ella Holt,

Congratulations.

You have won the chance to meet your perfect man. A representative of the Perfect Agency will arrive on your doorstep this Saturday at 10.30 am. You will then be escorted to our London headquarters for the partner selection process to begin.

Yours sincerely
Dr Lara Stein

This is obviously a practical joke and it has Maddie Hatfield's pawmarks all over it. I storm back through the flat, dodging Pip's sidekicks, and head straight for Maddie's bedroom.

Maddie is a very lovely and kind person but she is also a total liability. She knows no shame, no fear, and absolutely no common sense.

She may be a teacher (of maths, which should, but does not, denote an instinct for logic), but she tends to act more like a child than any of her pupils.

She wants life to be a never-ending carnival of music and matchmaking and Margaritas, spiced up with the occasional kinky tussle in the sheets with a total stranger.

But to understand the full madness of Maddie you should perhaps know a bit about her past.

She lost her parents in a car accident when she was five and was raised by her Aunt Cynthia, a retired history teacher with chronic osteoporosis and an allergy to fun in any form.

As a result, Maddie grew up in a house with no TV, with a radio that was forbidden from playing anything other than Beethoven, and in a village that was still convinced it was 1856.

So as soon as she hit teacher training college she went off like a bomb, exploding into lectures and nightclubs with equal energy and leaving a trail of vodka and hairdye and shagged-out men behind her.

17

Someone at work once called her a 'human cyclone', and that certainly sums up how she leaves her bedroom. It also helps to sum up what you can get caught up in if you're mad enough to be friends with her. Get too close and you end up being whisked away to her own little Land of Oz.

I have been known to get angry with her sometimes. Like when she hosted a school assembly two days after I'd finished Rob, and she sang a song 'about a close friend'. The first verse went:

Ella –
She's got no fella
Won't you tell her
It'll be OK
Ella –
You've got no fella
Perhaps you'd betta
Become a *gay!*

And then there was the time she signed us both up to appear in the school production of *Grease* (I was Sandy, while Maddie played Rizzo with more relish than a hot dog). We were the only two members of staff in the whole production, which was fine for Maddie who, five-foot high and giddy as anything, is still essentially a teenager. But at five nine and surrounded by a crop of perky pink Year Eights I stood out like a sunflower in a bed of roses.

I open her bedroom door to find her jigging about on Boring Steve.

'Oh my God,' I say, covering my eyes and walking back out the room.

'Sorry.'

Maddie's body defies the laws of science. She's the size of a pepperpot. She drank at least seven Tequila Mockingbirds last night. She's had about four hours sleep. She's got to go to work. And she still has the energy for a quick kinky bronco ride on Boring Steve (who still manages to look boring even when he is handcuffed to a bed).

Within the space of a minute she is out on the hallway, giggling.

'This just came in the post,' I say, thrusting the white card towards her.

She starts to read, her eyes widening with every word. By the time she's finished, they look ready to drop straight out of their sockets.

'Oh my God!' she says, bouncing like a rabbit. 'Oh my God! Oh my God! . . .' And she carries on saying it like she's a malfunctioning robot with a three word vocabulary.

'Oh my God, *what?*' I ask her.

'You've won!' She acts as though this is a full and detailed explanation.

'Maddie, please, start speaking sense. What is it? What've you gone and done this time? You know what I said about dating agencies.'

'Yes, yes. I do. Yes. Yes. But this is completely different.' And then the malfunctioning robot returns. 'Oh my God! Oh my God! Oh my God! . . .'

After about seven hundred 'Oh my Gods!' she eventually calms down and explains herself.

'Can you remember about a month ago when I made you do that questionnaire?'

A month is a very long time in Maddie-land. 'What questionnaire?'

19

'It was in *Gloss* magazine. One hundred questions about your ideal man. I read it aloud and ticked your answers.'

The memory comes back. It was nearly two months ago. It was a few days after I broke up with Rob and Maddie had been asking me questions about my perfect man to highlight just how hideously imperfect Rob had been.

'I remember,' I tell her.

'*Well . . .*'

Uh-oh. I know that 'well'. It's the same well that goes before a major confession.

As in:

'Well, I've accidentally broken your hair straighteners . . .'

or 'Well, there's a cigarette burn in the top I borrowed . . .'

or 'Well, I signed us both up for the school trip to Stonehenge . . .'

And here it comes: 'Well, apparently it was this, er, competition. And I just thought I'd send it off.'

'What competition?'

She leads me into the living room, where Pip has started doing some sado-masochist version of a stomach crunch, and roots out last month's *Gloss* magazine.

We go into the kitchen and she finds the right page.

'There,' she says. 'Look'.

21

'Maddie, what the hell have you done?'

'Answered your prayers, by the looks of it. You always say that men never meet your standards and now you're going to have one who does.'

'I don't . . . I . . . but . . .' I am still dreaming. That is the only explanation. I'm sleepwalking again, and this is all a dream.

Pip walks into the room, glossed with sweat, and pulls an Evian bottle from the fridge.

Maddie gives me the 'ssh' gesture.

'Good night last night?' Pip asks, intensely.

'Yes,' Maddie says, while I'm still dazed. 'It was a laugh. What about you?'

'Marking papers all night. I've just got so much to catch up on at the moment.

It's a fucking nightmare.' She glugs back on her Evian, washes her hands and starts to prepare her salad, burning holes in the chopping board with her stare.

Maddie makes inane chit-chat for ten minutes then Pip heads for the shower.

'But it sounds totally weird,' I say to Maddie, when I hear Pip turn the shower on.

'I know,' she says, chomping on a raw piece of carrot pinched from Pip's lunch. 'But it's all one hundred per cent factuality Ella Holt. One-hundred per cent fact-u-al-it-y.'

'But what if it doesn't work out?'

Maddie bends double and starts to laugh. 'Of course it'll work out. He'll be *your* perfect man.'

Rising smoke

During the next two days at school, I can hardly concentrate.

'OK,' I say, looking around at the blank faces of Year eleven. 'What do you think that tells us about Romeo's character?'

Nothing.

Not so much as a flicker of a suggestion that anyone is going to raise a hand. I tell you, teaching this class always feels like taking part in an uneven staring contest that I am always destined to lose.

'OK, I'll read it this time.' I clear my throat. Then read aloud:

Love is a smoke rais'd with the fume of sighs;
Being purg'd, a fire sparkling in lovers' eyes;
Being vex'd; a sea nourish'd with lovers' tears;
What is it else? A madness most discreet,
A choking gall, and a preserving sweet.

I look up and see the same blank faces.

'What is interesting about this,' I say. 'Is that even before he has met Juliet, Romeo is obsessed with the idea of love. He is apparently infatuated with another girl, Rosalind, but he hardly ever mentions her name. Instead, he always talks about love and lovers. He talks in a language of extremes that is so over-the-top as to almost mean nothing. He is obsessed with the idea of love, and talks in this very flowery language about it. But when he later experiences love for real he has that idea challenged.'

A hand goes up. It is the last hand in the world you ever want to see go up. It is the ink-stained, nail chewed, scab-ridden hand of Darren Bentley. The teenage father, former arsonist, petrol sniffer and boy found guilty of setting the fire alarm off two weeks ago.

'Yes Darren?'

'You know how you was saying like how Romeo was talking all the flowery stuff like and he never mentioned his woman's name?'

'Yes,' I say, waiting with dread for whatever is about to exit his mouth.

'Do you think he was, like, a shirt-lifter?'

A clatter of laughter fills the room.

'No, I don't think that Darren.'

'Do you think he had a secret crush on his mate, that Bendovio geezer?'

'Ben*volio*.'

'Cos he like asks Bendovio if he wants to hear him groan.' He glances around at his receptive audience, then reads from the text. 'He says *"What, shall I groan and tell thee?"* Now that's some crazy stuff man innit? He wants to groan for him.'

'Darren, I don't think he –'

'And then like he says, "In sadness, cousin, I do love a woman", as if he's sad for loving a woman,

24

because really he's a quimbo and fancies his cousin.'

'It's an, erm, interesting and creative interpretation of the text, Darren. It really is. But I think the point is not that Romeo loves a man or a woman, but that he is in love with love itself. He thinks he's a bit of a Casanova, but at this point in the play he's still too immature to understand what love really means.'

'Like Darren, miss,' says Chantal Farrell, chewing gum and playing with her hair.

'Like a lot of men, I'm afraid, Chantal,' I say, nodding.

'Not like Dobbo,' Darren says. Mark Dobson, Darren's best friend, is a shy blonde boy with emerald eyes and an astute intelligence that he hides like a guilty secret or an unwanted erection (which he's also been known to visibly suffer from on occasion). An intelligence that makes its way onto essay papers but never into the classroom.

'He fancies you miss,' Darren chortles.

Mark's head hits the desk and the class turns into a pack of manic hyenas.

'Oh,' I say, suddenly taken aback. 'I'm sure that's not really –'

The bell goes and I am saved, but judging by the colour of Mark's cheeks, his torment isn't over. I watch him sway like an embarrassed monkey out of the room, and tell myself off for feeling strangely flattered.

Slobometrics

That evening I do a Google on the Perfect Agency to see what comes up. One news site has an interview with Dr Lara Stein, who talks about how they found one million potentially perfect men.

Q: So what sort of men were you looking for?
A: The sort of men women want. Men who had made something of themselves. Men who understand a woman's needs. Of course, women have different ideals and so we have to cater for those different ideals. Some want young, some want old. Some want creative, some want corporate. Some want rich, some want very rich. It's all to do with our genetic make-up. We've got a whole range of guys on the menu here. Lawyers, doctors, CEOs, sports professionals, musicians, airline pilots, male models – you name it. What we have on offer here is a total cross-section of attractive, eligible men. Well, almost a total cross-section.
Q: What do you mean by 'almost a total cross-section'?
A: Well, women have different tastes in men, but

generally there is one type of man we never fanta-
sise about.
Q: Oh. And what type is that?
A: The slobby type. I have yet to come across a
woman who says, 'Hey, Lara, there are just too
many millionaire go-getters on the market. What I'm
really looking for is a fat, lazy couch potato.'
Q: No, I guess not. So how do you manage to
screen out the slobs?
A: Good question. Well, firstly, it's to do with where
we advertised. If we'd stuck the ad in PlayStation
Magazine *or a lad's magazine the slobometer would*
have been pretty high. So we chose magazines and
newspapers very carefully. The Financial Times,
Fortune, Professional Athlete, Airline International,
Space Magazine, Entrepreneur, Law Magazine, *the*
Medicine Journal ... *By targeting these sort of*
publications we knew we'd be aiming at alpha
males. And from these adverts we had about five
million entries which we eventually managed down
to one million.
Q: How did you do that?
A: Well, as well as all our scientific tests, we had a
team of psychologists who designed a special test. A
variation of a psychometric test. I suppose you could
call it a slobometric test. We also had professional
astrologers analysing their birthdays, and they
screened out all the Sagittarian males straight away.
Very high slob potential apparently. And, slowly but
surely, we got our million men.
Q: My husband's a Sagittarius.
A: Oh dear. I'm so sorry for you.

I log off and get into bed and try to think of the

questionnaire Maddie filled in for me.

Why would any of these people be interested in me? I doubt I'd be anyone's one in a million. Or one in ten, for that matter. I mean, look at my hair. And my stupid grey skin. And my arse the size of Latvia. OK, so it's not technically the size of Latvia – not that I know the size of Latvia. Or where it is.

Oh my God. I don't know where Latvia is. What if some uber-male with an IQ of 258 is my one in a million and I don't know where bloody Latvia is! Is it even a country?

What if he's Latvian? Or what if he's this hotshot property developer and he's just bought lots of Latvian land?

OK, I tell myself, calm down.

The worst that can happen is we won't hit it off and if that happens he's not my Mr Perfect anyway.

The Fairy Godmother

Saturday morning.

'Ella!' Pip's voice. 'Someone here for you.'

I told her about the Perfect Agency last night and she wasn't impressed.

'I don't believe in fairytales,' she said, 'life's always got an unhappy ending.'

A skinny woman with scraped-back black hair and an even more scraped-back face is standing in my doorway, wearing an expensive-looking smart grey trouser suit and a smile that probably cost just as much.

'Oh hi. Ella Holt?' The woman's voice is American sounding.

'Yes,' I say.

'Oh *hi*. I'm Jessica Perk. The Perfect Agency's representative. Congratulations on becoming the first person to meet her perfect date.' She says it with all the conviction of a robot.

'Oh,' I say, feeling strangely nervous. 'Thanks.'

'Are you all ready?'

'I think so.'

I say 'Bye' to Maddie, who waves and crosses her fingers from the bay window.

I follow Jessica out into the warm sunshine and head to her car. A Mercedes. Tinted glass. She gets in the back seat. I wonder who's going to drive, when I notice a man with a flat cap in the front seat.

'Now, listen,' Jessica says, all hand gestures as the car pulls out. 'There is just one tiny little thing we would like you to do for us.'

'OK,' I say, not awake enough to cope with full sentences.

'Now, as you are the first woman who is going to use this service, Dr Lara would like to use you as a kind of case study. You know, to promote the service to our paying clients. A kind of Cinderella meets her perfect Prince kind of piece with me as your Fairy Godmother.'

This is all too much to take in. It's not only the fact that she's speaking way over the Saturday morning noise limit or that her robotic voice seems to come out of her nose rather than her mouth, it's also because it seems to be assuming too much.

How does she know there'll be a fairytale-ending? And where does she get this Cinderella idea from? I may not be the seventh or even seven millionth richest woman in the world, but I'm not scraping out fire-places to earn my rent either.

But my breakfastless stomach is too weak to let me say anything other than, 'Sure, of course.'

'I knew you would,' she says, blasting New York confidence.

The car turns through a maze of streets until we end up on Tooting High Street, heading direct for the City. Jessica keeps babbling at hyperspeed, but I only catch pieces of what she is saying.

30

... genetically proven ...
... top scientist ...
... press conference ...
... guaranteed to work ...

When she reaches her first full stop I ask her 'But what if my perfect man doesn't like me?'

Jessica Perk closes her eyes and shakes her head. A fake smile tries to fight the botox. 'Not going to happen sweetheart. You see, I'm no scientist or anything, but the way I understand it is that because all the tests are based on genetics, if you are attracted to him, he will be attracted to you. After all, it's only perfection if it works both ways.'

'Right, I see.'

Ten minutes later the car pulls into an anonymous entrance and slows to a stop. 'OK Cinderella,' says Jessica. 'We're here.'

The Perfect Agency

The headquarters of the Perfect Agency and Slim-2–Win look rather strange from outside. Ten storeys of uninterrupted reflective glass. The building rises out of the pavement like a giant mirror, reflecting the Spring sunshine.

I get out of the car and follow Jessica through the revolving doors, and down a long series of white steps heading into the ground.

Once down the steps we arrive in a vast white windowless space. On one of the white walls, in off-white letters, is written Slim-2–Win's call-to-arms in broad block capitals.

WAIST NOT. WANT LOTS.

We wait by the lifts.

'The Perfect Agency's on the top floor,' Jessica tells me. 'Floor Eleven.'

Jessica has a strange face. Botoxed into blandness. I try to guess her age, but in reality it could be anywhere between thirty and sixty. I start to forget what she looks like even as I stare straight at her.

Ping!

The lift doors open.

We step inside. Jessica rabbits.

'The whole building is taken over by Dr Lara's empire. Slim-2–Win. That's where I worked before Lara shifted me over to the Perfect Agency. I was like you,' she says, with a tinge of bitterness. 'A case study. Slim-2–Win's dieter of the year. Followed the Slim-2–Win diet for twelve months. Ate nothing but Slim-2–Win shakes and cereal bars. Lost eleven stone.' Her voice starts to drift. 'Used to be as big as a house. Comfort eater. I lost my twin sister in a roller-blading incident. Ate Ben and Jerry's out of stock. But I'm in control now. In control ... in control ...'

Ping!

The lift doors open.

I follow Jessica's non-existent arse down a long corridor, a wall of glass to my left. London sprawls out to the horizon.

We reach a black door with a gold plaque. The plaque says: Dr LARA STEIN, CEO AND FOUNDER, SLIM-2–WIN/THE PERFECT AGENCY.

Jessica knocks, but there is no reply.

We just stand there, overhearing Dr Lara on the phone. She's got a posh voice. A British voice. I don't know why, but I thought Dr Lara Stein would be American.

I get the feeling from her tone of voice that this is a conversation I shouldn't be listening to.

'Tell those bastard lawyers their clients' daughter should have read the small print. It says "PLEASE CONSULT YOUR DOCTOR BEFORE TAKING THE SLIM-2–WIN CARBLESS DIET". And did

33

she? Did she consult her doctor? No. She didn't. It's not our fault she had bad arteries before she started the diet. Is it? Is it? No. It's not. We offered to pay for the funeral. We've sent the whole family a year's supply of cereal. You know, what can we do? Resurrect the dead? She was size twenty-eight for Christ's sake. She was on a flaming treadmill. She was a walking time bomb ... If they want to fight dirty, we can fight dirty ... get something on her ... talk to every fast food place in her area ... if we can find she broke the diet we're laughing ... Do it. OK?'

She puts the phone down. Jessica knocks again.

'What is it?'

'The girl,' says Jessica, through the wood. 'You know, who won the competition.'

'Ah,' says Dr Lara, sounding much more professional. 'Bring her in.'

We walk in the room just in time to catch her face change. The cat's-arse pout she is still wearing from the phonecall becomes a Cheshire cat smile.

'Ah, yes, of course. The girl. Our very own Cinderella.'

Dr Lara Stein moves round her desk and crosses the room.

She doesn't look like a business woman. She looks like a Stepford Wife. Or a Sloane Ranger. Upturned collar. Riviera tan. Big hair, big pearls, big scary smile.

'Hi, Cinders,' she says.

'Ella,' I say.

'Yes, Hella. Pleased to meet you.' She shakes my hand.

'No, *Ella*. That's my name.'

Dr Lara's smile slips. I hear Jessica gulp next to me. Clearly Dr Lara is not the type of woman who is used to being corrected.

But it's only a blip.

The smile returns and Dr Lara Stein says, 'You look absolutely perfect.'

'Thank you.'

'So girl-next-door. So *normal*. You could be anyone.'

'Er, thanks.'

She turns to Jessica. 'Have you told her about the press conference?'

'Yes. I briefed her on the way here.'

Press conference?

What press conference?

I wasn't even listening to her in the car. I tried, but it was like trying to get on a roundabout that was moving too fast.

'Good,' says Dr Lara. 'Perfect. It starts in twenty minutes.'

She looks at me again, her eyes scanning up and down over my outfit.

'You must be so excited,' she says. From her tone it's difficult to tell if it's a query or a command.

'Yes,' I say. 'I am.'

'It's like *Charlie and the Chocolate Factory*! I feel like Willy Wonka!' She looks at Jessica. 'And you can be my chief Umpa-Lumpa!'

It's becoming increasingly apparent that Dr Lara Stein is clinically insane. It's becoming equally apparent that Jessica Perk isn't happy about this whole thing. She sees me as a rival – after all, she started off as a case study. Just like me. Only I didn't have to live on snacks that come in three flavours of cardboard.

One of Dr Lara's perfectly manicured hands arrives on my shoulder. She leans in close and whispers: 'This is going to be big. Really big. This agency is the biggest and most important thing I have ever done in my life, and I don't think it's over boastful to say that I've done quite a few big and important things. And you are at the centre of it. How does that feel?'

'Good,' I say, scared out of my mind.

'You are going to meet your perfect man. No woman in the world has been able to know that with as much certainty as you do right now. And after you've met him, you can be our spokesperson. We'll pay you of course.' I see Jessica glaring at me behind Dr Lara's shoulder. 'What job do you do now?' Lara asks.

'I'm a teacher.'

'A teacher! Adorable! A teacher! That's so ... so ... everygirl. Which is perfect. Because that's what the whole point of this is. I mean, the point of you. Here. It's great for you and it's great for us. It trials the service and it makes excellent PR. The humble schoolteacher meets her dashing prince. Who said romance was dead? Jessica, what time is it?'

'Ten to twelve.'

'OK, we'd better get going.'

The press conference

I follow Dr Lara and Jessica out into the room.

Cameras flash.

Chairs shuffle.

There is a long table, behind which is a giant projection of the Perfect Agency's logo.

**THE PERFECT AGENCY
YOUR LOVE LIFE. SOLVED.**

Jessica directs me to a chair and whispers in my ear: 'Only speak when they ask you a direct question. And keep your answers as short as possible. OK?'

'OK.'

I look out at the audience of journalists, ready with the notepads and dictaphones and serious faces. I hate this sort of thing. That's why I'm the only teacher in the whole of Thistlemead Comp who has never led a school assembly.

Surely there must be an easier way to find a decent man. Hell, who am I kidding?

Dr Lara stands up and instantly the room goes quiet.

I've always admired those sort of people. The sort who only have to stand up to shut people's mouths. It must feel good, having that kind of power.

'Hello everyone,' she says, flashing the smile. 'Thanks for coming along to the launch of the most revolutionary concept in relationships since the invention of marriage. Ladies and gentleman, I give you the Perfect Agency.'

She clicks something in her hand. Something connected to a wire. Then some music starts. The lights dim. All the journalists stare at the screen behind us. I turn round and watch it too, without having a clue about what is going on.

'It's a promo,' Jessica whispers in my ear. 'It lasts about ten minutes. Then there'll be the Q and A session.'

I nod and look behind at the screen.

Footage of notorious celebrity couples appears on the screen. Charles and Diana. Brad and Jen. Tom and Nicole. Angelina and Billy Bob. J-Lo and P. Diddy. J-Lo and Ben Affleck. J-Lo and that other bloke ... All to the sound of that crap Roxette song from *Pretty Woman*.

It must have been love, but it's over now ... After that, it cuts to a soft focus Lara Stein against a dreamy peach background.

'These are sad times for believers in true love,' she says, all sincerity as she stares straight to camera. 'The breakdown of celebrity marriages is just the most visible sign of a trend that is affecting the entire Western World.

'Love simply isn't working anymore. In the US and the UK increasing numbers of people are beginning to doubt the whole concept of marriage. After all, if it isn't for life, it isn't for anything, right?

'Well, I'm an optimist. I may be three divorces down the line, but I'm still a believer. Which is why I decided to set up the Perfect Agency.'

There's some more cheesy music. Shots of couples holding hands. Feeding each other ice cream. Snogging on park benches. A man giving his girl-friend a piggyback as he runs through a field.

Then a close up of the ugliest man on the planet. He's got three strands of hair combed–over his bald head. Skin that is flakier than our front door. And he's wearing a suit that looks like it has been worn every day since 1973, the same year he probably acquired his thick-rimmed glasses. A subtitle slides under his face.

It says:

Dr Ludwig Fischer, Emeritus Professor of Genetics, University of Bern, Switzerland.

He starts to speak with the kind of clipped German accent you get in old war comedies.

'Love is a science. It is in the genes. We have been aware of this for some time, but now we are able to put the theory into practice. Using research from the fields of mathematics, genetics and biomedical science, it is now possible to find your perfect match.'

Then it cuts back to Dr Lara.

'The human species has evolved,' she says, with the same Oscar-worthy sense of meaning. 'And so too have relationships. Five thousand years ago, marriage was invented. This revolutionised relationships between men and women. But in the beginning, marriage wasn't exactly working in the woman's favour. Among the Sumerian people who invented marriage, the "Best Man" got that name because he helped the groom to kidnap the bride and beat up relatives if they tried to rescue her.'

There are titters from the journalists as Lara keeps on talking on the film . . .

'The Romans advanced things three thousand years later by making sure that both the bride and groom entered into marriage of their own free will. And, over the years, women have gained more and more freedom within relationships. Ever since the female orgasm was finally recognised a century ago, women demand as much as men from a loving relationship.

'The trouble is that with increased demands, there comes increased pressure. Women and men now expect a hell of a lot from each other. Good looks. Good sex. Good orgasms. Good conversation. Mutual understanding. Nothing short of total compatibility . . .'

The journalists bow their heads as they scribble 'total compatibility' into their notepads.

'. . . But people have less time and are surrounded by temptation, week in and week out. They watch romantic movies. They read romantic books. They see all those couples in the magazines. And it all feeds the desire for a perfect love life.'

She leans in forward. The camera zooms in. Her tanned face is now gigantic on the screen.

'But I do not condemn these people,' she says, sounding posher than ever. 'I am not one of those who believe we should not expect things to be perfect, or that women should get realistic and back to faking orgasms and marital bliss until the end of time.' She shakes her head. 'No, I believe that women and men

40

should have their expectations matched. They should have their one in a million partner, without having to suffer the lottery of blind dates, web dates, or speed dates or, for that matter, a traditional dating agency.'

Soft violins play over the soundtrack as Dr Lara reaches her conclusion.

'What the Perfect Agency does is work on the science of true love, to find a perfect match that would otherwise take a hundred lifetimes to find,' she says. 'And the modern single barely has a free evening a week, let alone a hundred lifetimes. So I really think what we are offering is the biggest revolution in relationships for five thousand years.'

More music.

A gravel-throated voiceover repeats the slogan.

'The Perfect Agency. Your Love Life. Solved.'

Then the lights come back and hands raise. Jessica points her skinny hand at friendly looking journalists. They ask friendly questions. Dr Lara answers, and her words and smile never falter.

Halfway through her spiel she introduces me. '. . . which leads us to our first lucky female member of the Perfect Agency, Miss Ella Holt. As you can see, Ella is not a millionairess for whom money is no object . . .'

To my dismay, half the room checks out my clothes and nods in agreement.

Lara continues, reading the cue cards Jessica gave her before we entered the room. 'She is a school-teacher. Twenty-nine years old. Starting to hear and fear the ticking of her biological clock . . .'

Hey, who told them that?

'. . . who so far has been very unlucky in love. Her last boyfriend even forgot her birthday!'

The room falls into sympathetic laughter.

I contemplate the various ways I can kill Maddie.

'... Anyway, her luck is about to change. Straight after this conference, Ella is going to enter Dr Ludwig Fischer's "love lab" on the top floor of this building, for the next part of the selection process, which involves the latest gene-matching technology.'

Jessica points to a man with ginger hair and a corduroy jacket on the back row.

He stands up and says, 'I'd like to ask Ella a question. If that's OK?'

'Sure,' Jessica says, nudging a bony elbow into me. 'Fire away.'

'How do you feel about being a human guinea pig?'

I look at Jessica, whose eyes widen as if to say *Go on, answer the question,* so I say, 'I feel great. I'm really happy to ... be a part of this.'

'And are you worried that your perfect man might fail to meet your expectations?' the journalist asks. 'I mean, if it doesn't work out, will you give up on dating all together?'

The room shrinks around me. My mouth is dry. In my head I keep seeing images of guinea pigs. 'Erm ... I ... don't ... I ...'

Dr Lara leans forward into her microphone, and speaks with smooth confidence.

'With the utmost respect, that is an irrelevant question,' she says. 'The Perfect Agency doesn't have "perfect" in its name for no reason. You can rest assured this will be one fairytale story with a very happy ending.'

A quick break

I have half an hour.

Jessica and Dr Lara have offered me a free lunch in the Slim-2-Win canteen, but I'm not hungry.

I go outside and phone Maddie.

'I'm going to kill you,' I tell her.

'I'm fine thank you. How are you?'

'This is a nightmare. I've just had to do a press conference.'

'A press conference? Wah-hey! You're a celebrity.'

'And who told them about Rob?'

'Oh ... er, yes ... I was going to tell you about that.'

'She's a maniac.'

'Who?'

'Dr Lara Stein. She's a maniac. Fat people die on her diets and she doesn't care! And I'm her guinea pig and she wants me to be her spokesperson.'

'Will you get paid?'

'Well yes but –'

'Cool.'

'No. Not cool. It's scary.'

'Well come home then.'

'What?'

'Leave,' she says

'What?'

'You haven't signed anything have you?'

'Er . . . no.'

'Then leave now. If you really don't like it.'

It's weird.

I phoned Maddie to bollock her for getting me into this, but now she's telling me to leave.

'You're meant to tell me to stick it out.'

'It's your life,' she says, out of character. 'It's not up to me to tell you to do anything.'

'I know. It's just . . . I thought you wanted me to do it.'

'I thought it would be fun, sure, but there's no point going to this much hassle is there?'

'I . . . er . . . I . . .'

'I mean, you could always go back to Rob.'

Back to Rob.

Words heavy enough to sink me into the ground.

'No,' I correct her. 'I couldn't.'

'Well, it looks like you're just going to have to get used to being single again. No one to snuggle up with.'

'All right, all right. I get your point.'

'Hey, seriously. It's up to you.'

'I'm sorry Mads. It's too much, I'm coming home.'

'All right, I'll get the kettle on. I'll expect to see you back in half an hour.'

'OK. Bye.'

'Bye.'

I am about to run for it. I could make Farringdon tube in two minutes from here and then I'd be back to my normal existence.

44

My normal manless existence.

Back to speed-dating with Maddie, screening a conveyor belt of losers and psychos who might as well have DYING FOR A SHAG tattooed on their Estonian-sized foreheads.

I look back at the building. The giant mirror sticking out of the ground.

I am tempted to leave. To go back and have the cup of tea Maddie is making for me. To walk out like I walk out of everything. A trend I started when I gave up my piano lessons when I was twelve years old.

But I don't.

I take a deep breath, as if I am about to dive underwater, and go back inside the revolving doors.

Dr Fischer's love detector

When Lara said something about a 'love lab', I saw a picture of a red coloured room with roses and heart-shaped cushions everywhere and test tubes full of pink potions.

But it isn't anything like that.

For a start, there's the smell.

There's nothing rosy about Dr Fischer's halitosis breath. And there's no pink. And no test tubes. Just lots of computers and printers and a projection screen and a weird contraption on a table in the middle of the room.

'OK, what I will have to do is to just attach pads to the cheeks and to the hands and to the chests,' says Dr Fischer, one of his three strands of combed-over hair lifting up and tickling my nose as he bends over me. 'These pads as you can see are wired up to the computers which are then programmed to read the data.'

It is surely an irony of Shakespearean proportions that the least attractive man on the planet is going to be in charge of finding my Mr Perfect.

He sticks the little white circles to my already

sweating palms and temples, before placing a hand inside my shirt, and sticking one on the top of my left breast.

'So er . . . how does it work?' I ask, feeling the need to talk.

'It works in many ways like a lie detector. It monitors changes in the pulse and the heartbeat and other external physical fluctuations. Only of course this is a *love* detector not a lie detector. Right, there we go, we are all set up.'

Dr Fischer sticks on the last pad and goes over to a computer on the other side of the room. He crouches over and starts to type.

'I don't understand,' I tell him. 'How can you tell that I'll fall in love with someone that I haven't met?'

'Love is not an art, Miss Holt. It is a science,' he says, turning his boggled, bespectacled eyes towards me. 'If you are attracted to someone, your body will release a group of neuro-transmitters called *monoamines*. There are three to look out for. The first is dopamine, which as well as love is also activated by cocaine and nicotine. The second is norepinephrine —'

'Nora-what?'

He looks over his thick-rimmed glasses. 'Norepinephrine. Or adrenalin, to use the layman's term. This is the chemical that makes the sweat and gets your heart racing. It is released by your body to let your brain know you are attracted to someone. When there is an upsurge of the adrenalin, you lose your appetite and need less sleep, symptoms found during the first few weeks of falling in love.'

I try to remember the early phase of my relationship with Rob. Our date at Pizza Heaven and his ability to eat an entire stuffed-crust pizza in front of

47

me. I certainly ate less. But that was because Rob stole it from my plate. I slept less as well. But who wouldn't lying next to a snoring rhinoceros.

'The third neuro-transmitter is seratonin,' he tells me, scratching the dry skin on his neck.

'Oh, I've heard of that one.'

'Yes. That is the real killer, Miss Holt. That is what made Antony give up the Roman Empire for Cleopatra. That is what made your King Edward give up the throne for Mrs Simpson. That is what made Romeo and Juliet commit the suicide. It is the chemical of madness, Miss Holt. It is what turns sane men and women into crazies. When people say you have fallen madly in love, they are speaking more of the truth than they realise. Love is madness, Miss Holt. Nothing more and nothing less.'

He finishes with the computer and walks over to the wall in front of where I am sitting. He pulls a string and a massive white screen falls down to cover most of the wall.

'Now, Miss Holt,' he says. 'I am going to project images onto this screen so I will need you to stay looking at it. Do not look at me or that will confuse the reading. Do you understand?

'Er, I think so. But what are the images going to be of?'

'Men, Miss Holt. Lots and lots of men.'

'Right.'

'This is the most important phase of finding your Mr Perfect. This is the Face Perception Test.'

I am starting to feel very sceptical. I might just be able to buy that love is a science. But there's no way you can tell who you are going to fall in love with just by looking at their face. I mean, if looks are everything, shouldn't someone tell Catherine Zeta Jones?

My scepticism is clearly visible because Dr Fischer says, 'Humans are very visual creatures Miss Holt. And the human face is what we are most responsive too. It tells us a lot. It tells us the age, race and gender of course, it tells us if someone is good-looking, but it also gives us a lot of clues about the personality. Big lips for instance tell us that someone is a sensual person. A face will also reveal to our subconscious if someone is an extrovert or an intro-vert. But this is only the first stage of the process Miss Holt. There will be other tests. But right now I will show you all the faces of the men we have selected as potential partners for you, Miss Holt. We have narrowed it down from the one million men to two hundred based on the answers you gave. You can be assured that the perfect man for you is going to be one of this two hundred so you must look at the screen at all times. Right, let us begin.'

I sit still in my chair, as Dr Fischer and his bad suit go over and dim the lights to start the slide show.

The 200 men

The first picture makes me jump out of my skin. It is Rob.

'This is your ex-boyfriend Miss Holt, is this correct?'

'Er ... yes ... yes ... it is ... where did you get that from?'

'From you, Miss Holt. Remember?'

'Er, no.'

'When you filled in the questionnaire we asked you to attach a picture of your most recent sexual partner. Do you remember?'

Of course I don't remember.

I didn't even fill in the questionnaire in the first place. Maddie must have gone into my room and got it from one of my drawers. The sneaky little ...

'Yes,' says Dr Fischer. 'As expected there is a very strong and violent reaction to this picture.'

'No, sorry,' I tell him. 'I wasn't thinking about Rob, I was thinking about someone else.'

Dr Fischer snaps his fingers behind me, causing me to jump again. 'You must concentrate on the images, Miss Holt! Only the images!'

'Sorry,' I say.

He calms down. 'It is all right. This is not a part of the test. This is just to show you why it did not work with your last boyfriend.'

'Oh.'

'In fact, it is clear from the picture that you had very little in common with this strange looking creature.'

Poor Rob. I stare at his fat face, filling the wall, as he stuffs his mouth full of pizza.

'His face shape is the near exact opposite of your face, Miss Holt. Look at the line of his jaw. Look at his chin, or should I say look at his chins? Ha ha ha. He has at least two of them. I might say four in fact.'

'It's a bad picture,' I say, feeling strangely protective.

'But if you look at his colouring and his eyes and those two weird little triangular ears you will see that he really has nothing in common with you, Miss Holt.'

'Does that matter?'

Dr Fischer laughs. 'Does that matter? That is a good one, Miss Holt. That is a very good one … Does that matter! Ha ha ha!'

The doctor types something into one of the computers behind me. Now all three strands of his hair are pointing towards the ceiling, exposing his pointy bald head. 'Your results for this image prove my point, Miss Holt. If you were to love this man everything would speed up, but what happens is in fact the opposite. Everything slows down. This indicates that the attachment you felt towards this man was not a positive one like love, but something more of the negative … like pity.'

Pity.

Could that really be true?

Could I really have wasted a year of my life with someone because I *pitied* them?

'I think you are a good person, Miss Holt. For good people like yourself it is sometimes hard to find the right partner because your feelings become very confused. Your brain might tell you that this man is a slob who loves pizza but you feel sorry for them and you feel like you can help them and you often think that these feelings are the love but they are not the love.' His weird voice is starting to give me a headache. 'And it is only when you understand that you cannot help them that you realise it is too late.'

I gulp.

He's right.

I stopped wanting to be with him the moment I knew he was never going to change.

I wasn't in love with Rob. I was in love with the idea of saving him. I was in love with the Rob he wanted to be. The Rob who walked out of his job and set up his own photography business. The Rob who was too busy and focused to be playing on PlayStation every night of the week. The Rob who inherited all the warmth and charm of his widowed taxi-driver father. I was in love, in other words, with a Rob who was a figment of my, and his, imagination.

'The two hundred men you are about to see are all much more suited to you Miss Holt. I can assure you this is the fact.'

So it begins.

Rob disappears and for the next ninety minutes I sit there and watch potential suitors beam down at me from giant photographs, while Dr Fischer types on keyboards and checks his findings behind me.

There are men in suits.

Men in T-shirts.

Slim men.

Muscle men.

Black.

White.

Blonde.

Dark.

Ginger.

Smiling.

Serious.

Earrings.

Nose rings.

No rings.

Shaved heads.

Slap heads.

Blackheads.

Thick lips.

No lips.

Dimples.

Pimples.

Clean-shaven.

Stubble.

Goatee.

Yeti.

On and on and on.

Face after face after face.

Most of them are good looking. Some of them are gorgeous. But my palms are dry and my heart feels pretty normal.

Beatbeat.

Beatbeat.

Beatbeat.

I am about 100 faces in and still can't believe I've seen my perfect man. I don't know why. They've all looked very nice, but they aren't doing anything for me.

This is confirmed by Dr Fischer, who keeps releasing disheartening sighs behind me, clearly disappointed by the readings on his computer screen.

The images keep on flicking.

My eyes get tired.

A headache starts to kick in below the pads on my temples.

And then it happens.

There is a face smiling at me with the most beautiful eyes I have ever seen. I feel like he is looking straight at me, even though he is just a photo projected onto the wall.

Despite the cool temperature of the room, my body suddenly feels warm. As if a heater has just been switched on inside me.

When every other picture flashed up on the wall, it was like playing a game of Guess Who? I was concentrating on their features. Their glasses or their curly hair.

But this picture is different. I see the person rather than just the packaging.

The only things I really notice about him are his smile and his eyes, but they are enough . . .

The smell test

The picture of the gorgeous man disappears. A tanned blonde surfer type replaces him up on the wall. The surfer is good-looking, but does nothing for me.

Nor do the other remaining ninety-eight images that flash before my eyes. It's back to Guess Who? Thick neck. Scar on upper-lid. No eyebrows.

That sort of thing.

When the last of the images has vanished into nothing, only one remains in my head.

Well OK, two. But Rob and his pizza don't count.

Dr Fischer switches the light back on, but doesn't take off the pads.

'OK, OK, Miss Holt, on to the next test.'

The tests continue for the rest of Saturday afternoon making me feel like a caged guinea pig. There are endless questions for compatibility, jealousy and biorhythmic something-or-other. By the time he starts measuring my face with a ruler for something to do with 'physical harmonism' I'm about to pass out with hunger. I wish I'd taken Dr Lara's offer up of some hydrogenated taste-free food from the Slim–2–Win canteen.

Dr Fischer ignores my rumbling stomach and widens his thin lips into a smile.

'There is one more test, Miss Holt.'

'I thought that was it?'

'No. I am sorry. But love isn't just about looks and personality.'

'No, I know. It's about –'

'Smell, Miss Holt.'

'Sorry?'

'In every species of mammal, Miss Holt, smell is a deciding factor when choosing a mate. It works for mice. It works for dogs. The human mammal is no different.'

If it's to do with smell God knows how you explain that wedding ring on your finger, Mr Halitosis breath.

'But I already know the man I like. Out of the pictures.'

'Yes, I must admit there was a man who did stimulate a very strong physical response from you in the Face Perception Test, Miss Holt. But we must check with the smell test that this is actually the perfect man for you.'

'Right. OK, but –'

'What this involves is finding your top ten matches from the tests and then finding their samples.'

For a minute I think there's something wrong with my hearing. *'Samples?* Did you just say samples?'

'Yes, Miss Holt. That is what I did just say.'

Now, I'm a believer in science. You know, Isaac Newton definitely had a point about gravity. And Einstein was definitely onto something when he said about time being relative (hell, anyone who has sat their way through our school's end of year concert has to agree that two hours can become two days).

But smelling someone's pee? That's a step too far.

Sure, it works for cocker spaniels. But I was never into the idea of golden showers. The only thing that turns me on about man piss is when it actually ends up in the toilet bowl. (Rob flaw No. 769: Little yellow puddles on the bathroom lino).

'Erm, Dr Fischer. It's okay, really. I can do without this test. I don't think it will work for me. Honestly.'

Dr Fischer isn't listening.

He is lost inside the walk-in cupboard. He emerges a minute later carrying a large shoebox.

'Dr Fischer, it's getting late. I really have to go. I don't think that –'

'Miss Holt, if we are to find you the perfect lifetime partner it is really worth taking an extra ten minutes don't you think? I mean, ten minutes is a very small amount of time when measured against a lifetime of loving union, you do not think?'

As Einstein said, ten minutes is not always ten minutes. And I could quite happily do without ten minutes with my nose hoovering heavy wafts of piss. Even Mr Perfect piss.

'Dr Fischer, the thing is, if I'm to fall in love with someone, I think it might, er ... jeopardise my chances if I smell their wee before I meet them. You know, it might put me off a little bit.'

Seratonin overloads Dr Fischer's brain and he laughs like a maniac. 'Ha ha ha, Miss Holt! You English girls are so funny. I am not talking about a sample of urine from the man.'

'You're not?'

'*Clothing* samples, Miss Holt. Not the mens pee pee. Ha ha ha. You English girls! Every man who is

part of the agency has to give a sample of their clothing that they have worn for two days. You do not
have to smell their pee pee. Only the sweat that drips
off their bodies and onto their clothes.'

I never thought I'd be relieved to hear I've got to
sniff the sweaty clothes of strangers, but I am. Sort of
'Sweat. Right. Great.'

He looks at my sour expression and laughs again.
'You English girls! Ha ha ha! Now, to make this all
the more effective I will have to blindfold you, Miss
Holt. That way I will know that no visual stimulus is
influencing the results.'

'I don't know if this –'

My words bounce off Dr Fischer's raised palm. 'In
the year two thousand and one some of my colleagues
at the University of Bern in the Switzerland discovered that human beings use smell to find the right
man. It is all about genetics, Miss Holt.'

'Genetics, right.'

Dr Fischer squints at me through his glasses, as if
I am a problem he can't quite solve. 'Yes, Miss Holt.
Genetics. I will explain.'

So he does.

He explains.

Not that I understand a word he says.

'The genes that cause this are a large cluster called
the major histocompatibility complex, or MHC for
the shortness. Every single human being in the world
has a unique combination of MHC genes and these
include the genes which help you fight off disease.'

'Disease?'

'I know what you are thinking. You want a man,
not a cure for the runny nose. Well, it just so happens
that the same genes that make up the immune system

58

also give the same olfactory cues that determine if you find someone sexy or not so sexy.'

'Olfactory cues?'

'The smell, Miss Holt. The *smell.*'

'Right, of course, the smell.'

His eyes appear massive through his thick lenses, as he explains the science. 'Humans are attracted to people with very different MHC genes to their own genes. And these are the smells your brain can smell when you are very close to someone when you are kissing or when you are ... when you are doing ... other things.' He scratches his neck and looks embarrassed.

'Right, erm, I see ... OK, I'll do it.'

'Right, Miss Holt. I will just place this blindfold around your head like so and then we can start the test. I will take the first sample out of the box and now it is under your nose. Sniff, Miss Holt. Sniff up the man.'

I sniff up the man and nearly choke on his BO. For a minute I wonder if Maddie had also cut up one of Rob's old T-shirts that he always wore in bed to send in with the photo.

There are nine more men to sniff and then Dr Fischer takes off the blindfold and claps his hands, as if he is a hypnotist telling me I'm back in the room.

'We are all done. That is the last of the tests.'

He peels off the pads from my temples and the palms of my hands and he is about to reach in and grab the one stuck to my left breast.

'It's okay,' I tell him. 'I'll get that one.'

Once I'm unwired, Dr Fischer goes back to his keyboard and starts typing away.

I try and sneak a peek at the screen but can't make

sense of the names and numbers.

Theo	46	55c	7	105
Mark	48	76c	5	236
James	50	72a	6	150
Danny	42	70b	7	130
Isham	49	85c	7	213
Philip	43	72c	5	118
Dominic	48	55c	6	201
Harry	41	76b	7	165
Tom	45	74d	7	148
Ross	47	72c	5	214

Dr Fischer prints out a piece of paper, then analyses it through his glasses. 'Yes, he says to himself, nodding his head. 'Yes ... yes ... yes ... yes.'

He then thumps the back of his free hand down on the sheet of paper.

'Miss Holt, this is quite amazing. The results are so clear.'

'What does that mean?' I ask him. I stand up, stretch my aching neck, and pick up my bag.

'Mean, Miss Holt? It means it is very good news. We have found you the perfect man!'

'Right.'

'I mean, I knew we were going to. Of course, that is why you are here. But I didn't know we were going to find you a man who was quite so compatible. Here, Miss Holt, take a look at this.'

I look to where his flaky hand is pointing on the sheet.

Per cent: 100

One hundred per cent? What's one hundred per cent?'

His face widens into a mad smile. He takes off his glasses.

'Why, Miss Holt. You. You are the one hundred per cent.'

'Me? I don't –'

'You, and the man. The perfect man for you. I was expecting a ninety-nine or ninety-eight, but not one hundred. This is incredible.'

'So what does it mean?'

'It means it is impossible not to work out with the man. Your science is perfect together. There is no way it can fail. This is the man you are going to marry.'

I gulp, and feel slightly scared.

'Right,' I say. 'I see.'

James Master

I see his fuzzy outline, behind the glass.

He looks slightly shorter than I'd imagined him to be. And fatter. Maybe they've got it wrong. Maybe they've got my Perfect Man mixed up with someone else's. Some weird pervert with a fetish for out-of-shape men in football shirts.

I open the door and see one of the most imperfect specimens of manhood imaginable.

That's right, it's Rob.

'Rob,' I say, looking desperately at my watch. 'Er, what do you want?'

He visibly deflates. 'Oh. Pleased to see you too.'

'No, it's just . . . I'm in a bit of a hurry.'

'Right. Of course. A hurry. That must be nice.'

(Something else I want to add to my unofficial reasons for dumping Rob: His ability to make me feel totally guilty for no reason whatsoever.)

'No, I mean, it's nice to see you. It's just a bit of an awkward time.'

'Oh well, don't worry. I only came to get my CD back.'

'What CD?'

'Chili Peppers. Greatest Hits. I lent it to you to tape.'

'Erm –'

'I know what you're thinking.'

'I doubt it.'

'But I'm not being petty. It's just ... you only like that one song and I like all of them. Well, apart from "Suck my Kiss" which is a totally stupid song and I don't even know what it means. So even if we had bought the CD together, mathematically it would be more fair for me to have it. But as the CD predates our relationship, technically speaking it is mine and it belongs to me and it is your obligation to return it.'

If this was some other time I would laugh at or question the fact that he has managed to motivate himself away from slaying PlayStation zombies to travel over here to get a CD of a band he decided he didn't like about a year ago. But this isn't some other time, so I go into the living room, find the bloody CD, and thrust it in his hand.

'Oh,' he says, sounding disappointed. 'Right. Thanks.'

'Was that it?'

His mouth twitches. It looks for a moment like it isn't it. Like he has something else to say. But instead he just nods and says, 'I'll be off then.'

'Right,' I say.

'Right.'

'Right.'

And I look nervously behind him as a silver car pulls up outside the gate, its windscreen glistening in the evening sun.

It's him.

I know it is.

Rob turns and walks away in an attempt to break the walking down a path slow-speed record. Before he's out the gate the door to the silver car opens and . . . and . . .

Oh. My. God.

I'm sorry, I'll come back to you in a second.

I'm back.

Just.

Trying to control my breathing as the most beautiful looking man I have ever seen is walking up my path – *my path* – towards me. He looks so much better than the photo.

He passes Rob, says 'Hello,' and Rob just stands there, scratching his arse, jaw to the floor, watching his complete antithesis walk towards me.

'Hello,' he says, and smiles a smile that could melt an iceberg. 'Are you Ella Holt?'

'Yes,' I say. Or try to. It comes out as a squeak.

'I'm James, James Master,' he says, in a voice I recognise from my dreams and which instantly turns me to butter. 'Your date.' He has an accent. Not quite British and not quite American, but floating somewhere in-between.

'Yes,' I say, and doubt that I'll ever be willing or able to say any other words again. Just 'Yes' for ever.

Rob is still standing on the path. Still gawping. Not moving, as if it's a garden gnome audition or something.

I gesture for him to leave, which he does, like a Basset Hound finding a Labrador lying in his basket.

And I am left there, staring up at someone I feel like I have known before, from some better lifetime, who looks absolutely perfect in every single way.

'Pizza-delivery man,' I say, gesturing towards the space Rob occupied thirty seconds ago. 'My flatmate lives on pizza. Hawaiian. You know, ham and pineapple ...' What am I talking about? Why does my mouth always let me down when I need it the most. 'Sorry,' I say. 'I'm rambling.'

He smiles, and says: 'Don't apologise. I've booked us a table at this new French restaurant. What do you say?'

I look at this tall, solid, sharp-suited wet dream of a man and cannot believe my luck. His perfectness looks so surreal against the backdrop of shabby cars and higgledy terrace houses that he seems cut out from some other reality.

'Yes,' I tell him. 'Yes.'

Well, what else can I say?

He holds out his arm, in the eighteenth-century style, and I take it and walk down the path and look behind at Maddie giving me the thumbs-up from her bedroom window.

I wave back, before walking out into a dream.

The food of love

He looks at me across the table with eyes I feel I have known in some other lifetime.

The waiter comes over and asks for our orders. I look hesitant so James decides to help me out.

'The duck confit is very good,' he assures me.

'I'm, er, vegetarian,' I say.

'Oh, in that case, you should have the asparagus soup followed by the gratin of red and yellow cherry tomatoes with a ricotta and basil topping.'

'OK, I'll have that.'

I remember my answer to the first question.

My Perfect man will know how to take control of a situation...

And I must admit. It is incredibly sexy. Watching him hand the menus over to the waiter with the smooth authority of a world leader. Turning back towards me and offering that caring, protective smile.

The wine arrives. A 1985 something-or-other. And as I take my first sip I wonder why I don't feel more nervous. I mean, this is the poshest restaurant I've ever been to in my life, which isn't saying much as Rob's idea of a night out at a restaurant usually involved taking the food home in a carrier bag.

OK, I'm being a bit hard.

He did take me out for a meal once. On our first date. Pizza Heaven. And he had certainly seemed like he was in heaven as he devoured the largest stuffed-crust pizza on the menu, topped with an entire pig's worth of pepperoni.

The conversation that night had been OK, but he hardly put Oscar Wilde to shame.

Most of the time he just commented on the food.

'Mmm, this is really good. . .'

Or 'What's yours like?'

Or 'Do you want the rest?'

Or 'You up for pudding?'

And when I asked him if we should leave a tip he said, 'Yeah, how about telling them to speed up the service.'

So being here, in a restaurant that uses gold leaf as liberally as other places use Dulux, is something of a new experience.

But strangely, I couldn't feel more relaxed. There's just something about James's face, his smile, that puts me instantly at ease. He's so perfectly beautiful, but it's not the kind of intimidating beauty that makes you speechless. It's the exact opposite, in fact.

He's got the sort of face that makes you want to reveal everything. So by the time my chilled asparagus soup arrives I'm onto chapter seven of my autobiography.

He knows about the time I nearly got squashed to death under a blackboard during sports day when I was eight years old.

He knows about my fear after spilling blackcurrant juice all over my mum and dad's new rug.

67

He knows about the time I sleepwalked and fell down the stairs.

He knows about the piano lessons I took when I was younger.

He knows everything. Well, nearly everything.

I didn't tell him about Rob.

I don't know why, it just didn't feel right. Maybe I didn't want to look stupid. Maybe I didn't want Rob to look stupid. Maybe I'd feel guilty telling Mr Perfect about Mr Very Incredibly Imperfect. It would be like talking about Vin Diesel's acting technique to Sir Ian McKellen.

But whatever the reason, Rob is edited out of the conversation.

And by the time I have finished telling James about my Rob-free life story, I realise I haven't asked him one thing about his past.

'I'm sorry,' I tell him. 'I've been rabbiting on about myself all night.'

'No, don't apologise. I want to know everything about you, Ella Holt. Absolutely everything.'

I remember another of my answers.

My perfect man will be interested in every part of my life.

And it feels so weird, seeing a male human being actually take such interest in me. I can remember Rob on our first date. I could picture him trying to calculate how many sentences he would have to utter before he could get into my knickers. But with James it seems totally different. It's almost as though – and I know this sounds crazy – it's almost as though he's making conversation because he likes making conversation. He doesn't see it as some necessary chore to get out of the way en route to getting his leg over.

'Oh,' I say. 'Thank you. But what do you do?'

He dabs the side of his mouth with a napkin, swallows, then says:

'I fly planes.'

'What, as a hobby or something?'

'No. As a living actually. I'm a pilot. Trans-Atlantic flights mainly.'

I suddenly picture him in his uniform, complete with cap. If anything, he looks even more gorgeous. To be honest, I'm not normally a uniform-type girl, but an airline pilot. Could you get any sexier than an airline pilot?

I suddenly want to ask him a million questions. What cities does he fly to? Does he get to see the places he visits? Where does he sleep when he gets there? Has he ever had to do an emergency landing?

As I said, a million questions.

And yet, the one I hear myself asking is this: 'Do your ears pop?'

'Sorry?'

'When you take off and land. Do you get popping ears? It's just, when I'm flying I always get bad ears. It's something to do with my sinuses.'

Sinuses? *Sinuses?* Did I just say sinuses? Why does my mouth hate me so much? Why does it want to tell my perfect man about the blocked-up tubes of dried gunk inside my head?

But he doesn't seem to mind. 'Yeah, actually, when I started my ears did crackle a bit. But I just suck sweets now. That's the best way. Just suck and keep swallowing.'

Just suck and keep swallowing? God, I really wish I'd asked a different question. My face is now so red,

69

the cherry tomatoes on my plate probably think I'm taking the piss out of them.

But the awkward moment rides itself out and I finish my meal.

The wine and conversation continue to flow.

He pays and leaves the tip.

I object, and almost read his refusal to accept any money as sexism. But then I remember something else from the questionnaire.

My perfect man will not be ashamed to spend his money on me...

As we drive home I watch his side profile as he concentrates on the road. An image of perfection glowing and fading under the fast-moving street-lamps.

The delicate waves of his hair. The strong line of his forehead, nose and chin. The lips that wait to be kissed, the way a swimming pool waits for you to dive in on a baking hot day. I try and guess his age, but it's as difficult to place as his accent. Somewhere in his thirties, probably, but he seems younger and older all at the same time.

He puts some music on. Alicia Keyes.

'She's such an incredible singer, isn't she?'

'Yes,' I tell him. 'She is.'

He pauses, listens to the music. Then he says: 'It's really amazing, what you do. To be able to teach people must be the most wonderful feeling. To be able to mould people and influence them, to shape them for life.'

'Er, well. I suppose so.'

'It must be a wonderful talent to have.'

I look to see if he's joking. He's not. 'I think

anyone could do it really. With the right training. It's hardly brain surgery. Or flying a plane.'

He laughs. 'I don't think I'd be able to stand up and talk about Shakespeare in front of a class of fifteen-year-olds if I was trained until the end of time. You shouldn't put yourself down. You are an incredible person. I know that sounds stupid after only one evening with you, but I can tell. You're a life-changer, I can feel it.'

A life-changer?

That sounds good. More than good, in fact.

He is the first person who has ever made me feel valued for being a teacher, and even if he looked like Quasimodo I could adore him for that. But he doesn't look like Quasimodo, so that's even better.

A few minutes later we park outside my flat. The engine and Alicia fall quiet, and I sit with James in a silence that should feel awkward but somehow doesn't.

'You can come inside,' I tell him. 'If you want.'

His lips are there, waiting for me to dive in. I have never wanted to kiss anyone so much in my whole life, but I wait for him to make the first move.

It doesn't happen.

Instead he says: 'I would love to, but I should really get back. I wouldn't want to take advantage of anything.'

The words fall like rain over my dream of wild rampant sex between the sheets. Right now, I want him to take advantage of *everything*.

My answer to question four: *My perfect man will never rush me into bed*.

'Oh,' I say. 'OK.'

'If you give me your number I'll call you,' he says,

and for once I can actually believe those words. 'I'm flying to Buenos Aires tomorrow and I'll be away for a few days, but when I come back I've got a fortnight off. So we can spend more time getting to know each other.'

He types my number into his phone and then plants a gentle peck on my lips. I feel myself dissolve, and want more, but know I'll have to wait.

'Goodbye then,' I say, fumbling with the door handle.

'Yes, bye Ella. I'll see you soon.'

I close the car door and watch his silver sports car pull away and drive off, and I stay there watching it disappear down the street. And even when it is completely out of view, my hand is still waving, and my body still warm and tingly.

Then a voice, behind me. 'Ella?'

It is Maddie. I turn and see her looking at me from the doorway.

'What are you doing?' she asks. 'You're getting soaked.'

She's right. I hadn't even noticed that for the last two minutes I had been standing in the rain.

'Oh,' I said, 'Yes, I'm coming.'

I walk up the path towards the warmth of the centrally-heated house and Maddie's raucous laugh.

'Good night I take it?'

'Yes,' I tell her, still in a trance. 'Absolutely perfect.'

Science helps lonely singleton

The dreamlike trance lasts all the next week.

Well, right up until Thursday, when it turns into one of those embarrassing dreams where you suddenly realise you aren't wearing any clothes.

Only the night before I had been dancing around the flat after James had phoned from Argentina to say he would be back on Friday, and that he wanted me to come round to his place.

But now, as I walk into the staffroom, any remaining euphoria has left me.

Everyone is staring.

I check my shoe.

No trail of toilet paper.

I check the side of my mouth.

No remains of breakfast.

I head over to where Pip and Maddie are sitting and whisper, 'What's going on?'

Pip nods over towards Brian Pemberton, the lecherous science teacher who is still wearing corduroy and tweed from the first time they were fashionable. 'He *knows*,' she says.

'Knows what?'

'About you. And the Agency. I told you it was a stupid idea,' says Pip.

I look over at Brian, who stops reading the *New Scientist* to turn it around and show me.

'Nice picture,' he says, gawping at me like I was something tasty on a menu.

Oh God.

It's a massive photo of me, in the magazine. It is next to an article with the headline SCIENCE HELPS LONELY SINGLETON.

The whole staffroom, with the exception of Maddie and Pip, are now stifling giggles. Or, as in the case of the Religious Education teacher Peter Fairchild, not stifling giggles.

'You lot are worse than the kids,' says Maddie, as Pip gives them all her Kung Fu death stare.

Lonely singleton?

My cheeks are on fire. This is as bad as the dream I have when I turn up at work with no clothes on. I try and say something to defuse the situation but my mouth is too dry and I can't think of anything.

I am about to spontaneously combust.

Next week's *New Scientist* will then be able to run it as a cover story.

LONELY SINGLETON SPONTANEOUSLY COMBUSTS.

Brian – who over the years has tried it on with every female member of staff – is tickled fluorescent pink by this. 'You could have always come to my love lab,' he tells me.

'No one's *that* lonely,' says Claudette Matthews, my colleague in the English department, with her raucous Jamaican laugh.

I stare at the floor, praying that it will open up any second now and swallow me whole.

I think about running out of the room. There's only fifteen teachers and two water coolers between me and the door.

'Ignore them,' Maddie says. 'They're just jealous.'

Jealous?

'What, does everybody want to be branded "lonely" in a leading international scientific journal?'

Oh no.

Just when I think this couldn't get any more painful in walks the head. Paul Loving. Yes, that's his name. Mr Loving. It is possibly the most inappropriate surname in the world. It's like Adolf Hitler had been called Adolf Nice or if Victoria Beckham had been called Victoria Talent or if Brad Pitt was called Brad Ugly.

He is staring straight at me in exactly the same way he stared at Darren Bentley after he was found guilty of setting off the fire alarm.

'Miss Holt,' he says, in his clipped voice. 'I'd like a word. In my office.'

Uh-oh.

He's cross with me.

The reason I know that he is cross with me is because he said 'Miss Holt'. When he says 'Ella' it means he is pleased with me, but when he uses the formality of 'Miss Holt' it always spells trouble.

I hear Maddie gulp on my behalf. 'Good luck,' she says.

'Kick his ass,' says Pip, rather unhelpfully.

I walk through the room – leaving a trail of giggles and gossipy murmurs behind me – and follow Paul's grey suit and grey head down the corridor.

He doesn't turn around or say anything to me as we pass examples of sixth-form art on the wall. Painted

75

and pencilled vampires and skulls and black crows looking down at me like omens of what awaits me in the head teacher's office.

'Sit,' he says, when I am inside the room.

I do so, like a guilty cocker spaniel after she has left a wet patch on the kitchen floor.

He shuts the door.

Sits down opposite me.

Takes off his glasses and rubs his weary eyes.

Once he's put his glasses back on he pulls out a newspaper from one of his desk drawers. It's the business supplement of the *Daily Telegraph*.

At first I wonder why he is showing it to me but then I see the picture. Or pictures. There's one of me and one of James.

This time the headline is a less offensive: 'TEACHER TRIALS STEIN SCI-FI DATING SERVICE'

Less offensive to me, that is.

My boss isn't looking too happy about it.

'Ella,' he says. 'What's going on?'

'Er... I've joined a dating agency.'

He's got one of those faces. That instantly makes you feel about five centimetres tall when it looks at you. I feel myself shrinking in my chair. 'Ella, most of the women in this school have joined a dating agency. But I don't wake up to see their face in the morning paper. I nearly spat out my cornflakes!'

'I'm sorry. About your cornflakes.'

'Never mind my cornflakes, Miss Holt! What on earth are you doing making a mockery of yourself and the school?'

'I didn't know I was making a mockery of anyone?'

He sighs. 'If a teacher of mine is dragging the name of Thistlemead Comprehensive School into the papers

76

don't you think I've got a right to know about it?'

'Er, . . . yes, . . . yes, I do . . . I'm sorry. I should
have told you.'

'Yes,' he says, swiftly. 'Yes, Miss Holt. You
should have told me. I have a right to know about
things such as this.'

'I know . . . I'm sorry. I didn't think it was going to
make the papers. There was a press conference but I –'

'A press conference?'

'Yes.'

'Oh my word, Miss Holt. This is a serious breach
of conduct.'

'It is?'

'What kind of example does it set to those young
fornicators out there?' he asks me, pointing his thumb
behind him at the window and the gladiatorial arena
commonly referred to as the school field.

'Er. . . I don't know. But I don't think they've
heard about it yet.'

'They will though, won't they?'

'I don't know. I don't think there'll be any more
publicity.'

'Oh they'll find out, Miss Holt.'

'Will they?'

'Yes,' he says, as the stern mask slips. 'Because
you'll tell them.'

He is laughing now. *Laughing*.

'I . . . don't . . . understand.'

'I'm not cross with you, Ella.'

'You're not?'

'Not at all.'

'But I thought you said it was a serious breach of
conduct.'

'I was pulling your leg. Even us head teachers have

77

a sense of humour, you know.'

Paul Loving has a sense of humour? Now that really is headline news.

'Oh, right. I see. That was very ... funny.'

'Yes. Yes it was, wasn't it? Anyway, I think all this is fantastic ... for the school. All publicity is good publicity and all that. And with a catchment area like this, and with our last OFSTED record, well, we need all the help we can get don't we?'

'Um ... yes. I suppose.'

He leans back in his chair, in the style of a Bond villain about to announce his plans for global domination. 'Why don't you do an assembly about it, tell the whole school.'

The words ring like an alarm bell inside my head. I've never led an assembly in my entire life, and I didn't imagine that my first time would involve talking about the embarrassing intricacies of my love life.

'I think it would be a great idea,' he tells me. 'I mean what better role-model for those kids than Lara Stein? You could talk about what she's like, about the Perfect Agency or whatever it's called, about all the science that was involved ... it would be educational.' He squeezes his lower lip thoughtfully and stares off towards some imaginary horizon. Then his eyes widen and says 'What about the half-term assembly?'

Uh-oh.

The half-term assembly. Half-term assemblies are a nightmare. They're the most notorious assemblies, when school is an open house, with parents and governors and the mayor and just about everyone is invited.

'Erm, well, I've only just met him. I've only had one date with him. I might not even be with him at the end of term.'

'But it's science, Ella. It's science. It says in the paper, there's a quote from Dr ... er, Fischer "The scientific chances of success are 100 per cent". Come on Ella, it would be great. And it's weeks away – you've got ages to prepare.'

'Er ... I ... I ... I don't ... er ...' Where are all the good excuses when you need them. 'I ... don't ... really ...'

He claps his hands.

'Great,' he says. 'That settles it. You can lead the half-term assembly. We could invite some members of the local press along ... have a little press conference of our own. Fantastic, Ella. Fantastic.'

'Yes,' I say, as the blood sucks out of me. 'Fantastic.'

Two to tango

Walking into James's apartment feels like walking into a magazine. I keep expecting to see some stork-legged model draped over his plush L-shaped sofa.

The sight of James, and his apartment, helps me forget all about my week and all the staffroom embarrassments and proposed school assemblies.

'What do you think?' he tells me.

'It's amazing,' I tell him, because that's the only word in my head. 'Amazing. Really. Amazing.'

He beckons me over to the window.

An entire wall of glass, complete with the most spectacular view of London I've ever seen.

'Amazing,' I say, for what I vow to be the last time.

'See that dome.'

'Yes.'

'That's St Paul's.'

'Wow.'

Between us and the dome the river carves the city in two. Lights in distant skyscrapers twinkle, as if answering the stars above them.

London. A mini-universe of possibility.

'Beautiful,' he says.

'Yes.'

But I can see out of the corner of my eye that he isn't looking out of the window any more. 'I wasn't talking about the view.'

I turn and meet his eyes. They are gleaming like the city lights.

'I was talking about you.'

His words should sound cheap. Like a come-on. Like a worn out chat-up line I should shrug off.

But there's something about him. Something real. Something true. Something that makes me melt each time he opens his mouth. He could read the back of a box of Crunchy Nut Corn Flakes and I'd still probably have to change my knickers.

'I'll get you something to drink.'

'Right. OK'

'Do you want some wine?'

'I'd love some.'

'Red? White?'

'Red please.' I don't know why I said red. I prefer white wine. In fact, I only ever drink white wine. Maybe I think that if I say I drink red I look less girly, more sophisticated.

On his way to get the drinks he picks up a remote control and puts on some music. Some old seventies soul album soothes its way out of his designer speakers.

While I wait for my wine I look back out of the window. My eyes head south of the river, towards an out-of-view Clapham. I wonder what Rob is doing right now.

Scratching his bollocks, probably.

Or wanking off in front of Channel 5.

I get a strange feeling in my stomach.

81

It's a feeling I've had before. I last got it when I was a teenager on a school trip to La Rochelle in France. The feeling is homesickness. Of missing something I used to take for granted.

The feeling evaporates as James walks out of his silver spaceship of a kitchen with two goldfish-bowl-sized glasses of red wine.

'There you go,' he says, handing me my glass.

'Thanks.'

I take a sip and try to like it. Or try to look like I like it. 'Lovely wine,' I lie.

'It's from Argentina.'

'Oh . . .'

I don't know why but I feel more nervous than the other night, at the restaurant. There's something about the swanky apartment that puts me on edge.

Maybe I want this to work *too much*.

Relax, I think to myself, it is going to work – we are perfectly matched. I try and say something but my mind is a blank.

'Our first awkward silence,' he says.

'Yes,' I say, with a giggle.

The awkward silence goes on and on and on and on for what feels like the length of *Titanic* and I try to say something but the only word I have in my head is iceberg because I am thinking about the length of *Titanic* and the silence builds and builds.

Of course, it isn't really a silence at all. The speakers are still sending seventies soul out into the apartment.

But I have to say something. If I don't say something soon we could probably make the *Guinness Book of Records*. The longest time a man and woman have stood looking at each other with a glass of wine without saying anything. If they have records for that kind of thing.

That was one thing about Rob. There were no awkward silences in his presence. Our silences were as comfy as beanbags.

And then I have it.

Something to say.

And so does James.

'What's –'

'You –'

We laugh. Awkwardly.

'You first.'

'No you first.'

'Honestly, you first.'

'No come on,' he says. 'It was nothing. What were you going to say?'

'I was just going to ask you what this music is. I really like it.'

He frowns and says, 'What's going on?'

'Nothing. I just wondered what it was.'

His frown becomes a smile. 'What's going on?'

'Seriously, nothing. I just –'

'No. That's what it's called. The music. *What's Going On?* That's the name of the album. It's by Marvin Gaye.'

'Oh yes. Of course. Sorry. I'm so –'

Stupid.

So so so stupid.

The easy confidence I felt in the neutral setting of our first date has completely disappeared.

But my brain decides I don't look stupid enough so it tells my heart to pump ninety per cent of my body's blood supply up to my cheeks.

'Don't be embarrassed,' he says. But it's about as

useless as telling an apple not to be a fruit. 'I'm always doing things like that.'

Somehow I doubt it. Six-foot-two airline pilots don't get to fly massive people-carriers at 30,000 feet above the ocean by acting stupid.

'It's a great album,' he says. 'One of the greatest.'

He then asks me the sort of question I dread. Namely: 'What sort of music are you into?'

I hate this question because I can never tell the truth.

'Oh, all sorts,' I say.

'That's a bit non-committal. What's your all-time favourite album?'

I run through possible answers.

Alicia Keyes.

Dirty Dancing soundtrack.

Grease.

I look at his serious Man Face and realise that none of these choices can emerge from my mouth.

'Erm, Elton John,' I say.

'Which one?'

'Sorry?'

'Which album?'

'Er . . . the, er, Greatest Hits.'

'I love Elton. What's your favourite song?'

Oh God.

'"Song for Guy", probably. When I was little I liked "Crocodile Rock"'

He smiles. No, wait a minute. That's not a smile. It's a *smirk*.

He's smirking at me!

My Perfect Man *smirks*.

'What other stuff do you like?'

'Oh . . . you know . . . I try desperately to look

84

cool. 'Er ... the Scissor Sisters, the Kings of Leon, the Killers...'

'They're from Las Vegas aren't they?'

'Er ... yes,' I say, blagging. 'I've always wanted to go there.'

The smirk becomes a smile. 'I'll take you one day,' he says. 'Do you want to go outside?'

'Outside?' I ask.

He nods his head towards the window, and the large balcony immediately beyond. 'It's a nice night.'

'Sure. I'd love to.'

He slides the window open and we step outside into the night.

As we stand there on the balcony the dark silhouette of a plane flies across the sky, erasing stars in its path.

I ask James where he flies to with the airline.

'All over,' he says. 'I mostly do the long haul stuff. My first routes used to be to Asia. Tokyo. Seoul. Singapore. Now they've got me on different routes. South and Central America.'

He starts talking about far-off cities.

Buenos Aires. Caracas. Rio. Montevideo. Sao Paulo.

'I've always wanted to go to Rio,' I tell him. And this is true. Ever since I heard the Duran Duran song. In truth, I don't know much about the place. Except that the people there love carnivals and hate pubic hairs.

'It's a crazy place. Last time I was there me and some of the crew saw a Samba concert on the beach. There were about 10,000 mad Brazilians partying on the sand as the sun went down behind the Sugar Loaf Mountain in the background.'

I see the memory shining in his eyes, and can't help but wonder if he slept alone that night.

'Wow,' I say. 'It sounds great. What was Buenos Aires like?'

'It's great. Quite different to the rest of South America really. It's like a European city. Like Paris or somewhere.'

'Did you go to any samba parties?'

'No. But I did do the tango.'

'The tango?'

I briefly wonder who his tango partner was. After all, it takes two . . .

He fnishes the last of his drink and places his glass on the outside table. 'I'll show you.'

'What?'

'The tango. Come on. It's easy.'

'But–'

'No buts. Come on. I'll show you.'

He takes my glass of wine and puts it on the table. Then he comes back and holds my stare.

'Eye contact. That's the important thing. The tango is about a close human connection, and that starts with the eyes.'

'Right.'

He places his hand on the small of my back and presses me gently towards him. His other hand hangs in the air, waiting for mine to join it.

Marvin Gaye has stopped singing. There is no sound but that of distant traffic on the streets below.

Words come back to haunt me.

My perfect man must be a good dancer.

'Left foot back.' His voice is soft, smooth. A kind of music itself.

I move back.

He moves forward. Pulls me closer. His eyes burrow deep into my soul.

86

'Feel it in your hips.'

As James keeps on instructing, a memory intrudes on what could be the perfect moment. An image of Rob on the dance floor from his birthday last year. It wasn't a pretty sight. In truth, it was the ugliest sight you could imagine. Sort of like watching an overweight ostrich having an epileptic fit to the sounds of a hyperactive Freddie Mercury.

Don't stop me now ...

I shake the image from my brain and try to enjoy the moment. *This* moment.

'You know what they say about the tango, don't you?'

'No,' I say, missing my step and treading on his toe.

'They say it's as close as two people can get without–'

A sudden modesty stops his sentence in its tracks. His body is less bashful.

I feel the firmness of his stomach as his hand holds me close.

As close as two people can get ...

Not close enough. I want to feel his skin against mine. I want to feel his warmth. I want ...

He carries on leading our dance. I don't know how he's doing it, but he's actually making me look kind of good at this.

It's like something out of *Dirty Dancing*. Or *Saturday Night Fever*. And he's become Patrick Swayze and John Travolta rolled into one.

'It might be London down there,' he says, with a deliberately cheesy smile. 'But up here it's Argentina.'

I laugh.

'Hook your right leg around the back of my left.'

He's getting ambitious now, but I go with it, enjoying the feel of his well-chiseled calf. I even throw my head back like a sultry senorita with a rose between her teeth.

'Wow,' he says. 'It's Carmen herself.'

We both laugh, but the laugh only seems to bring us closer. It's the same laugh, shared by two people.

The laugh fades and there is a different kind of moment. I stand still and look into the eyes that have seen the world, that almost seem to contain it within that bluegreen sphere.

I want to see what those eyes have seen. I want him to take me to all the countries he has been to.

His hand touches my face, brushes my cheek.

His touch is strong and gentle all at once. He leans in for the kiss.

My lips meet his halfway, and my hands move over his back. I feel safe, warm, suddenly immune to the cool evening breeze.

His phone goes.

'Sorry,' he says, pulling away.

He gets the phone out of his pocket, and his eyes flinch as they see the display screen. He switches the phone off and puts it back in his pocket.

'It was just ... someone from work ... Now, where were we?' James asks me.

'Right about here,' I say.

Before our lips meet again, another phone goes inside his apartment.

'It's OK,' he says, somewhat sheepishly. 'It can wait.'

We carry on kissing, and I carry on feeling like a teenager on a first date.

The kiss is intense now, as the tenderness turns to lust. But yet again we are interrupted, this time by my phone.

I pull it out of my pocket and see MADDIE on the display. If James isn't taking calls, then neither should I.

'It's OK,' I say, echoing James. 'It can wait.'

We talk.

We drink more wine.

There are silences, but they are no longer awkward.

My phone beeps in my pocket to tell me I've received a text message. I'll check it later, I think to myself

But then I hear something else.

Something twenty floors below. Something different from the distant swooshes of traffic.

A voice, rising up.

The balcony scene – part one

I look at James, but he doesn't seem to be able to hear it. Perhaps it's in my head.

'Ella! Ella!'

There it was again. I'm almost sure someone was calling my name.

I am about to say something when James – who still hasn't noticed – says, 'Wait there. I'll just put more music on.'

'OK.'

He goes back inside the apartment and starts fiddling about with his CD collection. While he's not looking I quickly turn to look over the balcony.

I feel a giddy tingle of vertigo as I look down at the car park. I strain my eyes but can't see anything but car roofs, neatly arranged in the grid of parking spaces.

'Ella! Ella!'

Then I see someone.

A dark dot with four shadows from the streetlights around the car park. I can't tell for sure, but he seems to be waving his arms at me.

'Ella! Ella!' he shouts.

I recognise the voice, and as I do so the feeling in my stomach switches from vertigo to horror.

It's Rob.

Rob.

'You're not thinking of jumping are you?'

I turn round and see James handing me my glass of red wine from the table, as some new music starts to play.

'I mean, I know my conversation can get pretty boring, but I've never had anyone commit suicide on me before.'

'No,' I say. 'I was just ... looking down ... to see ... how high up we are ... that's all.'

'Pretty high,' he says.

'Yes.'

'I sometimes think I must have a phobia with the ground,' he says. 'What with my job, and this apartment.'

I pray he doesn't look down over the balcony, and I decide to quickly change the conversation.

'So, erm, when are you back flying planes?'

I take a sip of my wine and try to hear Rob's cries above the sounds of opera now coming from the stereo, but they are drowned out.

'Two weeks,' he says. 'But it's going to be with a different airline.'

'Really?' I say, wondering what on earth Rob is playing at.

'Well, it's the sister airline. I'll still be doing Transatlantic routes. North America mainly. New York. Boston. Vegas. LAX. I've got a better contract now. One month on. One month off. That means I'll have more time to see you. And I might be able to get you on some flights to New York. Treat you to a shopping spree on Fifth Avenue.'

I nod my head and smile, but not even the promise of New York shopping heaven is enough to stop me worrying about what Rob is up to.

Maybe I got it wrong.

Maybe it wasn't Rob. After all, I've had a bit to drink and I'm twenty storeys up.

There's a knock on the door. A loud knock. Loud enough to be heard over the opera and out on the balcony.

James raises his eyebrows, and looks slightly worried.

'That's weird,' he says 'No one buzzed the intercom.'

While he goes to get the door, I check my mobile to see who sent me a text. It was Maddie.

I click open the message and my stomach sinks as I start to read.

Robs been round – wouldnt leave till I told him where u are – think hes on his way M XXX

Nevermind XXX, what the hell does she think she's playing at? James can't meet Rob. It can't happen.

Too late.

James opens the door and Rob is standing there out on the landing. Rob, like James, is wearing jeans and what I know to be his best black shirt. (It's his only black shirt. In fact, it's his only shirt of any colour). This is a weird coincidence, and an even weirder sight.

The similar clothes and dissimilar physiques make it look like James is standing in front of one of those bendy fairground mirrors that stretch and fatten all the wrong body parts.

'Hello?' says James.

'Is Ella there?' grunts Rob.

Oh no.

This can't be happening.

'I'm sorry, but who exactly are you?'

'Rob.'

I hide behind the wall and pray that James is a good liar.

'Rob?'

'Rob. Ella's ex-boyfriend.'

'Oh,' James says, probably wondering why I've never told him about Rob. 'Ella's ex-boyfriend.'

'Yeah.'

There is a silence. James is probably wondering why Rob is so different to how he imagined my ex-boyfriends. (Rob is always different to what people imagine. Worse, generally. So whatever you see him as in your mind, downgrade your mental image by at least two notches).

I start to say my prayer aloud. 'Please say I'm not in. Please say I'm not in. Please say I'm–'

'Ella! Ella!'

It's James. He's calling me.

I grab my glass of red wine that's on the outside table and down it in one go, before heading back into the apartment.

They are both looking at me.

Rob the slob.

James the pilot.

I feel embarrassed but I don't know why. After all, it's not like I asked Rob to come around here.

Am I ashamed of him? Do I think James will go off me if he sees my normal standards?

Bad questions. Bad thoughts. But I can't help them.

93

I look at James and say, 'Sorry about this. But I'd better just talk to him.'

James is about to say something, but thinks twice. I go out on the landing with Rob and close the door behind me.

Rob gets a newsflash

I look at Rob, and wonder how his fear of heights got him up to the twentieth floor.

'What on earth are you doing here?' I ask him, trying to decide where you draw the line between 'Ex-boyfriend Who Can't Let Go' and 'Stalker'.

'I . . . er, don't know.'

'You don't know?'

'No.'

O Rob, Rob, wherefore art thou such a total loser?

'So why bully Maddie into giving you James's address and drive across London to shout at me from a car park?'

'So, he's Mr Perfect is he?'

'What?'

'I read about it in the paper. I was about to check the football results and there you were.'

'Oh,' I say. 'Yeah.'

'James? *James?* What kind of a name is that?'

He's acting like he's just found out my new boyfriend is called Cecil or Tarquin or Moses or something. 'It's a perfectly normal name,' I tell him. 'Anyway, what *are* you doing here?'

'Who is he?'

'What?'

'What does he do?' Rob looks around at the lush sofa on the communal landing. 'Is he a bank robber?'

'He's an airline pilot. Not that it's any of your–'

'An airline pilot.' His mouth laughs, but his eyes look desperate as he measures 'airline pilot' against 'recruitment consultant' in his mind.

'Rob, go home,' I tell him. 'If you haven't come over here for any other reason than to submit your entry into the World's Biggest Dickhead competition, then I'd like to get on with my life.'

'What do you see in him?'

'Why aren't you at home? On your PlayStation? Why tonight? Why not yesterday? Why not the night before? Why tonight do you feel suddenly compelled to see me?'

The answer twitches his lips, but never comes. His eyes look hurt. 'Is it serious?'

'What?'

'With Mr Airline Pilot. Mr Perfect Scientific Match.'

'I don't know.'

'But won't he be away all the time?'

'Sometimes, he will. Sometimes I'll go with him.'

This will wind Rob up. You see, Rob and air travel get on like President Bush at a peace rally.

'Tosser,' Rob says.

'What?'

'He's a tosser.'

I can't believe how immature he's acting. Well, I suppose I can. This is Rob, after all. 'You don't know him. Now, if you haven't got–'

'Dump him.'

'What?'

'Dump him.'

'No.'

'Why?'

'I like him,' I say. Then I get furious: 'I can't believe I'm even having this conversation. Why are you here? Have you been drinking? Have you got your car?'

He isn't listening. 'No, trust me. Whatever that stupid dating thing said, it was wrong. He's not your perfect man. He's bad news. You can tell. Men know these things. We can pick it up on our ... our ... bad news radar.'

'Bad news radar. Right.'

He scratches his cheek. He wants to say something, I can see that, but I'm only going to give him two more minutes.

'What's so fucking special about him?'

'He's strong. He's gentle.'

Rob snorts. 'He sounds like toilet paper.'

'Rob, please. Just listen to me. If I mean anything to you then you'd want the best for me. You'd want me to be happy. And I am. I really am.'

He looks at me as if I am speaking a foreign language.

'Bollocks,' he says.

'Rob, please. If you're going to be like that there's really no point–'

'Bollocks. Bollocks. Bollocks.'

'Rob, you really better go.'

He looks lost. 'Just tell me what *he's* got that I haven't?'

He pauses, considering his own question. 'I mean, apart from money. And a posh flat. And the ability to

97

fly a Boeing 747. And stupid white teeth.'

'Stupid white teeth? What colour are teeth meant to be?'

'I bet he's had them done. He looks like ... like ... like ... like a lighthouse!'

Rob does a big fake smile and starts to wiggle his fingers near his mouth which makes him look even weirder than usual.

'Rob, what are you doing?'

'A lighthouse.' He points with his free hand to the wiggling fingers. 'These are rays of light.'

I hear a noise in James's apartment and wonder for a moment if he is listening at the door so I move us a bit further down the corridor. Out of view of the peep-hole. Just in case.

'Rob, why are you doing this?' I ask, in a whisper. 'I mean, haven't you got more important things to be doing. Like watching TV.'

He bites his lip. There are words inside his head that he doesn't seem to be able to let out. Like bad children stuck in for detention.

'I ... I ... I ...'

He is two words away from where he wants to be. Two tiny little words. But he still can't manage it.

'I just want it to be back to the way it was. Just you know, just us two.'

I think for a moment he might be joking. I really do. So I laugh. But the laugh is not a shared one. It bounces back off his serious face like a squash ball.

'Oh,' I say. 'You mean it.'

'Course I mean it. It was great.'

'Great? Great? What was great about it? It was OK, sure. Sometimes. But we weren't right together. Surely, you can't think we were right together?

He shrugs. 'Why not?'

I try to be as tactful as I possibly can. 'We want different things out of life.'

'What different things?'

For a second I pity him. He genuinely doesn't know. We were in a relationship for a year. A *year*. And our now obvious and blatant incompatibility is reaching his ears like a newsflash.

So I explain.

'Well, I want to travel. I want to do things. See the world. You can't even get on a plane for God's sake. I don't want to spend every night in the pub. Or in front of your PlayStation. Or watching *Match of the Day*. Or being ignored.'

'Ignored?' he asks, shaking the word out of his head.

'I used to feel like the Invisible Woman. You forgot my birthday. You forgot to meet my parents. You hardly spoke to me when you were with your mates. Other than to explain the offside rule.'

Rob looks at me as if that's all beside the point. 'But ... but ... I miss you.'

'No you don't.'

'I do.'

'You don't.'

'I do.'

I shake my head. 'No. You don't. You think you miss me. But you miss having someone around. That's what you miss. Someone to share a drink with so you don't feel like a lonely alcoholic. I was just your Player Two on the PlayStation. A familiar face. A regular shag. I could have been anyone. I could have been any girl on the street. And the only reason you're round here now is because you think it would be easier than to go to the hassle of finding someone new.'

'That's not true,' he says, with total sincerity.

'Maybe you're right. Maybe it's not true. Maybe you're here because you're miserable and you can't stand the thought of me being happy. Maybe you're here because you think this is some big man game where you have to fight the Airline Pilot to win the girl. But I'm not a computer game Rob. I'm a real person. And I want to be happy. I want to be with someone who understands me. Who wants to get to know me better. Not someone who takes me for granted.'

His eyes sting me.

I've just killed Bambi.

'I didn't take you for granted,' he says.

'Rob, this isn't your fault. It's just, we weren't right. We didn't fit. It's like pineapple and pasta. Both perfectly nice, but you wouldn't want them on the same plate.'

It's sinking in. His shoulders slump. I'm chomping into a Bambi steak sandwich.

I try and make things better by telling him, 'It's *science*. Our brains and bodies are too far apart from each other for it to ever work. If you want to go left, I go right. If you want to go up, I go down. It's just the way it is. It's programmed into our genes. Somewhere out there is your perfect woman. But it isn't me Rob. It really isn't.'

The lift door pings open and a couple in matching raincoats step out after a night at a restaurant or the theatre or the opera. They walk past and head to their apartment without acknowledging us, wearing love's happy blinkers.

'I could change,' Rob says.

'How?'

'I don't know. I could stop going to the pub. We could go away. We could travel.'

'But Rob, you can't even fly. You can't get on a plane.'

'We could get a coach. Or the Eurostar. We could drive to France and get a ferry. Roll on roll off.'

For a cruel second I think he is providing an accurate description of his sexual technique.

'Rob, please.'

The Bambi eyes return as I hear James's door open behind me.

A silly agreement

James's face is a picture of concern.

'Ella, are you all right?' he asks.

For a second I feel sorry for Rob. But then he blows it by saying 'Oi mate, piss off would you? We're trying to sort things out.'

I look back at James and see his eyes harden. He steps out onto the landing and says, 'I was talking to Ella.'

'I was talking to Ella,' mimics Rob, in a posh voice.

Uh-oh.

All of a sudden I feel like I've been beamed up to Planet Testosterone.

I look at Rob. His eyes switch from bravado to fear as he takes in James's tall, muscular build. Rob's never been in a fight in his life but if his fighting is in anyway comparable to his dancing, he'll be in serious trouble.

'Wait,' I say, turning back to James. 'Look, just give us another minute. I'll sort it out. Just one minute. I'm sorry.'

'It's not a problem,' he says, before heading back

inside his apartment and closing the door.

'It's not a problem,' Rob says, once he's made sure James has gone, in the same stupid posh voice.

'Stop doing that,' I tell him.

'Sorry. It's just . . . I don't think he's right for you.'

How can I get through to him. 'He. Makes. Me. Happy.'

'I made you happy.'

'No. You made me cups of tea. And the odd ready meal. If I was lucky. Now Rob, go home. Please.'

'I . . . I . . . want to see you.'

'You've seen me.'

'No. I want to talk to you properly,' he says with a pained expression. 'I've got to tell you something.'

'I've got to go.'

'I know. I know. It's just . . . Please. I just want one hour that's all. I'll meet you anywhere.'

This is incredible. I spent a year of my life trying to get him off a sofa or a barstool and now he's practically begging to go to the ends of the Earth just to talk to me.

'OK,' says a voice. It is my voice.

I can't believe I'm agreeing to this.

'OK. I'll meet you. Saturday. At one.'

'Where?'

I try and think of somewhere neutral. Somewhere anonymous. 'All Bar One in Soho.'

We'd been there before. In our first month as a couple. Back when we got out of Rob's flat or the pub.

'Right,' he says, visibly buoyed up. 'Saturday. One o'clock.'

'Just to talk.'

'Yeah. Sure. Just to talk.'

'I'd better go back inside.'

He looks at the door to James's apartmnent as if it was the source of all the world's evil.

'OK,' he says.

I reach over and press for the lift. The doors open and Rob reluctantly steps inside.

'See you Saturday,' he says.

'Yes. See you.'

I watch Rob disappear behind the lift doors and feel myself sinking with the numbers in the display, as my ex heads down to the car park.

20. 19. 18. 17 . . .

What was I thinking?

Why on earth did I agree to meet him?

OK, so I know why I agreed to meet him. To get him to leave. To stop those Bambi eyes. To hear the 'something' he has to tell me.

I go back inside the apartment.

'Hi,' I say, trying to deflect the questions in James's stare. 'Sorry about that.'

'Don't worry, we've all got our skeletons . . . It's lucky I'm not the insecure type,' he smiles, or half-smiles. The smile of a liar . . . but my perfect man doesn't lie.

'Yes,' I say.

'He's not stalking you is he?' he says, with unconvincing flippancy, as he pours me another glass of red wine.

'No,' I say. 'He's just, I don't know, I just think he finds it hard me being with someone else when he's still stuck on his own. But don't worry. I told him we're scientifically incompatible and he took it well. I don't think I'll be seeing him again any time soon.'

I take my wine, and swallow the taste of lies out of my mouth.

The empty chair

It's Saturday.

It's one o clock.

And here I am, sitting in All Bar One, by the window.

I sip my drink. White wine. Well, white wine vinegar would probably be a more accurate description.

I can't believe I'm doing this. But then, maybe Rob does deserve some kind of explanation. After all, it was kind of messy when we finished. I never gave him my reasons. Well, not all of them anyway. If I can properly explain to Rob the scientific fact of our incompatibility then maybe he will understand. He will be able to move on and find someone else, like I have.

For a few seconds I try to imagine exactly who Rob's perfect partner would be. Someone who is quite happy going to the pub every night, listening contentedly to his dreams of setting up his own business while he spends all his non-pub time in front of his PlayStation. Someone who doesn't have parents, or a birthday, who never has to fly on a plane, who can reach a climax within one minute and thirty-five seconds, who is quite happy to swap meaningful fore-play for five minutes of breast massage and nipple licking.

I look around the bar for any suitable candidates. That Italian student behind the bar? Those two giggling blondes eating the potato wedges?

Nah.

It's impossible imagining any woman in their right mind choosing Rob as their ideal partner.

Here he comes now. Walking through the–

No. It's another fat bloke with a shirt that hasn't been ironed this millennium.

I look at my watch. 1.15. I look at the empty chair opposite me.

Where the hell is he?

'You would like another drink?' the Italian girl asks, as she takes my glass.

'Er, yes please. The same again.'

My drink arrives. Rob doesn't.

I'm starting to look majorly stood up.

1.22.

I get my mobile out and phone him. After three rings it clicks over to voicemail.

'Rob? It's me. Ella. Where are you?'

I try his home number and get his answer machine. 'Hi this is Rob,' it says, in Rob's usual lethargic tone. 'Leave a message if you want.'

'Rob, it's nearly half past one. I've been in All Bar One for nearly half an hour. Was this all a big prac-tical joke? If it was it's not that funny. Rob? Are you there? Rob?'

1.25.

The two blondes have finished their potato wedges and now seem to be giggling at me.

106

1.27.

This is unbelievable. He nearly breaks his neck trying to ruin my evening with James because he's apparently so desperate to talk to me and tell me something and when I agree to meet him on neutral ground he doesn't show.

1.28.

I finish my drink and send him a text message.

where R U?

1.31.

I wait five more minutes before I remember exactly why I dumped him in the first place.

1.36.

The Italian girl comes back. 'You would like the same wine again?'

'No,' I tell her. 'I'm finished.'

I give her a ten-pound note, which just about covers the two glasses of vinegar, and leave.

As soon as I am out of the door, I phone the man I know would never let me down like this.

My perfect man will never stand me up . . .

'Hello?' His perfect voice.

'James, it's me. Ella.'

'Oh Ella, hi,' he says.

'I just wondered if I could come round and see you.'

'Now?' he sounds panicked.

'Well, if it's okay. I mean, if you're not–'

'No, now's fine,' he says, sounding less panicked. 'Now's great. I'd love to see you. In fact, I was just thinking about you.'

'Great.'

'Where are you now?'

'Soho. I did some window shopping in Covent Garden and stopped for a drink. I'm heading for the tube. I'll be there in about twenty minutes.'

'Perfect,' he says.

'See you.'

'Yes, see you.'

Perfect sex

He opens the door, and stands there looking more gorgeous than ever.

His hair is scruffy and towel-dried, fresh from the shower. He's wearing neat-fitting jeans, a tight black T-shirt, and no shoes. His arms are pumped from a workout.

He tries to speak: 'Hi, I've just–'

My lips swallow his words, as I kiss him and push him back into the apartment.

I've been stupid. Whatever was holding me back before?

He shuts the door without breaking the kiss. My hands head inside his T-shirt, greedily charting their way over his chiseled physique.

He unbuttons my shirt, the kiss still alive – getting more alive with every lust-fueled second.

We only break for a moment, when he decides to lift me up and carry me into the bedroom. If his arms are struggling with the weight, his face is kind enough not to show it.

I land on the bed and he rises over me.

'Lets get naked,' he says, playfully.

I happily oblige. After all, this is my captain speaking.

He leaves the blinds open, but I don't care. We're twenty storeys up, after all. Out of view of everyone, except any passing police helicopters or curious sparrows.

It's been a while since I've had sex. Even longer since I've had it in daylight – or any kind of light, now I come to think about it.

He peels back the sheets and we slide under the crisp Egyptian cotton. I tingle as I feel his smooth skin next to mine.

It feels so natural. Every kiss, every touch, every taste feels new and familiar all at once, as though we have been together in some former lifetime.

'Your skin feels cold. Let me warm you up.'

'Thanks,' I tell him. 'You're very–'

My words sink into his kiss. The perfect kiss.

My hands navigate his body. Muscles flicker under his skin at my touch.

He kisses my neck, then I watch the top of his head as he goes lower and disappears under the sheets.

Lower …

Lower …

Lower …

I don't want this to stop. Ever.

Every inch of my body tickles with pleasure as I stare out of the window at the clouds, thin white scratches across the sky.

Don't stop.

'Don't stop.'

I say it aloud. I don't care. He doesn't care. I place my hands through the top of his hair, feel the smooth, soft, broad strokes of his tongue.

I bite my lip.

It is too much.

My body doesn't know how to control or contain so many sensations.

An hour ago I was sitting on my own in All Bar One, waiting for Rob to stand me up and let me down for the seven hundredth time in his life. Now, lost in unimaginable pleasure, I have well and truly come to my senses.

There is only one man in my life now. And he is the only man in the world who could make me feel like this.

He charts his way back up my body, kissing me as he rises. There is a giggly condom moment and then he is inside me, moving with the kind of smooth confidence you would expect from a man who spends his life flying people over the clouds.

I close my eyes, and dig my nails into his bum, pulling him deeper.

Deeper . . .

I open my eyes and lock his stare.

'You're beautiful,' he says. 'Beautiful.'

I try to return the compliment, but talking is no longer an option.

He rolls onto his back, and brings me onto his front. I sit, on top of him, and lift my head towards the ceiling.

There is a skylight, a small rectangle framing a slab of clear, cloudless blue.

I feel sexy and strangely powerful all at once as we climax together, as the pleasure overwhelms us, before escaping our bodies.

I fall onto him, feel his rapid breath and heartbeat, enjoy the stickiness of our skin.

After a long, breathless silence he kisses my forehead. 'What better way to spend a Saturday afternoon?'

I smile and say nothing, because nothing needs to be said.

The friend test

My answer to question fifty-five.

My perfect man will be able to get on with my friends ...

This is the clincher, really.

I know what magazines say. All those articles about how boyfriends and girly friends shouldn't mix. But I'm sorry, it's hard enough balancing a work life and a home life without having to split yourself between a friend life and a boyfriend life.

And, so far, James is definitely passing the test.

Last night: After he'd managed to turn me into strawberry jelly after a second hour-long sex marathon, he stroked my hair in bed and said: 'This is it isn't it ... we're an item now aren't we?'

'Yes,' I said. 'I hope so.'

'So when am I going to meet your friends?'

'My friends?' I asked, in a post-coital daze, as I drew invisible circles on his chest.

'Yes. I want to meet them. I want to get to know the whole you.'

This caught me completely off-guard.

You see, I didn't think men could say those things.

I thought it wasn't programmed into their DNA, not unless they were thinking of group sex possibilities.

'Why?' I ask him.

'Ella, don't be so suspicious,' he tells me, as if reading my mind. 'I'm a one woman man now. You know, some men are capable of talking to women without imagining what they'd look like having an orgasm.'

'I never said anything about imagining a woman having an orgasm,' I said.

'Oh,' he said quickly, checking himself. 'Oh, I know. I know you didn't. It's just there are men like that, and I'm not one of them.'

'I know you're not.'

I remember what Rob used to be like. His allergy to meeting my friends was only marginally less severe than his allergy to meeting my parents. He always had something of more pressing importance to do. Like scratch his balls or play the new version of Grand Theft Auto or, on really busy nights, scratch his balls while playing the new version of Grand Theft Auto.

And then, when Rob did eventually meet my friends (in the pub, I hasten to add – beer had to be involved, needless to say) he spent the entire time gazing into the dark valley of Maddie's cleavage. Oh no, actually I'm wrong. He averted his gaze to look at Pip's tight Tae-Bo buttocks when she went to the bar to order her fifth Slimline Tonic.

Not that I ever had to worry too much about Rob's fidelity.

There was only ever one Other Woman in Rob's life. The girl with the golden touch. A Belgian called Stella. Surname: Artois. She got him drunk every night and gave him bad gas.

Anyway, where was I?

That's right. In bed with James. Yesterday.

'So,' he said, 'when can I meet them? When can I spend an evening at your place?'

Er ...

I panicked.

It wasn't that I was worried about him meeting Pip and Maddie. After all, I'm as proud of them as I am of James. It's just that I suddenly realised James hasn't seen the inside of our apartment.

And our apartment, compared to James's swank palace, leaves a lot to be desired. For a start, there's the space problem. We rent what has to be one of the most deluxe and expensive shoeboxes in the whole of South London. Every time Pip does a workout we lose another £50 on our deposit as she puts her foot through something or smashes another Ikea vase.

Then there's the carpet, and the settee, and the wall-paper, and the strange smell of cabbage, and the wannabe Jimi Hendrix who lives upstairs, and the kitchen, and the brown cupboards, and the hall with the mystery bike always in it, and the bars on the back windows, and the kettle, and the bed, and the embar-rassing poster of lots of cocks on Maddie's door that says NATIONAL PENIS GALLERY, and the even more embarrassing poster of lots of cocks on Pip's door that says MAROON 5, and the soggy walls, and the twelve-year-old gangsters who loiter outside the off-licence at the end of our street, and the sense of total and near-apocalyptic despair that sinks in after five minutes in the darkest living room this side of the Death Star.

But hey, apart from that it's great.

'Er ... I don't know,' I told him, 'er ... when do you want to meet them?'

I was going to suggest going to the pub, but even a cabbage-smelling shoebox is better than the bear pits that double as the public houses of Tooting.

'What about tomorrow?' he asked me.

'What about it?'

'I could come around tomorrow evening.'

'Tomorrow evening?' I tapped my brain's excuse bank but realised I'd used them all up after getting out of going to that arty Dutch movie he wants to go and see (my answer to question twelve: *My perfect man will be interested in international culture, especially obscure European arthouse movies which are called things like* My Life As an Apple, *and which bore me into a state of unconsciousness but which I know I should like* – or something). 'Er ... yeah ... why not? Tomorrow evening's great.'

Fast-forward twenty hours and I am here, briefing Maddie and Pip on how to behave.

'No burping,' I tell Maddie. 'It's not very lady-like.'

This is her new thing. Musical burps. It's not very attractive.

'And no third degree,' I warn Pip.

You see, Pip has man issues. You only have to walk into her room and see the dart-board covered with pictures of her ex – a dickhead called Greg who dumped her because she had a flabby backside – to realise that. The night he dumped her she cut out a picture of his face and stuck it on an Action Man to make a voodoo doll of him. Which was fine, although she kept complaining there were no balls for her to do some real damage.

For the record, since I have known her, Pip's backside has never been the remotest bit flabby. But it still

116

hasn't stopped her working out like a psycho every single morning since he dumped her. And now she wants as little to do with men as possible. She is, she has decided, a 'manorexic' and wants only the smallest portions of male company.

James's car pulls up.

Tooting's hardest twelve-year-old gangsters gather around it, like bees to honey.

He gets out.

Locks it. Switches on the state-of-art alarm system that Tooting's finest will find harder to crack than *The Da Vinci* code.

'God, I can't remember him being *that* gorgeous,' says Maddie, as he walks to the door. 'You lucky cow.'

Maddie's hamster story (and other embarrassing moments)

Knock knock.

I go and get the door.

'Hi, beautiful,' he says, kissing me on the lips.

'Hi.'

He holds out his hand and mimes the shakes.

'Come on through,' I tell him. 'The jury's waiting.'

'Very funny,' he says.

'Oh, and er mind the bicycle.'

'Who's is it?'

'Haven't a clue. It's been there since we moved in.'

I open the door to our flat and Maddie is there waiting for him, cleavage and big smile at the ready.

'Hello,' she says, almost leaking excitement. 'I'm Mad.'

'Oh.'

'I mean, that's my name,' she prattles. 'Mad. Mads. Maddie. Madeleine. Mad. And sometimes I am Mad as well. I mean not hearing-voices-of-dead-aliens mad ... I'm not on tablets or anything ... well, I was when I a teenager ... after Danny Zuco died ...'

'Who was Danny Zuco?'

Uh-oh.

We've lost her.

'My hamster. I left the cage door open. He walked out and walked over the desk ... and my desk was by the window ... and ... and ... and it was summer ... a hot summer ... my aunt had left the window open and he ... he ... I always thought it was ... everyone said it was an accident but I always thought it was ... you know ... that he'd had enough ... of the cage ... of the wheel ... of the dry flaky food ... of me ...'

Oh dear. This isn't good. She is nearly crying.

She hasn't brought up the hamster story for three years.

Maddie stares forlornly at the carpet, as memories of Danny Zuco scamper through her mind. She pulls it together, just in time.

'Sorry,' she says.

'It's fine,' he assures her. 'I remember when my dog got run over. I still get flashbacks.'

I decide to move things on. 'Right ... and this is Pip ...'

I've already warned him about Pip. I told him she can be kind of intense.

'Hi Pip,' he says. 'Heard a lot about you.'

He smiles at Pip and she sort-of-smiles back. I guide James to the sofa and sit down next to him.

He sniffs up. 'Is that cabbage?'

'It's just our flat ... it always smells like that,' Maddie tells him. 'There's a phantom cabbage-cooker in the kitchen.'

I notice that Pip is giving James the laser-eye treatment.

119

'You're an airline pilot, aren't you?' she asks him, with a deadpan expression.

'Yes ... yes, I am.'

'You must spend a lot of time away.'

James nods. 'Quite a bit ... yes.'

'You must get lonely.'

'Er ...' James starts to wonder where this is going.

'It must be hard to remember your responsibilities.'

'Er ... not really.'

'Good,' Pip says. 'Because a lot of men would. A lot of men might lose track of what was important. They might do something stupid.'

Oh God.

She's doing the kind of face that makes Robert De Niro in *Taxi Driver* look positively cuddly.

'James won't do anything stupid,' I assure her, and offer a giggle to lighten the atmosphere.

'No,' says the psycho who has now taken over Pip's body. 'No, I can see that ... But if he was the type to do something stupid, it wouldn't just be his heart that would be broken. I'd see to that.'

'Right,' James says. 'That's ... er ... comforting.'

'Would you like anything to drink?' Maddie asks him, doing her best impression of Joan Cusack in *Working Girl* (her third favourite film ever – after *When Harry Met Sally* and, er, *Babe: Pig in the City*). 'Coffee? Tea? Me?'

'I wouldn't mind a cup of tea,' he asks her. And, while he is looking at Maddie, I gesture wildly at Pip for her to chill out. Then, when Pip's looking back down at her work, I turn to James.

'I'm sorry,' I whisper.

'They're great,' he mouths back.
And, like a nutcase, he genuinely seems to mean it.
Ah well, that's my perfect man for you.

The Channel Four News

Scared of any further conversation, I switch on the TV and flick through the channels.

When I reach Channel Four I nearly jump out of my skin.

Right there, on the screen, is Dr Ludwig Fischer.

'Oh my God ... I know him ...'

'Oh yes, look. It's that Swiss doctor,' says James. 'From the love lab.'

' ... all this time human beings have been tormenting themselves about love and in the future there shall be no need ... there will be no misery ... no unrequited love ... my apologies to Mister William Shakespeare ... and with the right technology we are able to guarantee that two people will be right for each other ... it is simple genetics.'

'He seems like a nutter,' Maddie says. The words 'pot' and 'kettle' inevitably spring to mind.

Then the TV cuts from Dr Fischer's love lab to the Channel Four News studio, where Jon Snow is interviewing Dr Lara Stein.

'Oh my God!' I yelp.

'It's Dr Lara,' says James.

'She looks like she's just stepped out of *Dynasty*,' says Maddie.

Jon Snow leans back in his chair.

'Simple genetics? But, if I can put this question to you now Dr Stein, can there really be such a thing as a simple genetic solution to something as abstract as love? I appreciate that you have invested millions in this technology, but are we really able to understand exactly what attracts people together?'

'Yes,' says Dr Lara, her usual vision of big hair, big pearls and big teeth. 'Yes. Absolutely. You may find it hard to believe Jon, but we are animals just like any other. We are sensual creatures in every sense – sorry – of the word. And if we can understand how our senses work, and how our brain perceives things, we can also understand love.'

'Oh my God,' says Maddie. 'Have you actually met her?'

'Yes.'

She looks star-struck. 'Wow.'

Jon Snow moves on to another question. 'All right, but even if we are to accept the scientific methods involved, that leaves us with another issue. You aren't a social philanthropist doing this for the good of the public's health, are you? You are a business woman, an entrepreneur, and people will have to pay extreme sums to become members of this service, won't they?'

Dr Lara smiles, to reveal a million pounds worth of cosmetic dentistry.

'You've read Darwin, haven't you Jon?'

'Er ... yes, but I don't quite see what that has to do with ...'

'Well then, you'll understand what I mean when I

123

say that love involves a process of natural selection. It isn't a fair or democratic or equal system. It's survival of the fittest. And, in a materialistic society, this often translates as survival of the wealthiest. But, I must say, that it is only the women who will pay for this service. To offer the widest pool possible, we have made it free for men to join. There are obvious reasons for this, of course?'

Jon Snow raises his eyebrows. 'Such as?'

'Well, only a man could ask that question, Jon,' Dr Lara says, with an accommodating smile.'Every woman knows that the ratio of suitable women to suitable men is weighed heavily against their favour.'

Pip snorts. 'She's not wrong there.'

Jon Snow looks perplexed. 'So only rich women will be able to find true love?'

Dr Lara clutches her white pearls and shines her pearly whites. 'With one exception, Jon.'

'Oh yes, this is the South London schoolteacher isn't it? Ella Holt?'

'Aaaaaagh,' squeals Maddie, pointing to footage of me at the press conference. 'It's you!!!'

She's right.

It is.

Oh my God.

I'm on telly.

The memory appears on the screen.

The ginger journalist: 'How do you feel about being a human guinea pig?'

The feeble reply: 'I feel great. I'm really happy to . . . be a part of this.'

'And are you worried that your perfect man might fail to meet your expectations? I mean, if it doesn't work out, will you give up on dating all together?'

'Oh God, look at me,' I say, to James and Maddie and Pip. 'I look like a frightened . .'

I'm interrupted by myself. The me on TV.

'Erm ... I ... don't ... I ...'

Then it cuts to Dr Lara, at the same press conference. 'With the utmost respect, that is an irrelevant question. The Perfect Agency doesn't have "perfect" in its name for no reason. You can rest assured this will be one fairytale with a happy ending.'

Back to the studio, and Dr Lara tells Jon Snow: 'There she is. There's our Cinderella, who I am sure is right now getting on very well with her Prince Charming.'

'Well,' says Jon, with a coy smile on his face as he looks straight to camera. 'There you have it. It looks like the Beatles were wrong. Can't buy me love? Not for much longer ... Now over to Samira for a round-up of our main headlines ...'

'You're famous!' says Maddie.

'Oh God!' I say. 'I was dreadful. I looked so pale. Do I look that pale normally?'

'You looked great,' lies Maddie.

Pip turns to me and curls her lip in wry amusement. 'So if you're Cinderella, and he's Prince Charming, what does that make me and Maddie?'

Maddie laughs. 'The two ugly sisters!'

A phonecall

Moments later, the phone rings.

Maddie gets it. 'Ella ... it's your mum.'

Uh-oh.

'Mum?' I stand up, leaving James to fend for himself on the sofa, as I take the phone into my bedroom.

She sounds cross. 'You were on the telly.'

'I know.'

'Ella ... what on earth were you doing on the telly? Your dad's nearly having a heart attack. He's had to take his tablets.'

'Yes. I know. But I didn't know I was going to be on the telly. If I'd have known I was going to be on TV I'd have told you.'

As you might be guessing right now, I haven't told my parents about the Perfect Agency. Or about James, for that matter. I was going to, it's just I've been waiting for the right moment. You see, my mum and dad always have a way of pouring water over every bit of good news. If there's a silver lining, they'll sure as hell be talking about the cloud.

And especially when it comes to my love life.

Not that it's all their fault.

I mean, after hyping up Rob to them for months, the stupid slob went and stood them up. Now they refuse to believe anything I say on the man front.

'Ella, what were you doing in that place? With all those photographers? We switched it on and thought you'd done something wrong. We thought you were in all sorts of trouble ... with the police. We thought you'd done something stupid.'

'Like what? Become a serial killer?'

She ignores my question and bulldozes on. 'Ella, what on earth have you got yourself involved in?'

'It's just this thing. This dating agency. It was on telly because it uses science ... genetics ... to match people together. And I'm doing their free trial.'

She tuts. Then scowls. Then tuts again. 'I could see that for myself. And so could half the blooming country!'

I'm missing something. 'So?'

'Well, it makes you look ridiculous. And us. What do you think Graham and Carole will say?'

Graham and Carole are Mum and Dad's next-door neighbours, and the world authority on everything as far as my parents are concerned. Caravans. Asylum seekers. The secret mysteries of the universe.

'I doubt that they saw it,' I say. 'But if they did, I don't have a clue what Graham and Carole would say. And, to be honest, I don't really care.'

'I can see that.'

'What's that supposed to mean?'

She makes more blustery sounds, then says: 'Well, you obviously don't care what people think of you, making yourself look cheap and desperate like that.'

127

'Cheap and desperate? Mum!'

'We didn't raise you like that.'

'Like *what?*'

She thinks twice about answering, and goes for another question instead.

'Why do you have to do it? You're a pretty girl.'

'*Mum.*'

'Me and your dad never had to do anything like that.'

No, I think to myself. *And what a blissful relationship that turned out to be.*

'Mum, I didn't *have* to do it. I wanted to. And the only reason I didn't tell you is because I knew how you'd both react.'

I can hear my dad clanking away in the kitchen in the background, in disgust.

'What's the matter with dad,' I ask Mum.

'He's upset.'

'Upset? Why?'

'He wants you to be happy.'

'*I am* happy.'

'We worry about you, love. That's all.'

Worry about Graham and Carole more like.

'Well, don't,' I tell her. 'There's nothing to worry about.'

'Men don't like women if they act desperate. You'll never find a man that way ...'

I sigh. 'I *have* found a man. And he does like me.'

'Since when? Why didn't you tell us?'

I pretend her question is rhetorical. 'He's called James. He's an airline pilot. And he's perfect for me.'

Mum's voice changes. 'An airline pilot?'

'Yes.'

'What? He flies planes?'

'Er ... yes he does ... That is quite an essential part of an airline pilot's job description.'

She tells my dad.

'She's met a man .. . an airline pilot.'

My dad falls silent in the background. I imagine him thinking that might be something to tell Graham: an airline pilot.

'Oh,' says my mum, suddenly forgetting that her cheap and desperate daughter has just embarrassed generations of the Holt family on national TV. 'When can we meet him?'

The I-love-you night

Later on, Boring Steve comes around to see Maddie. This has now become a regular occurrence. Ever since the speed dating night Maddie's been shagging the poor lad senseless on a daily basis. I think it must be getting pretty serious.

He sits on the sofa and asks James five-hundred questions about the computer technology and radar systems used on aeroplanes.

Pip, out of depth in coupledom, disappears into her room to mark work and listen to Maroon 5, and so me and Maddie meet in the kitchen for the requisite what-do-you-think-of-my-man conversation.

'Oh he's fantastic,' Maddie assures me. 'So what's he like?'

'Like?'

'In *bed,*' she says, as if I was stupid.

'Erm ... nice,' I say, coyly.

She puts the palms of her hands together, then moves them wider apart to indicate the possible length of, er, something. 'Tell me when to stop,' she says.

I slap her shoulder. 'Shut up you rude thing.'

'I'm only joking,' she says, then nods her head to

the two men talking radars in the living room. 'But Steve's about there,' she says, her palms roughly seven inches apart.

'That's ... erm ... useful to know Maddie. Thanks.'

'And he can go for hours.'

'I know,' I tell her. 'You're in the next room. I'm thinking of coating the walls with eggboxes.'

'Eggboxes?'

'They're soundproof.'

Her hand covers her mouth. 'Oh ... are we really that loud?'

I nod, solemnly. 'You can probably hear it in Clapham. No, I'm only joking. It's not that bad.'

Two hours later, I am eating my words. And I wouldn't like to hazard a guess at what Maddie's eating.

'Oh that's good, that's good.'

That was Steve. His voice (and only his *voice* thankfully) is coming through the wall, as Maddie pleasures him in some unseen way.

I am lying in my grotty bed, apologising to James. I think about how different it is at his flat. With the sky-high balcony, and the view, and the soundproof walls, and the bed the size of my entire room.

'Don't worry,' he says, with his arm around me.

'James ...'

'Yes?'

I hesitate, before asking, 'What do you see in me? I mean, I know we're the perfect match and everything, and I know you're right for me, I just wondered what on earth someone like you sees in someone like me.'

He looks at me with sweet, puzzled eyes and asks,

131

'What are you talking about?'

'Well, you're rich and gorgeous and you've seen the world ... and, well, I'm poor and not-gorgeous and I've seen Disneyworld when I was about eight, and I've been to Spain a few times, but other than that I've been nowhere and ... and ... I just don't understand why you would fancy me?'

He smiles as if I am being ridiculous, as if the answer speaks for itself (which it doesn't, or I wouldn't be asking).

He is about to tell me when Steve and Maddie's bed starts banging against the wall like a battering-ram.

'More!' squeals Maddie. 'More! More! More!'

'Ella,' he says, trying to ignore the sounds of shagging next door. 'It may sound strange to you, but I don't measure a woman's attractiveness in wealth or air-miles ... and as for you saying you're not gorgeous ... well, that's just a–'

His mobile goes.

His hand digs into his crumpled trousers, lying on the floor and he looks at the screen. I can't see the name of whoever is calling him but I can see pain in his eyes as they reflect the lit-up LED display.

'Who is it?' I ask him.

He switches off his phone. 'No one.'

Maddie starts squealing her way to orgasm in the next room. 'Oh ... oh ... oh ...' Each oh getting higher and higher until she can almost smash a window.

James goes to kiss me, but the moment's been lost. There's nothing less sexy than hearing other people having sex, and I've got no intention of playing Battle of the Orgasms with Maddie. Because she'd win, hands down. Or hands handcuffed to the bedposts. Whatever.

I lie with my head on his chest as he plays with my hair.

'So,' I ask him, 'you were saying?'

'About what?'

'About what you see in me.'

'Oh ... he says, his voice still tight. 'Yes. Right, well ... you *are* gorgeous and you not knowing you're gorgeous makes you even more gorgeous. And you're funny. And you're intelligent.'

He stops.

That can't be it.

'More,' I tell him. 'Give me more.'

So he carries on feeding my ego.

'Well ... you're well read ... you like books ... which is a turn-on ... you can quote Shakespeare ...'

'More!'

'You're warm ... and sensitive ... and you've got a sexy voice ... and your eyes sparkle when you smile ... and you've got the cutest button nose ... and when I'm with you ...'

He suddenly sounds shy.

' ... when I'm with you ... this sounds stupid, but when I'm with you I suddenly feel *real.*'

'Real?'

'I feel like the whole of life is an act, and half the time I am even acting to myself, and the whole world seems a fraud – including me. But when I'm with you, it pulls the covers off everything ... off me ... and in seeing who you are I can suddenly see myself. It's like my whole life has been one long escape from something ... and you're right, I have seen the world, but I've lost sight of other things in the process.' He gently taps the side of my head. 'There's a whole world locked inside here, and that's the world I want to explore now.'

133

His words heat me from inside.

I feel myself melting.

Why didn't Rob ever say anything like that?

'Ella,' James says, stroking my cheek with the back of his hand, as if I was something precious. 'Ella ... And then he says it: 'Ella, I know we haven't known each other long, but I feel so connected to you. It's like my whole life was just building up to the point we'd meet. When I signed up to the Perfect Agency I was a bit sceptical ... I did it because I sometimes find it hard to meet people ... with my job ... I never thought I was going to meet anyone like you.'

'Oh,' I say. 'That's nice.'

That's nice? That's *nice?* Bloody hell, is that the best I can do?

James carries on talking. 'I know it's early ... I know we haven't spent long together but I already feel it, when we're not together. I feel it ... like every single second not spent with you is a wasted moment – a moment we won't get back.'

His words give me goosebumps, and raise the hairs on my arm.

'Ella,' he says, looking straight into my eyes. 'Ella, I love you.'

The three words Rob could never say.

'I know it's quick ... and I don't want to scare you ... but I felt it from the first time I saw you ...'

My perfect man will believe in love at first sight ...

There is a strand of hair on my face. He strokes it back and tucks it behind my ear.

'Love isn't something that builds slowly over time,' he says. 'Love is all or nothing. It's either there or it's not, and when it happens it happens totally and I know I love you Ella. I know it.'

134

His words instantly cancel out sounds of shagging and smells of cabbage.

And I say it, for the first time: 'I love you too.'

We kiss, and hold each other tight in my tiny bed. And it feels great.

James loves me.

I love James.

Of course I do. He's my one in a million. The Prince Charming with the only glass slipper that fits.

But love is blind, and lovers cannot *see*
The pretty follies that themselves commit.

Maybe Shakespeare was right. Maybe the course of true love never did run smooth. But as I try and stop myself worrying about James's mystery caller, I decide to put my faith in science, not Shakespeare.

We kiss again.

I hold his wrist, direct his hand towards my knickers. Nothing else exists. Just me and him. We kiss deeper, longer, as if eating a sweet fruit that teases but doesn't satisfy our appetite. Every taste just makes us more hungry.

My roving hands move their way over his skin.

Behind, between, above, below.

His touch, inside.

'I love you,' I breathe the words into his ear.

'I love you.' He breathes them back, his breath sending warm tingles of pleasure to every part of me.

In the dark we could be anywhere. Anywhere other than a dingy flat in South London.

We could be in Rio.

In Buenos Aires.

In New York.

In Venice.

In Rome.

Or Paris.

I get on top, lean forward.

Kiss.

Lose my breath as I feel his body inside me.

The sweet mix of love and lust passing like electricity between us as we lose ourselves into each other.

And into the night.

The relationship fairy

There is a moment in every relationship when something switches.

You wake up in the morning and something has changed. Something magical has happened in your sleep, and you realise it with the kind of happiness you had when you were seven-years-old and discovered a tooth had turned into a silver coin.

And when I wake up, I can feel it. The switch. No longer are we just two individuals who like each other's company, and enjoy rubbing our bodies together.

No.

We are no longer a couple. We are a Couple, capital C.

Two is dissolving into one.

The need to shine and be continually impressive in his company has suddenly lifted, and I sense that from now on there will only be natural silences, not awkward ones.

I kiss his shoulder, breathe his scent.

He is still sleeping.

What time is it? Light is creeping into the room,

bringing the mirror and the chest of drawers and the whole physical world of objects back into existence.

I stare at him, in the half-light. The light that occurs somewhere between the sun and the moon.

'I love you,' I whisper into his ear.

He smiles in his sleep, in his dream.

I watch him. I lie there for an hour doing nothing, just watching. Studying his face. The soft rise and fall of his breathing. And as I watch it comes to me.

This is the man I am going to marry.

The thought arrives not as a hope or a wish or a prayer, but as an absolute certainty, like a voice from the future telling me that it will be so. It sounds stupid, but it feels like the most logical and reasonable thing in the world.

I imagine what he will look like in ten, twenty, thirty years time. He will get better with age, there's no doubt about it. He has one of those strong, classic faces that suit lines and creases.

We'll be one of those couples that age as one. You see them all the time. Men and women who have spent so long together they actually start to look like each other, the way a dog can resemble its owner.

Every smile and frown line on our faces will belong to the other person. It will be beautiful, as part of some mutual memory or just as a token of our shared existence. Maybe James will one day want me to botox away all my creases and imperfections but I doubt it.

When it happens it happens totally ...

That is what he told me last night.

And total love isn't scared of a few lines or physical imperfections.

No, we are going to grow old together, I can feel it in my bones.

He wakes. His eyes flicker and hatch, like something coming out of an egg.

I worry for a second that I have been deluding myself. Maybe we're still a lower-case couple, not a Couple.

But my worry eases as soon as he opens his mouth.

'Morning,' he says, puckering up for a kiss.

I kiss him and stroke his hair.

'You've got nice friends,' he says, with still-sleepy eyes.

'Thanks.'

'Now it's time for your parents.'

'What?'

'I've met your friends. So when can I meet your parents?'

I smile. The relationship fairy has been busy under his pillow as well.

'Why?' I ask him.

'I want to know everything about you. And I want to meet everyone who is important to you. I assume your parents are on that list somewhere.'

'Yes,' I say. 'They're on there ... but you don't have to meet them just yet.'

I should be dreading it. After all, the last thing I want is for James to think I'm going to turn out like mum. But it's weird – I'm not scared at all. Suddenly, James meeting my parents makes perfect sense. Even yesterday, the idea would have probably terrified me, but that was before the relationship fairy switched the switch. Now I no longer feel I am auditioning for his love, there is nothing to fear.

'I want to meet them,' he says. 'What about the weekend after next? We could drive up to Leeds and see them.'

'Well, I'd have to ring them and check that they

aren't busy but as they haven't had a busy weekend since nineteen-eighty-three I'd imagine it will be fine. So long as you're sure.'

'Sure I'm sure,' he says, propping himself up on the mattress with his elbow.

'We're a Couple now.'

'Capital C or lower-case c?'

'Capital C, of course.'

'Good,' I say. 'Just checking.'

And the relationship fairy works her invisible magic for the next fortnight, turning us into the kind of Couple that inspires psychopathic side-glances from single people.

I've always wanted to be one of those Couples. You know the ones. That seem to walk around with a kind of glow, and who seem to be so genuinely happy in each other's company.

And that is us. At the cinema. Hand-in-hand walking around the park. In bed. We are becoming the kind of Couple I always hated . . . and, I have to say, it feels great.

Every minute we are together helps cement our Couple status. We are now known, officially, as Ella and James, like Ella-and-James is one person and I am half of that person, as if people realise something is missing when I am on my own.

This is how it's always going to be, I tell myself. Me and him. Him and me.

And I catch myself saying it in my head, over and over.

Ella-and-James. Ella-and-James. Ella-and-James.

The parent test

I spend the five hours on the motorway up to Leeds briefing James about my parents.

'My mum and dad can be a bit ... er, ...' I search my brain for the right word '... *protective* over me.'

'Protective? Well, that's what parents are for isn't it?'

He doesn't get it. 'Yes, I know. It's just that *my* mum can be a bit intense.'

'Intense?'

'Be prepared for questions.'

He takes his eye off the road. 'What kind of questions?'

'Oh, you know. Have you been married? Have you got a criminal record? Have you ever had thoughts of a sexual nature in relation to my daughter? That sort of thing.'

'I might get stuck on that last one.'

'My mum still thinks I'm fifteen years old. She finds it hard ... to let go.'

'And your dad?'

'He's a bit better. I mean, he still thinks I'm fifteen, but he's a bit less intense on the Jeremy

Paxman routine. He's just a bit of a worrier. He hates me living in London. He says it's too dirty. I think if he could have his way he'd roll me up in bubble wrap and lock me in the attic. But he keeps quiet most of the time. Mind you, he can't get a word in edgeways with mum rabbiting on. Do you know what they got me for my last birthday?'

'Tell me.'

'A doll. A *doll!* I mean, it was a nice doll, as dolls go. But still, it's not what you expect for your twenty-ninth birthday, is it?'

'They sound sweet.'

I nod. 'So are jelly babies. But you can have too much.'

'I love jelly babies.'

'You don't strike me as a jelly babies person.'

'I'm full of surprises.'

'Anyway, all I'm saying is be prepared.'

'OK, OK. I'll be prepared.'

My mum is at the door, while my dad is at the window, parting the blinds.

I feel their stares on us as we open the doors. My dad will already be pricing up James's car, while my mum will be watching the scene through the neighbours' eyes, checking that James meets the high behavioural standards and oppressive dress code of Shakespeare Drive.

It's always weird, coming back home. I spent eighteen years under that roof, with these two people who fed me and raised me and changed my nappies (well, OK, it was only one person who did all that).

'Hello love,' it's my mum, clenching the world between her hands as she walks up to greet us.

142

James takes the suitcase out of the boot and places it on the pavement. He flashes the smile. Makes the eyes. 'Mrs Holt. Hello, I'm James. So pleased to meet you.'

'Oh hello,' my mum says, flush-cheeked. My dad is behind her. He walks over, shakes James's hand.

The firm handshake test.

'Dad, this is James.'

'Mr Holt,' says James.

My dad has temporarily lost the ability to speak. His mouth wobbles, but nothing comes out.

'Hello,' he manages eventually. 'I'm Ella's father.'

Perhaps he fancies him.

(When I was a teenager I was convinced my dad was gay. It would certainly explain a few things. Like the Shirley Bassey/Elton John/Anastasia axis within his CD collection. Like the immaculate iron-line and pleats in his trousers. Like the love of dusting. And alphabetical ordering – CDS, DVDs, cook books, aftershaves, you name it.)

We go inside, into the house. To James, it is just like walking into any other identikit 1970s suburban semi, complete with white walls, naff carpet, and that waiting-to-grow-old-and-die kind of feel.

But for me, every sight is a heavy cocktail of memories. It's less like walking into a house, and more like walking into a museum of my childhood.

Nothing has changed. It's like time froze when I left for teacher training college. Like my mum and dad don't want to accept that I no longer live here, as if putting some new wallpaper up or repainting the place would be some kind of betrayal.

Not that it looks tatty. Far from it. Dust doesn't stand a chance when my dad's around. His attitude towards cleanliness makes Howard Hughes look positively laid back.

And there is one change, at least. The beige three-piece suite in the living-room has been replaced by, well, a beige three-piece suite. Only this one has got a bit of floral embroidery on it and, as it's under a year old, Mum and Dad still haven't taken the clear plastic cover off.

James spots the neat row of shoes and slippers by the front door, and quickly unlaces his size elevens and parks them alongside.

'Right, shall I take this upstairs?' he asks my dad, with a nod down to our suitcase.

'Yes,' my mum says, answering on Dad's behalf. 'Ella's room is the first on the right.'

I am in it only five days a year, but to my mum it will always be 'Ella's room'.

James pads up the stairs in his socks, lugging the suitcase with him.

My mum lifts up her shoulders and says in a whisper, 'By love, he's smashing.'

My dad looks out to the car and says, 'Must have cost a pretty penny. By, Graham and Carole will think we've gone up in the world with that parked outside.'

Graham and Carole live next-door, and provide my dad with a handy yardstick by which he can measure his own wealth and happiness.

'Mind you,' he says, sadness falling over his features. 'They won't see it will they? They're off on that Mediterranean Cruise.'

'So James, Ella tells me you're a pilot,' my mum says, an hour after we arrive, as we are sitting in the living room.

144

'Yes,' James says. 'Yes, I am.'

Mum looks out of the window, at my dad mowing the front lawn. 'I always said your dad would make a good pilot.'

Did she? When? I remember her saying he would make a good policeman, but never a good pilot. 'Why?' I say, reverting back to my sixteen-year-old self.

'He's a good driver. I mean, I'm sure driving a car is very different to flying a plane, but look how neatly he's cutting the grass,' mum says, with an assuming look to James. 'He's a very safe pair of hands.'

I look out at dad sliding the Flymo from side to side, and try to work out the connection between mowing a patch of grass and international air travel.

'Yes,' says James before sipping his tea. 'A safe pair of hands is certainly important.'

'It's so glamorous, isn't it? An airline pilot.'

'Well, the reality's not always so exciting,' says James.

'Oh?' my mum raises her eyebrows and tilts her head and hangs on his every word.

'I mainly do long-haul flights. So that means spending very long hours sitting in a flight deck, which is a very confined space. And then there's the jet-lag.'

'Oh I get jet-lag,' my mum says. 'I got it when we went to Florida when Ella was smaller. We took her to Disney World. She cried when she saw Donald Duck, didn't you love. I said to her "It's only Donald Duck", but she wasn't having it. Took her for the best day of her life and spent the whole time hiding in my skirt.'

If it was possible to kill someone of embarrassment, my mum would be a convicted murderer by now.

'Donald Duck *is* pretty scary,' James says, smiling at me.

'She liked Snow White though. You liked Snow White, didn't you Ella? Didn't you'

'Yes mum,' I say, 'I liked Snow White.'

The smiling maniacs

An hour of humiliation later and I've got a headache.

Maybe the wine is too much. Or maybe I can't take much more of my mum and dad's James-worship.

Don't get me wrong. I'm glad they like him – of course I am. It's just that there's approval and there's approval. I've never seen my dad like this. In James's presence he seems to be too awestruck to speak.

'This lasagne is really good, Mrs Holt,' James says. 'I can see where Ella gets her culinary skills from.'

What culinary skills? The most I've ever cooked him was two slices of toast and marmite. And even then I managed to turn the toast into charcoal.

But I guess he knows his audience. He senses that my mum isn't a hardline feminist who might take offence at the idea of her daughter cooking for her man. Indeed, quite the opposite.

'Oh, I'm glad you like it. Yes, I taught Ella everything she knows. We used to make flapjacks together didn't we?'

I shrug. 'Did we?'

'You probably can't remember. It was before you went

to school. You made a mess of the whole kitchen!'

'Awwww,' says James.

'She was always such a messy thing, wasn't she Peter?'

My dad nods, and looks at me for about five minutes, before making his first contribution to the conversation, 'Oh ay, she was a messy thing all right.'

James elbows me. 'You messy girl.'

My headache is getting worse, moving up the headache career ladder to become a fully qualified migraine, complete with blurred vision and that nice needle sticking through the eye sensation.

'Erm, I've got a bit of a headache,' I tell them.

'Are you all right?' James asks me, his face etched with the kind of concern you'd expect if you'd just told him you've got six days to live.

'Yes. I'm fine. I just think I'll go upstairs and have a bit of a lie down for an hour. I'm sorry to leave you.' That last bit is directed at James, but he seems to be genuinely unfazed at the idea of spending an hour in my mum and dad's company. In fact, for some strange reason he seems to be looking forward to it.

'Right then,' I say. 'See you in a bit.'

Oh no.

I sense it as I walk in the room.

Something has definitely happened. They are all sitting there, smiling up at me like maniacs.

Either James has spiked my mum and dad's cups of tea with some happy pills or I'm the one who is tripping.

'Hiya,' James says.

'Hello,' my mum and dad chime in unison.

'Er, hello,' I say. 'All right?'

'Oh yes,' my mum says. 'We're all right. We're all right aren't we, Peter?'

'Yes, we're all right.'

My mum turns to James. 'We're all right aren't we, James?'

'Yes, Kathleen, we're very much all right.'

And then my mum and dad burst out laughing, as if auditioning for My Wacko Parents Flew Over the Cuckoo's Nest.

'We're just watching the TV.'

'*Who wants to be a Millionaire*,' adds my dad, helpfully.

'And that's why you're all smiling?'

'It's the best thing on the telly,' says mum, her head about to burst with something.

'What's going on?'

James looks at me and says, 'I told them about next weekend?'

'Next weekend?'

'About what we're going to do.'

He winks at my mum.

My headache is already coming back. 'What we're going to do?' I ask.

'We're going to Rome.'

'What?'

'I wangled us free flights. With the airline.'

'Rome?'

My headache disappears. Rome. *Rome!*

'Yes,' he says. 'I've booked the hotel and everything.'

I still have a feeling that there's something else the three of them aren't telling me. Something contained

149

within the wink. But for the moment, I don't care. I'm going to Rome! The eternal city. The closest Rob ever got to surprising me with a trip to Rome was when he ordered me an extra garlic bread from De Niro's Pizzeria and Takeaway (slogan: You ring-a, De Niro's will bring-a).

'I mean, if you don't want to go I can always cancel it.'

He sits there on the settee. In the home I grew up in. Like a long-awaited answer to all my teenage prayers.

'No, no. Don't cancel. It's amazing. I can't wait.'

The elephant theory

James looks at me from my childhood bed as I put on my night cream. 'Why do you use that? he asks me, quiet enough to keep the words contained in the room.

'What?'

'That anti-ageing stuff.'

'Because I'm starting to look old.'

'Old? You're twenty-nine!'

'I know, but I look old.' If I'm going to Rome I've got to keep up with all those sexy young Italian women.

I turn around, see his rarely displayed you're-talking-rubbish face, and decide to show him the evidence on my forehead. 'Look . . . look at all those lines. And look at that one between my eyebrows. It's like a slot you put coins in. I look like a piggy bank.'

'You can hardly see it. And anyway, it's beautiful. I think it's cute.'

'It's ugly. I need botox.'

'Twenty-nine and you need botox?!'

'Uh-huh.'

'How do you work that out.'

'Well, twenty-nine's my real age,' I say. 'Like, my

biological age. But it's not my worry age.'

'Your worry age?'

So I tell him. 'I'm a neurotic. I worry about everything. And if you worry you get old quicker.'

What is up with me? Why am I telling him this? Why am I letting him know he is dating a neurotic who will look like a dried-up prune by the time she hits forty.

'What do you worry about?'

'Oh just silly things.'

I can't tell him the truth. I can't tell him that my biggest fear is growing old and dying an old spinster.

'What sort of silly things?'

OK, what else do I worry about?

'Swallowing,' I tell him.

'What?'

Uh-oh. I should have probably just given him the growing old and dying on my own thing. At least then I'd have looked less like a weirdo. 'Yes, you see sometimes when I swallow, like when I've had a drink, I keep thinking about it and I keep on swallowing. And like I can go on for days swallowing every six seconds because I'm thinking about it. And the more I tell myself to stop swallowing the more I swallow. It's not like I've got like a compulsive disorder or anything. I mean, I'm pretty normal in other ways.' I swallow. 'Well, apart from the blinking.'

'Blinking?'

'Yes. It's like if you really tell yourself not to do something you really want to do it don't you?'

I swallow again. And blink.

'It's like the elephant theory,' James says.

'The elephant theory?'

'I read a lot of Freud when I was at uni. Basically,

152

the elephant theory says we can't help disobeying ourselves. Our subconscious always overrules our conscious self.'

'Why's it called the elephant theory?'

I blink and swallow.

And blink.

'Close your eyes and really try hard not to think of an elephant.'

I close my eyes and see an elephant. It's an elephant dressed in a pink tutu, standing on its hind legs.

'I bet you're thinking of an elephant.'

'I am,' I say, still with my eyes closed. 'It's wearing a pink tutu. It's standing up. It's doing a dance and playing a tune out of its trunk. Like a trumpet.'

James laughs. I hear my mum roll over in the next room. James says, 'What's the tune? "Nelly the elephant".?'

'No. No it's not actually. It's ... Oh, what's that one from *Flashdance*? By that woman. You know, who did the *Fame* song.'

'"What a Feeling"?'

'Yes, that's it.'

I open my eyes, and see James's broad smile.

'So there you go,' he says. 'You tell yourself not to think about an elephant and what happens? You think of an elephant. And not just any elephant, a dancing tutu-wearing elephant blowing an eighties pop classic out of its trunk. That's the elephant theory for you.'

I've never been able to do this before. Let someone inside my mad circus of a brain. Not a man, at any rate. I mean, I tell Maddie stuff. But that's only because she's even more insane than I am. Normally, with men, I have to check each sentence in my head first before letting it out in the open. As if there's a big bouncer guarding my tongue, checking nothing unsuitable gets past. But when I'm with James, my mouth-bouncer's off duty. It's a free party. Any sentence, however weird it sounds, is allowed through.

'However much we try and obey ourselves,' he goes on. 'We always let ourselves down. It's like your conscious is a strict parent and your subconscious is a rebellious teenager. Whatever you *think* you want, whatever you *think* is good for you, your subconscious always knows better.'

'Not always.'

'Oh?'

'I think *you're* good for me.'

'Well, okay. Every rule has an exception.'

I pull back the duvet and climb in next to him.

It's a no sex night, obviously. My parents like to pretend that sexual intercourse doesn't exist, at least on their planet, so I don't want to dispel the illusion.

His arm goes around me. His chest becomes my pillow. He kisses my forehead the way a father might kiss his child.

No-sex nights are underrated, in my opinion. Don't get me wrong, sex nights are good. Hey, sex nights are great. All those tingles he makes me feel. All that panting. All that discovery as we try something new. Two bodies getting as close as two bodies can get. The breathless urgency of it, cancelling out the rest of the world. All those sweet nothings that pass between us.

But no-sex nights can be just as good.

There are different ways to get close to someone,

to get inside them. You can shag. Or you can talk. Sweet nothings are nice, but so are sweet somethings.

And there is no denying it. No-sex nights are incredibly ... well, sexy. Stripping yourself bare in front of someone. Letting them see bits of you no one else gets to see.

I'm not talking about nipples, or birth-marks in rude places.

I'm talking about the parts of your brain you normally keep locked up inside your head. The bits no one knows about. Not your mum. Not your dad. Not your best friend.

No one. And as we spend the night talking in my old bed, I feel like I am thirteen again, talking to my best friend at a sleepover. Because that's what love does, it sends you back to childhood, when everything was new.

'I want to know everything about you,' he says.

'There's not much to know.'

'Of course there is. There's everything.'

'OK, what do you want to know?'

'Oh ... OK .... can you play a musical instrument?'

'No,' I say. 'Well, not really. The piano, a tiny bit.'

'The piano? Wow, I'd love to be able to play the piano.'

My mum rolls over again so I lower the volume further. 'Well, I'm not very good. When I was little I used to listen to Elton John. He's my dad's favourite. Apparently, I used to dance around the room to "Crocodile Rock" That was when I was really little ... when I was –'

'Sixteen?'

I slap his tummy. 'Shut up, you cheeky bugger. When I was about five or something. No, but after that I used to pester my mum and dad for piano lessons. You know how kids go on about getting a dog or a cat or a PlayStation, well I was like that about piano lessons. I used to go on and on and on. I used to sit here in my room, playing an imaginary piano. But really *believing* it, you know. With my eyes closed like I was a concert pianist or something.'

'So, did you break them? Did you get the lessons?'

'Well, it took some time. When I was eight they tried to appease me with one of those Casio keyboard jobbies. But even when I was eight I couldn't escape the fact that I didn't have a clue how to play a tune. But there used to be an automatic setting. It automatically played "Gold" by Spandau Ballet. It didn't play the words. Just the music. But I'd do concerts for my mum and dad and Nan at Christmas and pretend I was playing. But then I got really bored of that and wanted to learn properly. So I eventually made my mum take me to a piano teacher.'

'How old were you?'

'About twelve. Went to this woman called Mrs Sharpe. She was about ninety-five. Or at least, she seemed about ninety-five. But she was a good teacher. Got me from nothing to Grade 2 in a year. I used to go back home and do this tune on my keyboard. It was Mozart, I think. It was quite a simple tune, but it didn't sound like Mozart when I played it. But I loved it. Going for lessons. I only did it for a year though. That's the thing I most regret in my whole life. Not sticking at the lessons.'

I listen to about five beatbeats of his heart, and then he asks me: 'So why did you stop going?'

156

Another memory I'd rather forget enters my head. Amanda Longthome and Lisa Blackwood sitting behind me in French lessons.

While the teacher was telling us how to ask '*pour aller à la gare*?' or '*pour aller à la bibliothèque*?', they were giggling and singing 'The Music Man' in a whisper behind me.

Pia-pia-piano piano piano!
Pia-pia-piano pia-pia-no!

'I used to get bullied. When I was in my first year of secondary school. And playing the piano didn't help. You know what it's like at that age. If you do anything vaguely different you're made to feel like a freak. And it was a pretty rough school. So after years of pestering my mum and dad to let me go to piano lessons I was now pestering them to let me leave.'

'Why didn't you just pretend?'

'What?'

'When I was at an international school in India I was made to go to cricket club, but I hated it. I thought it was the most stupid game in the world. Well it is, if you think about it. Those three stupid sticks in the ground and all that LBW stuff.'

'What's LBW?'

'Leg before wicket. If you're batting and the ball hits your leg when it's in the way of a wicket then you're out.'

I don't have a clue what he is talking about but I nod and say, 'Right.'

'So I just used to pretend I went and walked around the streets of Bombay or went and sat in some sweltering cinema and watched some Bollywood film I couldn't understand. I used to stand out like a sore thumb. This white kid in his school uniform. But it was a friendly area, a posh area. Malabar. So I never got into any trouble.'

I find it amazing that James is interested in my life. His life is like a book. A big glossy travel book.

I try and imagine him as a child.

Running in his school uniform under a hot Indian sun. Part of another world.

My life is so boring in comparison.

A few holidays on the Costa Brava.

One in Orlando.

But I was hardly a globetrotter. My life was just school-TV-bed with the odd piano lesson thrown in, or the occasional hour reading magazines.

('Have you seen what she's reading?' my dad would say to my mum, after catching me with the latest copy of *More!* magazine. 'It's *pornography*.')

James strokes my hair, kisses my forehead again. 'So what happened about the piano lessons?'

'Well, I couldn't pretend not to go because Mum used to drive me around to Mrs Sharpe's house. So I just had to pester her until she eventually gave in. My dad wasn't very happy about it. "The amount of money we've wasted on giving you lessons." But I'd rather have my dad shout at me than have trouble at school. So I stopped playing. I can still play that Mozart tune though. Gavotte in B Minor I think it's called.'

I dum-dum the tune.

'Dum-dee-dee-dum-dum-Dum-dee-dee-dum-dum-Dum-deedy-dum-deedy- dum-dum-dum.'

'Nice rendition.'

'Thanks.'

'So do you wish you still played?'

'What?' I ask him. 'The piano?'

No, you idiot. The banjo. What do you think?

'Yeah. Do you wish you'd kept up the lessons?'

Rob asked me the same question once. In one of his rare flashes of interest.

And I gave the same answer.

'Yes, I do.'

James look at me for a while, still stroking my hair. 'You could always take them up again,' he says.

'I suppose.'

'Why not?'

'Oh, I don't know. Perhaps I'm old enough to realise I'll never be Elton John.'

'Oh, I don't know. I can see you in one of those outfits.'

He starts humming 'Your Song'. You know the one Ewan MacGregor sings in *Moulin Rouge*.

'I suppose I just feel there's no point,' I say, as sleep begins to weigh heavy on my eyes.

'In what?'

'In going back to something.'

Even as I say this, I don't believe it. Of course, there's not a point in going back to everything. Rob, for instance. But the piano is something I always wish I'd stuck with, and if I had a push I'd probably pick it up again.

But James doesn't push.

He just keeps on humming Elton until I sink into a deep, child-like sleep.

Roman Holiday

He knows the captain. That's why we're here, on the flight deck.

Trained with him apparently.

He's called Francis. He's probably about forty-five, but he looks like a chubby little boy that's just been blown-up to adult size, along with his toy aeroplane.

Francis seems nice. So does the co-pilot.

'What do you think?' James asks me, as we fly into another cloud.

I look at the control panel. A million buttons and switches and dials.

'Do you understand what they all mean?'

'Most of them,' he says. Then he starts to point at different dials and buttons. 'Air pressure ... fuel gauge ... altitude ... ejector seat ...'

'Ejector seat?'

Francis laughs. So does the co-pilot, a skinny blonde guy who has one of those laughs that doubles as an impression of a pig.

'It was a joke.'

'Oh yes,' I say. 'Funny.'

For the first time since I've met James I am seeing another side of him. A side that is prepared to make me the butt of his jokes in front of his friends. Maybe him and Rob have more in common than I suspected.

I look out of the window as we hit another cloud. 'So how high up are we now?'

James says to Francis, 'What are we at? Thirty-thousand.'

'Doing twenty-eight at the moment,' Francis tells him.

'Twenty-eight-thosand feet?' I ask.

'That's right,' James says. 'Twenty-eight thou.'

Twenty eight thou? What sort of stupid language is that?

'We'd better go back to our seats,' James tells me. 'They're going to start to head down now.'

I can already feel it in my ears.

The popping.

I'm not good on planes. Don't get me wrong, I'm not Rob. I don't end up hyperventilating in the sick bag the moment I set foot on them, or anything like that. It's just my ears. They don't seem to have been engineered for intemational air travel.

We get back to our seats.

Clip on our seat-belts.

The popping gets worse.

I get my chewing gum out and start to move my jaws like an Ibiza raver at five in the moming.

Then, on top of the popping, there comes the pain. Like something is drilling through both of my ears to get to my brain.

'Are you all right?' James asks me.

'I get bad ears,' I tell him.

'I hope they don't explode.'

161

'What?'

'Your eardrums. I hope they don't explode. It can happen. When I made my first flight to Rio. This poor guy started screaming then blood splattered all over his window. Lost his hearing in his left ear. One of the cabin crew fainted. It's to do with the pressure, you see. If you have to make a steep drop because there are too many planes around some ears just can't cope.'

I stare at him and suddenly realise the full disadvantages of dating an airline pilot.

'Could we talk about something else?' I ask him. 'To take my mind off it.'

'Sure. Sure.' He pauses for a while. 'Do you know that ninety per cent of airline disasters happen in the ten minutes before they land? In fact, the most dangerous moment is –'

Fortunately my ears are now so blocked with the air pressure that I can no longer hear a word he is saying.

The Hotel de Russie

As soon as we have landed, James reverts to his normal, romantic self. He talks to the taxi driver in Italian, and kisses my ears better as we drive through the ancient city.

'Is it like you expected?' he asks, as I stare out of the window.

'Better,' I say.

Halfway to the hotel we pass the Colosseum.

'*Il Colosseo*,' points out the taxi driver.

I stare up at the ancient arches and the pink evening sky peeping through.

'It's funny isn't it?' says James. 'It looks so peaceful. The place where Christians were fed to the lions. Where gladiators fought to the death. And it seems so calm, as if nothing had ever happened there.'

The taxi driver, on the other hand, is far from calm. He leans out of the window, makes unfathomable hand gestures, and honks his way through the traffic.

We eventually arrive at a gorgeous pink building, and the car pulls up.

'Here we are,' says James.

'What? *That's* our hotel.'

'The Hotel de Russie. It's meant to be the best.'

'Wow. It's amazing.'

By the time I get out of the car a man in a stylish uniform and neat little cap is taking our suitcases out of the boot.

'It's where all the stars stay,' James tells me. 'Leonardo di Caprio and Cameron Diaz were here while they filmed *Gangs of New York,* dontcha know?'

'Thank you, Mr Tour Guide.'

Inside, it's even more impressive. Beautiful antiques line the foyer. Beautiful people line the reception desk.

James does the talking, sounding even more sexy than normal as the Italian words trip off his tongue.

'OhmyGodohmyGodohmyGod,' is the only reasonable response to our room.

The bed! The TV! The bottle of champagne! The fresh fruit! The bathroom! The towels! The Jacuzzi! The bath! The shampoos! The other-little-bottles-of-things- I-can't-read.

'Ella!'

'Yes?'

'Take a look at this.'

I head out of the bathroom and see James out on the balcony.

'Look at the view,' he tells me.

So I do.

'They are said to be the most beautiful gardens in the whole of Italy.'

Now, to be honest, I'm not really a garden sort of girl. Too many early memories of my dad's arse as he bent over his flowerbeds I think. But these gardens

164

are pretty bloody impressive, even at night.

Under the nightlights, I can see the grass going up a hill in massive steps, with flowerbeds inbetween. Posh old men and their high maintenance wives sit out for evening drinks under Dom Perignon parasols on the garden terrace.

Look up 'luxury' in your illustrated dictionary and don't be surprised if you see a picture of this.

'It's amazing,' I say. 'Like a fairytale. You must have broke the bank.'

He turns and looks at me. Holds my head in his hands as though it is the most precious thing in the world. 'You are worth it.'

He kisses me.

It's a gentle kiss. Gentle, but deep and special.

The kind of kiss that reminds you that you are in love. And I feel it. I'm falling all over again . . .

I want him.

I pull him back into the bedroom.

Rome can wait, he can fly me to the moon first.

He pulls back.

'We can't,' he says, smiling sheepishly.

'Why not?'

'We have to eat.'

'We can eat later,' I say, nibbling on his lower lip. 'We can work up an appetite.'

My hand heads trouserwards, but he grabs my wrist.

'I've booked somewhere.'

'Booked somewhere.'

'Somewhere special.'

Curiouser and curiouser.

'Where is it?'

'You'll see. But we'd better get changed. Quickly.'

'What shall I wear?'

'Something . . . um . . . special.'

'What are you up to?'

'Nothing,' he smiles. 'Nothing at all.'

James's surprise

While I get ready I hear James on the phone, talking Italian. By the time I get out James is ready. In fact, ready doesn't do it justice. He's wearing a tux. A tux! Best-dress time I think.

I do my make-up and wear my earrings and feel all spangly.

'You look good enough to eat,' he says.

'Save your appetite,' I tell him.

We get in the lift and he presses the button.

'You've pressed the wrong button,' I tell him. 'We're going up. Look, the lift's going up.'

'I know.'

'But –'

The lift reaches the top floor and the doors slide back to reveal a room full of roses and white flowers. An engraved sign on the wall says *Suite Popolo* in ornate lettering.

I follow James as he walks out of some French doors and onto the roof terrace.

The roof terrace is vast, filled with pots of more white flowers and one, solitary table in the centre. It has a white tablecloth, beautifully laid cutlery and a single red rose in a vase.

'I don't think this is the restaurant,' I tell James.

But then a man appears from nowhere. Well, he must have appeared from *somewhere,* it's just I'm in such a state of amazement I didn't notice him.

'Good eve-a-ning Mr James and Miss Ella,' he says, in voice that makes me feel like royalty.

His black hair is so slick it seems to be painted onto his head. He is wearing a black and grey uniform and white gloves. The gloves are holding a large silver tray with one of those big silver dome-shaped covers on top of it.

'He knows our names,' I whisper to James.

He doesn't say anything.

He knows he knows our names.

James pulls out one of the chairs at the table for me to sit down.

It starts to dawn on me.

'Oh my God, this is for us.'

'I though it would be something different,' James says.

Something different!

As understatements go, that's on a par with 'I'm just going to trek the Sahara to stretch my legs.'

When Rob used to say we should do something different, he meant we should get a curry rather than a pizza.

But James really is a man of surprises. And then I remember, from the questionnaire.

Which element do you believe is most important in a relationship?

And my answer?

I believe the most important element in a relationship is SURPRISE.

168

James sits down in front of me.

'Do you like it?' he sips the champagne that has just been poured.

'It's amazing. I can't believe it's real. It feels like a dream.'

And it does feel like a dream. As the white gloves next to me open up the tray to reveal our starter, I feel genuinely frightened that I will wake up.

But as I look around at the lights from cars and buildings on the seven hills I realise this is beyond anything I've dreamt before.

The white gloves serve plates of food.

'Your starters,' says the man from the hotel. 'For the lady who not eat meat we have the pink Russian salad.'

Wow.

Pink Russian salad!

I have no idea what it is but it looks gorgeous.

'It's like a work of art,' I say.

'A work of art for a work of art,' says James.

It's a smooth line, but I'm in the mood for smooth – perhaps it's my earrings.

We eat our starters.

We sip our champagne.

We gaze into each other's eyes.

We generally act like we're in some 1980s Spandau Ballet video. I even start seeing James in soft focus, or maybe that's just the champagne.

If there's anything lacking, it's the conversation.

James's mind seems to be somewhere else. Now don't get me wrong, my mind is *always* somewhere else. But where on earth could James's mind be that is better than right here and now. After all, he's the one who has gone to all this trouble – booking the whole roof terrace. It must have cost a fortune. I mean, he may work for an airline, but he doesn't *own* one.

'So,' I say, trying to jump-start the conversation. 'What shall we do tomorrow? There's so much isn't there ... The Sistine Chapel ... the Pantheon ... the Spanish Steps ... the Trevi fountain ... the Villa Borghese ... the Via Veneto ... the Vatican ... St Peters ... the shops!'

'Yes,' he says.

'What, all of them?'

'Yes.'

But he's not listening. I can tell.

We finish our starters. The white gloves take away our plates. Then another man arrives – a smartly dressed old man with a big smile and a violin.

'Oh my God ... what's this?'

James shrugs under a nervous smile. 'Music, I guess.'

So the music starts.

Soft, beautiful music. Each stroke of the violin sending tingles down my spine. The food of love.

The main meal arrives. It looks like art on my plate. I hardly want to touch it. I don't want to spoil it, or move the moment on.

And James seems to feel the same. He is playing with his steak.

But we eat the meal, passing the occasional mono-syllable back and forth. The plates disappear, then James takes a deep breath and looks at me. The violin player has moved further into the background, but the music plays on.

James is trying to say something.

After about a minute he manages 'Ella', as if it's

the hardest word in the English language.

'Yes? What ... what is it?'

'Ella ...' And then it starts. 'Ella ... I know we haven't known each other for that long, but over the last few weeks I've felt something change inside me ...'

Oh my God.

'... you see, all my life I've been moving around. My dad, as I've told you, worked for the British government. He was a diplomat. After my mum died, when I was eight, I followed dad wherever he went. Kenya. Saudi Arabia. Portugal. All over. I'd been to about ten different international schools by the time I left for university. And I loved it. I know that sounds weird but I did. I loved the travel aspect ... seeing new places. My dad died when I was twenty-one. He was only in his fifties. Died of a stroke. Stress of the job. But even after he was gone I wanted to keep moving. I mean, that's what made me want to be an airline pilot. When your home isn't anywhere, it becomes everywhere. If you stay in one place for too long, you start to feel home-sick for everywhere else. And that's how it's always been.'

He holds my hands over the table.

'The thing is Ella ... You've changed me. Before I met you, I thought home was a place. Always a different place, but a place all the same. But I know now that I could feel at home anywhere so long as I've got you.'

I gulp.

Suddenly I'm the one who is lost for words.

Anywhere else, that line would sound cheesier than a Quattro Formaggio, but trust me, when you hear it over the sounds of a violin on the roof terrace of the

171

Hotel de Russie, it sounds just right.

He leans closer, over the table. 'I know, deep in my heart, we were meant to be together,' he continues, with hushed urgency. 'It's not just science, it's about fate. We were *meant* to be together. I feel it stronger than I feel anything. I dreamed about you before I met you ... someone who could make me feel like this. I never thought it could happen, not really. But now I realise I was always going to meet you. You are the point of my life ... you are why I'm here.'

Time is away and somewhere else.

In the Eternal City, this is our eternal moment.

I feel a pulse in our joined hands. I can't tell if it is his or mine. It makes no difference. Right now, within this moment, we might as well be the same person.

I remember something from an old poem.

> *There were two glasses and two chairs*
> *And two people with one pulse.*

It could have been written for us. It could have been written for right now.

'Ella, I don't want to leave you. I don't want to ever leave you. I know it's going to be difficult ... with my job. But we can work it out, I know we can. And it's not going to be forever, and I'll quit tomorrow if you ask me to. I'd do anything ... *anything* for you Ella. Anything at all.'

He takes a hand from mine, places it in his pocket.

A second later he pulls out a satin pouch.

'What's that?' I ask him.

But he doesn't answer.

172

Instead, he opens the pouch and pulls out a dark blue box. A dark blue *jeweller's* box. The kind of box that might contain earrings.

Or a ring.

The happiest girl in the world

Oh no.

He pulls back his chair. The music soars, as if knowing what is about to happen.

'I want to do this properly,' he says.

And he does.

He picks up the box.

Gets down on one knee.

The violin stops, along with my heart.

'Ella, I love you. I want to be by your side for ever.'

He opens the box.

His hand is shaking as he takes out the ring.

It's an emerald.

The light is refracted green and white in it. Light from the three-quarter moon, the candle and the glow of the Suite Popolo across the terrace.

'I chose it because it matches your eyes,' he says.

The ring trembles expectantly between his fingers.

I look at James. He looks in torture, dreading what my lips still might say.

The man with the violin is there watching. So is the man with white gloves. Both are standing there like statues, scared any movement could change my reply.

Back to James's eyes.

A lifetime of wanting contained in one gaze.

This is the only man in the world for me. It's a scientific fact.

They say that when you die your whole past flashes before your eyes.

When you are proposed to, the exact opposite happens.

Your whole future flashes in front of you. The future as you imagine it. How it might be.

The wedding.

The house.

The babies.

The holidays.

The school runs.

The fights.

The making up.

Growing old. Together.

For the first time in forever, the future isn't something to dread. James says he will always love me, and I believe him. Growing old and wrinkly isn't so scary when you've got someone to grow old and wrinkly with.

He is still there.

Still in the moment.

Waiting.

'Will you, Ella . . . Will you marry me?'

He looks so scared.

Why, I have no idea.

There is only one answer.

There is only one possible word.

So I put him out of his misery.

I give him the word.

'Yes.'

His eyes don't believe me. 'Yes?'

'Yes. *Yes.*'

'Yes.'

'Yes.'

'You're saying Yes?'

The yeses burst in the night air like fireworks.

'Yes.'

'Yes!'

'Yes.'

And as he slides the ring onto my finger, the gentle patter of applause comes from our waiter and violin player.

'She said yes!' James tell them.

'Si!'

'Yes! Si! Yes!'

The violin starts.

James rises for a kiss, our lips meet in the middle.

I hold his head in my hands and know, beyond all doubt, that right now I am the happiest girl in the world.

A non-parent moment

Marriage proposals happen all the time. I will not be the only girl in the world to be proposed to this evening. I will not even be the only girl in Rome having a ring placed tentatively on her finger.

But although an engagement is not a bizarre, happens-to-you-only kind of thing – like growing a third breast or discovering you fancy Donald Rumsfeld – the moment it happens you feel utterly unique.

Because think about it. There are over three billion women on the planet.

Three billion. And over two and three-quarter billion of them definitely would not say no to a sexy airline pilot and a gorgeous emerald ring. No way.

So for someone like James, there's a lot of choice out there. It's a buyer's market. And he chose me.

And that makes you feel kind of special. Like you've got something that no one else has. Something irreplaceable.

I want to save this feeling. Bottle it and store it away like some fine wine, so I can take a sip of it on some miserable Monday morning in the future.

But then I think, maybe they won't ever exist again. Miserable Monday mornings. Okay, there'll be times when James is away and I've got to go to school, but all I'll have to do is look down at the glinting, green-eyed beauty on my ring finger and I'll be all right.

I'll be able to say 'He's mine.'

He's mine.

Mine all mine.

And then I'll remember everything is perfect.

Nothing can go wrong.

'You'd better phone your mum and dad,' James tells me, when we are back in our room.

'Mum and Dad?'

'Remember when you came down after your headache and you wondered why they were smiling?'

I remember my mum's face, a swollen tomato of happiness. 'Yes, I remember. I thought it was because you told them about taking me to Rome.'

'Well, I did. And then I asked for your dad's permission.'

I look at his face to see if he is joking.

Nope, not a flicker.

'My dad's permission?'

What year is this? 1786?

'Sure. I thought I'd do it the old-fashioned way. Get his permission first.'

This is sweet, I tell myself.

Not weird. Not, like, three centuries out of date. Not like I'm a secondhand car, passed on for sale.

It will have made my dad's day. Month. Year. Life.

'Right,' I say. 'That was ... lovely.'

'Are you sure?'

'Sure?'

'Yes. It was nice of you. Sweet. Really.'

'So do you want to phone them?'

Some moments are for parents. And some moment simply aren't. I look at the phone. My mum's yelping congratulations only ten numbers away. Hardly the world's greatest aphrodisiac.

'Erm, it can wait till the morning,' I tell him.

Everything can wait till the morning.

I kiss him, tugging his shirt towards the bed, and think of all the perfection that lies ahead.

The reactions

It's weird, when you get engaged.

When you are proposed to it is the most wonderful feeling in the world, because the moment belongs to you. And that's how it was in Italy, throughout our Roman Holiday. We were in a bubble, our own little lovestruck world.

The trouble with bubbles though is that they burst.

Now we are back from Rome it's a different story.

Everyone knows.

Which is fine, really. I mean, that's sort of the whole point of getting engaged.

To make your love official and public. It's just that, with every new person you tell, the news seems to diminish.

There is a law of diminishing returns.

With each new reaction, the inner glow I felt in Rome fades just slightly.

First up, there was my parents' reaction:

'Dad?' my mum said to my father while I was on the phone. 'Dad? Dad? Guess what, she said yes ...

180

Ella said yes!!'

Most of the phonecall was just my mum making excited noises that bore little or no resemblance to anything approaching words. 'Eee ... oooh ... aaah ... eeeh ...'

Then my dad got on the line.

'That's fantastic love. Smashing news. We're chuffed to bits.'

Don't get me wrong. I'm glad they were pleased for me. But I mean, there have been socks in my washing basket that have been there longer than they've known James. I thought they might be just a little hesitant. They were obviously so amazed that someone like James wanted to marry someone like me, that they happily dispelled all doubts.

After all, when it comes to James, anything goes. I could probably tell them that James likes to have sex with farmyard animals and mum's only reaction would be: 'Well, your dad's partial to a bit of chicken.'

Maddie was next on the list:

'Wow!' she said, with eyes as wide as saucers as she looked at the ring. 'Look at that beauty! Oh, was it romantic? Was it? Tell me! How did he ask? Did he ask during sex? Did he? Tell me every single detail!!!'

Then Pip:

'Well, he better be good to you. If he cheats on you ... if he criticises your arse ... just tell me and I'll give him a roundhouse kick to the head so fast he'll be sucking his meals out of a straw for the rest of his life.'

'Thanks Pip,' I told her. 'That means a lot.'
Then I got a phonecall:

'Is that Cinderella?'

'Dr Lara?'

'I've just heard the news.'

'The news?'

'I just phoned Prince Charming. He told me the news about your engagement.'

'Oh ... right ... did he?'

'Of course, it's not really news. We knew this was going to happen. But even I had to admit our fairytale is moving faster than expected. This is great PR. Simply great. We'll put it up on our website. Oh ... and you must tell us when the Big Day is going to be. Those pictures will be priceless publicity.'

And that was it.

The final reaction.

That was when I first thought that, from now on, my love life was out of my control. And, on the following evening I had my suspicion confirmed.

That sinking feeling

I am on my own in the flat. Maddie is being wined and dined by Steve and Pip is at her Boxercise class at the gym.

James is due round at eight. He's taking me out for a meal. *Again*. It's 7.36 and I am halfway through Maddie's DVD of *When Harry Met Sally* when there is a knock on the door.

James must be so eager to see me, he couldn't wait.

I open the door with a big welcoming smile and say 'Hi.'

'Say it again,' he tells me. 'Only this time say "Hi *captain*,"'

'Captain?' I ask, grabbing my coat and heading with James towards the car.

'The airline just phoned. They've made me a captain. I can't believe it! I mean, I knew they would. I've been with the company for six years now, but I wasn't expecting them to do it so soon.'

'That's fantastic,' I say.

He starts singing 'Money, Money, Money' as we get into his car.

'So ... er ... when do you start, er, captain-ing?'

'Two weeks. And I'm going to be flying all North American routes now. Guess where I fly to first?'

'I don't know.'

'Go on. Guess. Guess!'

'Er ... New York.'

We drive off. 'Further west.'

'LA?'

He starts singing. 'Viva Las Vegas.'

'Wow, that's great.'

'You could come with,' he says.

'What?'

'On my first flight as captain. I could wangle you a ticket.'

'Are you allowed to do that?'

'I've got a friend who can sort it out. What do you think? Do you fancy a Vegas institution? You break up in two weeks don't you? So you'll be off school. Come on, what do you say?'

It's weird.

I'm being offered a free fantastic holiday with the man I am going to marry and all I have is a sinking feeling.

'Yes, it sounds great,' I find myself saying.

'You know what we could do in Las Vegas?' James asks, when we are at the restaurant.

'Gamble?'

He shakes his head. 'There's no gamble involved. It's a safe bet. We could do it there.'

'What?'

'Get *married*.'

I stare at him, waiting for him to tell me he is joking. I keep waiting.

Oh.

He's not joking.

'Married? In Vegas?'

'Why not?'

'Well,' I say, trying not to sound too flabber-gasted. 'When I pictured my wedding day, you know, when I was little, I always imagined the perfect English country wedding in some church near my parents. I didn't imagine some tacky Elvis-themed, conveyor belt, drive thru, ten-minute, Vegas wedding in some tiny naff chapel of love. It's what runaways do and celebrities who get divorced after five hours.'

He looks at me, and raises his arms in front of him in the 'calm down' gesture.

'It doesn't have to be like that,' he says. 'There's a hotel. The Bellagio. It's the most luxurious hotel in the world. It's amazing, apparently. And they do weddings. Real, classy, expensive wedding. No Elvis impersonators. It could be great.'

I can't believe it. He is dead serious.

Why doesn't my perfect man want my perfect wedding?

'No,' I say.

'What?'

'No. I don't want to.'

'What do you mean you don't want to?'

My heart is up to anger speed. I feel like I'm about to say something stupid.

'I'd rather eat my own sick.'

'Ella. What are you talking about?'

'I can't believe you want me to get married without my parents there.' I feel bad as soon as I have said this. After all, James has no choice about his parents not being there.

'I'll get free tickets for them as well. They can come. And your friends.'

Uh-oh.

I'm about to do something stupid. I can feel it coming. Any minute now ...

'Fine,' I snap, as a waitress places a plate of bruschetta down on the table.

'Fine. Fine. Fine. It sounds like you've got it all sorted out. I tell you what: perhaps I don't need to turn up at all. Why don't you do it without me? Get my dad to fill in for me.'

I place my wine down and storm my way to the toilets.

What the hell is the matter with me?

It's not even the time of the month. Okay, so James's idea of a perfect wedding is different to mine. So what? It's not the Big Day that's so important. It's the two-hundred thousand little days that follow.

Las Vegas.

Does it really matter that much?

I eventually pull myself together and go back into the restaurant.

'Ella?'

'What?'

'I'm sorry. Silly idea. I won't suggest it again.'

His mobile goes. He looks at the screen. Switches it off. 'It's no one,' he tells me.

'No,' I tell him. 'I'm *sorry*. It sounds great. Really. I'd love to do it.'

He holds my chin in his hand across the table, lifts it up to see my eyes. 'Are you sure?'

'Sure,' I say, wondering how my mum and dad will react to a Vegas wedding.

'Sure I'm sure.'

*

Dear Mum and Dad,

How are you both? Hopefully well!
I am writing with fantastic news. We have decided to get married in Las Vegas on the 25th of this month. Don't worry – it's not going to be a tacky wedding. It's going to be in a very posh hotel called the Bellagio (Dad – it's where they filmed Ocean's 11*!). I've popped in a little brochure with this letter to show you exactly what it's like.*

Anyway, the really exciting news is that James is flying both of you out and putting you up in the hotel so you'll be there for the Big Day!!

I hope you don't think we're rushing into anything. I know we haven't known each other for that long, but it feels like we've been together for years. And he really is my Mr Perfect – it's a scientific fact!

I'm so glad you get on with him, and I can't wait to see you . . .
Thanks for being the best parents ever.

Love and hugs,
Ella (and James!)
XXX

A visit to the library

If you ever want to make the loudest noise humanly possible, take a class full of Year Eleven pupils and drag them to the quietest part of Tooting Public Lending Library in South London.

'Miss! Miss!' shouts Darren Bentley. He holds up a copy of *Where Do I Come From?* 'Could you explain this to Dobbo? He wants to know where he comes from Miss. He's clueless Miss. He wonders if you could show him.'

The whole library looks up from their books to see exactly who is invading their silence.

'Sssssh,' says the stern-faced librarian, who looks like she hasn't been outside since 1954.

'Sssssh,' I repeat, to Darren Bentley, and try to desperately dampen the wildfire giggles he has started. I beckon Mark Dobson and Darren out of the children's section and direct everyone towards the section marked Newspapers and Periodicals.

'Sorry,' I whisper, to all the miserable tutters I walk passed. 'Sorry . . . sorry . . . sorry . . .'

This wasn't my idea.

Mr Loving is very keen for us to find ways to

stretch the curriculum beyond the school gates, meaning he can get on with his paperwork while the actual pupils are as far away from him as possible. And so I am here in one of the largest quiet spaces in the whole of South London, trying to interest Year Eleven in stories from copies of *The Times* newspaper dating from the 1800s.

As well as *Romeo and Juliet*, the other text Year Eleven are pretending to read is Mary Shelley's *Frankenstein*. The idea is to get them to see what world events were happening at the time it was written.

Once we reach the right alcove I flick desperately through the old, yellowing pages for something that might stimulate their interest.

Napoleon's retreat from Moscow.

The world's first blood transfusions conducted at Guy's hospital, London.

Hmm, that's going to excite them.

'Right,' I say, 'look at this everyone. The invention of the wooden stethoscope. This was in eighteen-sixteen, a year before Mary Shelley started writing Frankenstein ... this was a time when a lot of amazing things were happening in medicine and science and ... *Darren, I saw that* ... as I was saying, this was a time of ... *Darren I mean it, if you don't stop flicking Minesh's ear you'll be seeing Mr Loving when you get back to school* ... right, anyway, this was a time when a lot of scientific changes were taking place, and people were getting very into the idea that electricity was the spark of life ... in fact, Mary's husband Percy conducted his own experiments and even managed to electrify the family cat ...'

189

All the Year Elevens start to giggle. Mind you, knowing them, they are probably just laughing at the name Percy.

That's when I see him.

He's standing in the alcove opposite, about twenty feet away. In the business books section.

'Er ... right ... everyone ... I'd like you to get into pairs ... and each pair could look at a different year ... from eighteen-ten onwards ... just take a different volume from the shelf and ... and ... I'll be back in a second ...'

I leave them and quickly make my way over to the business books section. I notice, halfway over, the books he is holding.

Starting Your Own Business.

The Photographer's Handbook.

The Small Business Guide.

101 Ways To Free Publicity.

Once I have reached him I turn to check my pupils aren't setting fire to anything, then tap him on his shoulder.

He nearly jumps out of his skin, then turns around.

God, he looks terrible. I briefly wonder why he isn't at work.

'Ella ... it's you,' he says, taking headphones out of his ears.

'Rob ... hi ... I saw you ... from over there ... I'm with a class from school.'

He nods. 'Right. I see.'

His voice is flat, dead. Is this the same Rob who came to see me at James's apartment?

I am smiling, but then I remember.

All Bar One.

An hour spent staring at an empty chair.

I remember I'm meant to be cross with him so I drop the smile. 'Rob? Where the hell were you? The other Saturday ... at All Bar One ... I waited ages for you but you didn't show?'

'I ... I ... I ...'

Oh God, we could be here till Christmas. 'Why weren't you there?'

'What?'

'Why weren't you at All Bar One? I waited there on my own for an hour. And you didn't turn up. You acted so desperate to see me and you weren't there.'

'That's what I'm trying to say ... I'm trying to tell you ... I wasn't there ... I wasn't there because ... I couldn't go ...'

'Why not?'

He looks vacant. 'It was ... difficult.'

'Difficult?' I'm furious, in a low-volume kind of way. '*Difficult?* You are so desperate to see me that you turn up on my boyfriend's doorstep and nearly start a fight and completely ruin the whole evening and then I have to keep this big secret about coming to see you and you didn't even bloody show up!'

'I'm ... sorry. It's just ... something happened.'

I turn around quickly to check I haven't managed to lose any of my pupils, and see Mark Dobson staring straight at me with smitten eyes while the rest of the pupils scour the pages for news stories from 200 years ago.

I turn back to Rob. 'Something happened? What ... you got stuck in traffic? You missed the bus? What? What was so bloody important?'

'Dad died.'

He says it just like that. 'Dad died.'

191

Matter of fact.

'He had a heart attack over a month ago. Before I last saw you. He was in hospital for two weeks. Too weak to come out. He had a second attack the day I was supposed to meet you. He died ... in the hospital.'

His voice breaks in the middle of 'hospital'.

I stare at Rob's face.

At the hurt buried just below the surface.

And, as I stare, I remember the last time I saw his father. He had been at the flat, for Rob's birthday. He'd been teasing me about what an easy life teachers must have with their long holidays. He said that before he retired, he'd spend six days a week in his taxi, twelve months a year. Knew South London like the back of his hand, he liked to boast. Every street. Every short-cut. Every greasy spoon. He always wondered what a 'sparky girl' like me was doing with a 'useless lump' like his son.

I can still hear his voice.

'Rob ... oh sorry ... I'm so sorry ...'

He locks emotion behind a tight smile. 'It's OK. Really. He'd had a bad heart for years. All those fry-ups. It's a wonder it didn't happen sooner.'

I remember what Rob said.

When I last saw him, outside James's apartment. 'I've got something to tell you.'

He was going to tell me about his dad being ill, but he never got the chance.

'I'm sorry I didn't tell you about the funeral,' Rob says, with the same glazed expression. 'I didn't want to put you in a ... situation. I didn't want you to feel like you had to come.'

'Don't worry,' I tell him, touching his arm. 'But of

course I wouldn't have felt like that. I'd have wanted to come.'

I want to hug him.

I want to stroke his head and tell him everything will be all right.

After all, who else has he got to do that now? He's got no parents left. No girlfriend. No one.

The hug doesn't happen.

We're in a library. He's holding books. A crowd of Year Elevens are behind me.

'He really liked you,' Rob said.

'Did he?' I say, hiding my left hand – and the engagement ring he hasn't yet noticed – behind my back.

'He told me to hold onto you ... something else I let him down about.'

'Rob, you didn't let him down. He was proud of you.'

Rob is about to disagree, but thinks better of it. 'Yeah,' he says, in a quiet voice. 'I know.'

'I'm sorry ... about what I said ... about you not meeting me ...'

'Don't be,' he says. 'You weren't to know.'

Right then, I see something in him I've never seen before. A maturity that didn't exist a month ago. A maturity that's been forced on him since his father's death.

I suddenly feel bad about not being with him. Not being there for him when he found out. I think about what he must have been going through while I was waiting for him in the bar getting angry.

'Rob, listen, if you want me to do anything ... if there's any way I can help ...'

He nods. 'I know.'

193

There's a sudden burst of noise behind me. Teenage laughter.

Rob looks over at my Year Elevens. 'You'd better go before they start a riot.'

'Right ... yeah ... OK ... Just ... er ... call me if there's anything I can do.'

He nods again. 'OK.'

There are million things left unsaid, and the unspoken words seem to change the air between us with a strange and suppressed energy.

'I'll go then,' I tell him.

'Yeah ... I'll see you.'

'Yeah ... bye ... I'm so sorry ... bye.'

I start walking over to my class.

Halfway there, Rob calls after me.

'Ella –'

'I turn and see him standing like a little boy lost, holding his business books.

'Yes?' I ask him.

He pauses. 'Thanks,' he says, and offers a slight, sad smile.

I have no idea what exactly he is thanking me for, but I smile back and tell him, 'It's OK.'

The invisible wall

I do something stupid, after school.

I go and see Rob.

It's weird. It wasn't like I had a conscious plan to go and see him. It was almost as if I was on automatic, watching myself from somewhere else, as I got on the tube and travelled three stops on the Northern Line.

A strange sadness falls over me as I head down the stone steps to his grotty basement flat. Steps I used to walk down almost every evening for a year of my life.

I knock on the door.

He takes so long to answer that at first I think he isn't in, that he's out at the pub, but then I see his face, like a ghost at the window.

'Ella,' he says, when he opens the door.

'I just thought I'd come round and see you. To see how you are ... you know ... it was a bit awkward in the library and I thought you might like a proper chat.'

He is wearing an old T-shirt with the brand of some Japanese beer on it.

'Oh,' he says. 'Right ... er ... come in.'

Inside, his living room is exactly as I remembered it. It's so bizarre. Like walking into the main exhibit at the Museum of My Failed Relationships.

The PlayStation. The TV that fills half the room. The unhoovered carpet. The unused camera on the floor. The posters worshipping footballers and football-sized breasts.

There are some differences though.

No empty beer cans.

And there are books on the table. The ones he was holding in the library. On business and photography. And an A4 pad, with writing in.

'I know we're not still together,' I tell him, 'but we're still friends aren't we? I just thought you might want ... a friend ... to talk to ...'

'What about James?'

'What about him?'

'Does he know you're round here?'

'*No* ... not yet ... but I'll tell him later ... he'll understand. He's not like *that*.'

Rob nods, then swallows, as if trying to get rid of the taste of something. 'Do you want anything?' he asks, changing the subject. 'Anything to drink, I mean. Like tea or something?'

'Yes. That would be nice.'

He disappears to the kitchen. Bangs about in cupboards. Then he says: 'I haven't got any ... tea ... I think I might have some coffee somewhere. I'm just looking.'

'It's all right,' I tell him. 'I'm fine.'

He comes back in the room. 'Sorry ... I'm just a bit all over the place.'

'You're bound to be.'

Oh God.

This is awkward.

I shouldn't have come.

I mean, all I'm doing is rubbing him up the wrong way.

I sit down on the sofa. He almost sits next to me, the way he always used to, but then plumps for the chair instead.

I think about the invisible wall that is built between people when their relationships end. You know someone so well, but have to force a distance between you, a distance that is even greater than when you first ever met.

After a long, impossible silence Rob speaks.

'I didn't tell him,' he says.

I don't understand. 'Sorry.'

'Dad. I didn't tell dad. About us. You know, about us breaking up. It sounds stupid but I never had the guts to tell him. I was going to tell him ... I was ... but then he was took into hospital and he kept asking about you, when he was wired into all these machines keeping him alive ... and I didn't tell him. I couldn't.' He releases a gentle laugh. 'He'd have killed me. Told me it was all my fault, which it was –'

'No,' I tell him. 'It wasn't your fault. It wasn't anyone's fault ... it just ... you know ...' My words fade out. I feel like I am pouring salt into an open wound.

And then he notices it, for the first time.

My ring.

Rob – the sequel

'You've got engaged,' Rob says, still staring at the ring.

'Yes.' I tell him.

'To that ...' He checks himself just in time '... man.'

'Yes. James. Yes.'

He slumps further into his chair, as if something has just been sucked out of him. 'But you've only just met him.'

'Rob, look come on, let's talk about something else ...'

But he's not really listening to me. 'Why?'

'Why what?'

'Why are you marrying him?'

He doesn't ask this the way I'd expect him to ask. There's no bitterness in his voice, just a genuine interest in what would motivate me to marry someone.

'Er ... I don't know ...' I look at Rob's face and realise this is the only topic he wants to talk about, or abuse himself with. Oh well, better just keep it as short as possible. 'It feels right.'

'Because of the science?'

'The science?'

'I saw you. I saw you on the news.'

Oh God. That couldn't have been good. 'Oh yes, the news. That was a bit embarrassing actually.'

'So is it true?'

'What?'

'Is he your Mr Perfect?' Again, no bitterness. I start to wonder if the old Rob is still there at all. It's like watching a sequel. He sort of looks the same (if a bit thinner), but the underlying structure has totally changed.

'Er ... he's right for me ... they did lots of tests ... I answered lots of questions ... and he's the right one for me.'

He absorbs my words, and looks again at the gleaming emerald on my finger.

'I'm pleased for you.'

No sarcasm. No anger. He genuinely seems to mean it.

'Are you really?' I ask, knocked off guard.

He nods. 'When you dumped me, I couldn't accept it. I didn't understand why you'd want to hurt me like that. That's why I kept phoning you. That's why I came round to see you. That's why I went to that ... man's ... flat. I wasn't thinking straight. I just wanted things to go back to the way they were. You and me. Round here every night. On the PlayStation. Or round the pub. Me boring your ears off moaning about my job and talking about setting up my own business but never doing anything about it.'

'Rob, you didn't bore –'

'No,' he says. 'I did. I bored myself as well. Deep down I knew nothing was going to change. I was going to be a recruitment consultant until I was sixty and that camera was going to stay unused in the corner ... but then, when dad got ill, when he was just lying there, plugged into machines, everything suddenly made sense. Nothing stays the same just because you want it to. You have to try. You have to work at it. And I was crap. I was fucking crap when we were together. I wasn't there for you ... I took you for granted. I was,' he struggles with the admission, 'a slob.'

'No,' I say, telling the whitest of lies. 'No you weren't. It wasn't all your fault Rob ... I expected too much. You know what I'm like with my sky-high standards.'

He smiles softly. 'I know ... and that's why I'm happy that you've found someone who lives up to your expectations. I mean, I can't kid myself, I'm no airline pilot.'

He laughs.

'What are you laughing at?' I ask him.

'The girl with sky-high standards ends up with an airline pilot.'

'Rob –

He raises his palm. 'No, I'm not feeling sorry for myself. That's the weird thing. I know that if I'm going to sort my life out I've got to be realistic. I was holding you back. I can't even get on a plane for God's sake. That's hardly the ideal partner for someone who wants to see the world. And if I wasn't right for you, then maybe you weren't right for me.'

It's irrational, but I feel hurt by these words. Don't get me wrong, I hated it when Rob was trying to break me and James up, but now I see that he has moved on I feel like I have lost something. It's like when my mum and dad had to have our old dog Baxter put down – I knew it was the right thing to do, but it still felt terrible realising he was no longer there in his basket.

'I'm getting on with my life now,' he says. 'When dad died I was tempted to drown myself in Stella, or something stronger ... but it's like he's there, you know. It's like he's watching me. And I want to make him proud. I'm getting out of the house. Seeing people. The world doesn't stop spinning.'

I nod, and look again at the business books on the table. I am about to ask him about them, and about work, when his phone rings.

He stands up and gets it, looking pleased that one of his friends is phoning. 'Hello ...'

I wonder who it is.

I wonder what he meant when he said 'seeing people'.

What people?

'Hello? Hello? Hello?' He puts the phone down. 'Some robot trying to sell me car insurance,' he explains.

'Listen, Ella ...' he says, sitting back down in his chair, the mask of indifference slipping just a little. 'I'm happy for you. If he's a good guy ... who's going to look after you then I'm happy ... He is a good guy, isn't he?'

'Yes.' I say. 'He's a good guy.'

Ten minutes later I am on his doorstep, saying goodbye.

I still have no idea whether Rob really meant what he said, about moving on, and about him being happy for me now I've found James. His voice was convincing, but his eyes might tell a different story.

We hug.

He kisses my cheek.

'Thanks for coming round.'

Part of me – part I thought was long buried – doesn't want to leave. It's the part that wants to stay soothing Rob, and stay being soothed.

His body feels warmer than James's. Softer sure, but warmer.

I wonder what I would be like in Rob's situation. If I'd lost a parent and had just found out he was engaged, while I was still single.

I doubt I'd be acting so strong.

And that's the weird thing.

In the list of adjectives I always used to describe Rob, strong never featured. Lazy. Lethargic. Hungry. Inconsiderate. Occasionally funny. But never strong.

It's like the warmth and quiet dignity that was always there in his dad had suddenly been born in him.

He holds me tight, rubs my back, then lets go.

'Look after yourself,' I tell him.

'Yeah. I will.'

'If you need anything, just call me ... or come round.'

He smiles. 'That might not be such a good idea.'

'No,' I say. 'Maybe not.'

'Bye, Ella.' His words have a finality that wrenches my heart.

'Yes,' I say, doing my best to ignore the part of me that wants to stay. 'Bye.'

How the other half live

I am late to see James.

'Did you get held up at school?'

'Yes,' I say but then I remember that perfect relationships aren't built on lies.

'No ... I, er, went to see Rob.'

James's eyes widen. 'As in ... your ex-boyfriend Rob?'

'Yes ... I saw him ... today ... in the library ... I went with a class from school ... and ... and ...' My heart is racing. Why do I feel I'm apologising? I've done nothing wrong. '... and he told me his dad died two weeks ago so I went to see him ... this evening ... after school ... to see how he was ...'

James is standing against the giant window at the back of the living area, with night-time London shining behind.

His arms are folded and his eyes are searching me for something.

'You went round to your ex-boyfriend's?'

'Yes.'

He turns his back on me and stares out of the window. I look at the glass, his reflection like a ghost.

'James? His dad died.'

'My dad died. Everyone's dad dies.'

I don't believe what I'm hearing. 'His dad died *two weeks ago.*'

My perfect man will want me all to himself ...

'James? What's the matter? You weren't like this before. When Rob came round here ... you were fine about it ... I don't understand.'

'Does that ring on your finger mean anything to you?'

My perfect man will understand the value of marriage ...

I look down at the ring. 'Of course it does ... it means everything.'

'It means so much you'd rather lend your ex a shoulder to cry on than be here with me? Is that it?'

'No, no it's not.'

'And what else did you lend him eh?'

'What? What's that supposed to mean?'

'Oh, come on Ella. You were fucking that slob only a few months ago. And I'm meant to believe he didn't try it on. That he didn't make a strike for a sympathy shag.'

'Yes,' I say. 'Yes, that is what you're meant to believe. Because it's the truth. And ... and ... even if he did nothing would have happened. I can't believe you don't trust me.'

My perfect man will be impulsive ...

I walk towards him, his back still turned away from me. I touch his shoulder.

'James?'

He shrugs my hand away. 'Get your dirty hands off me.'

There is hatred in his voice.

Hatred, and disgust.

My perfect man will be able to make quick decisions and stick with them ...

He turns around. The sight of his face, and the burning rage it contains, makes me jump. It's like a stranger has walked into the room. I've never seen him like this, and I never thought I would.

I feel like Dr Frankenstein when he discovers that the perfect being he has created is in fact a monster.

I run an Ella-and-James mantra in my head, in the hope that the Relationship Fairy hasn't just reversed her magic.

Ella-and-James. Ella-and-James. Ella-and-James.

He is everything I wanted. The complete and total opposite of Rob. But, all of a sudden, I'm starting to realise that the total opposite of Rob comes with its own problems.

And I can't even blame the Perfect Agency.

After all, this is what I asked for.

A romantic, strong-minded, hot-blooded, impulsive man who wants to have me all to himself.

In short, my Mr Perfect.

'James? James? Please ... nothing happened ... for *fuck's* sake, his dad died ... and I don't even have to explain myself. I've done nothing wrong.'

He looks down at me with the sternest eyes imaginable. 'When we are married you will never see that stupid ugly slob again.'

This isn't a question.

This is a statement of fact.

'James, you can't tell me what to ...'

He storms off to his bedroom. Slams the door.

Needing air, I go out onto the balcony. My heart is racing as I look out at the city lights.

205

Why is he so jealous? So unreasonable?

I look down at the ring, the emerald gleaming like a green-eyed monster. How can a jewel that looked so beautiful now look so ugly?

For a moment I am tempted to take it off my finger and let it drop twenty storeys. I inch the ring slowly off and pinch it between my fingers as I contemplate its fate.

Then my mobile goes.

'Ella?'

It's mum.

I wipe away the uninvited tear that has started to roll down my cheek. 'Mum, hi ...'

'I tried to call you on your other number.'

'I'm at James's,' I tell her.

Her voice lifts. 'We got your letter.'

'What?'

'It came today. The letter. About the wedding.'

'Oh.'

I remember the gushing letter I wrote, desperately praying they wouldn't hit the roof. As it turns out, the letter more than did the trick.

'Isn't it fantastic? Doesn't the hotel look wonderful?'

I place the phone between my shoulder and my ear and slide the ring back on my finger.

'Yes,' I say. 'It does.'

'Oh Ella, we're so *proud* of you ... I've never seen your dad so happy.'

I close my eyes, bite my lip. 'Oh.'

'It was such a wonderful surprise ... your dad's always wanted to go to Las Vegas! Ooh, and the hotel! Doesn't it look posh?! How the other half live, eh? Well, you're the other half now aren't you?

206

You've gone right up in the world! Anyway, I can't stay on long. It's your mobile. I just had to say how happy you've made us. We're the proudest parents in the world! ... Just need the grandkids now.'

My mum is high as a kite. Her happiness and my present unhappiness seem to be in direct correlation with each other. Suddenly, I realise this is about more than me and James. It's about Mum and Dad. It's about everyone. The moment you declare you are getting married is the moment your love becomes public property, floated on the emotional stock exchange which your friends and family all have shares in.

And Mum's share value is going up at the precise moment mine is going down.

But I'm not about to let one row ruin everything.

'Anyway,' Mum says, 'I'd better go. Bye love.'

'Bye.'

I put the mobile back in my pocket, and breathe the night air into my lungs.

'Ella.'

It's James, behind me.

I turn around. The apology is there on his face before he says it. 'I'm sorry.'

'It's OK,' I tell him. 'It's OK.'

'I'll make it up to you,' he says. 'You'll see, on your birthday. I'll make it up to you.'

We hug, he strokes my back. I am still ready to believe it.

I'm still ready to believe it can be perfection.

Gentleman callers

It is two nights before my birthday. I am already acting like a five-year-old on Christmas Eve after too much Sunny Delight. You see, James has got something secret planned. Something big. What exactly it is, I'm not quite sure, but when he says 'something big' I take him at face value. After all, this is the man for whom 'going out for an Italian' means going out for an Italian *in Italy*.

So when James knocks on the door to our flat this evening I am almost wetting myself with excitement.

'I'll get it,' I say, to Maddie and Pip as I run to the door.

But it's not James.

It's Rob, sporting a black eye.

'Oh my God. Rob. What happened?'

'Are you ... are you on your own?'

'Yes.'

'Ella,' he says. 'I've got to tell you something?'

'Your eye. Were you in a fight? Were you mugged? What happened?' I feel a pang of hurt. I mean, Rob is many things but Rambo isn't one of them. His proudest boast used to be that he'd never got into a physical fight in his entire life. Hell, he even used to flinch at the boxing.

'*Ella* . . . listen to me . . . I've got to say something and . . . and . . . you're not going to like it . . .'

He stalls. Looks desperate. Even more desperate than usual.

'Rob, what is it?' I ask.

'I'm not meant to be here . . . He looks over his shoulder. 'I just . . . I'm not . . . I've got to tell you . . . something . . . Ella, it's about . . .'

Headlights.

The smooth purr of James's engine.

'James is here,' I tell Rob.

Rob's eyes swell with terror. 'James? Oh no . . .'

I mean, I'm not too happy about this situation either, but Rob's acting like I've just told him the sky is about to fall on his head.

'We're not doing anything wrong,' I tell Rob, although after James's over-the-top reaction the other night, I'm secretly worried. I close my eyes, trying to think of the best excuse. 'James knows there's nothing going on between us, Rob . . . ' I open my eyes. 'Rob? Rob?'

He's gone.

Vanished into thin air.

I peep my head out of the open door and look down the street. I hear the sound of Rob's feet clip-clopping at hyperspeed down the pavement towards his car.

I am about to call his name when I realise that James is now only three metres away on the footpath, walking towards me with a broad, face-wide grin.

He obviously has no idea that one minute ago Rob was standing right where he is now.

'Hi,' I say, as I hear Rob's car cough its way down the street.

'Would you like a cup of tea James?' Maddie asks, in her posh in-front-of-James voice.

'No, thanks, I'm fine.'

'Vodka?' she asks, reverting to her old self. 'We've got some vodka.'

'No really, I'm *fine*. Have you told them yet?'

'Sorry?' I ask him. I'm miles away, still thinking about Rob's mystery black eye and his sharp exit.

Pip, who is stroppily marking work on the sofa, looks up and says, 'Told us what?'

'Well . . . we've set a date for the wedding,' James tells them. 'Saturday the twenty-fifth of May.'

'It's May now,' Pip says.

'Yes, I know.'

'*This* May?'

'Yup. In half-term.'

Pip looks stunned, which isn't really surprising for someone who lives her whole life ten months in advance.

'. . .in Las Vegas.'

'Las Vegas? Bloody hell.'

'Wow. Fantastic,' Maddie says.

I nod, and try to push Rob out of my mind. But even as I speak, anxiety chews my stomach.

'James can wangle two extra tickets with the airline,' I say. 'So I'd like you both to come. To be there. There's not going to be bridesmaids or anything, because it's not that sort of service, but I'd really love it if you were there with me.'

Maddie is hopping up and down and yelping like

210

she's won the lottery. Pip, on the other hand, looks like she's won the lottery and lost the ticket.

'That's really kind, El. It's just that I'm so behind with everything ... and it's only a week before Ofsted ... and I don't think I'll be able to take any time off ... I'm sorry ... if I'd have known about it sooner I might have been able to rearrange my schedule but honestly I've got so much work to do. There's no way I can ...'

'It's all right,' I tell her. 'Honestly. It's fine. Really.'

God, what is the matter with her? A free holiday to Vegas to go to her friend's wedding and she says no because of bloody Ofsted. She's so desperately in need of a shag that I'm sometimes tempted to strap on a dildo and do the job myself, just to hear her go on about something other than lesson plans and exam papers.

'OK' says James. 'Well ... that leaves us with an extra ticket.'

I look at Maddie, who is still a bubbling saucepan of excitement. 'What about Steve?' I ask her.

Her eyes shine with joy. Although I have to admit that I was sceptical at first, Maddie and Boring Steve are now an official item. And Maddie is well and truly smitten. Two months ago, Maddie said all men were interchangeable 'walking willies', and yet now she is a one man, one willy woman.

'Steve? Honestly?' she beams. 'Steve can come? Wow! Wow! That's brilliant. I'll phone him.'

She hops out of the room to call him from the hallway, and me and James leave Pip to her work and go to my bedroom, with the knot of anxiety still in my stomach.

The good and bad surprises

James sits on the bed next to me and puts his hand on my knee. 'Ella, I've got to tell you something. It's about your birthday.'

'What?' I ask, wondering where in the world he's going to whisk me off to.

'I won't be able to be with you.'

For a minute, I don't understand. 'What? What do you mean?'

'They want me to do a flight to LA.'

'Can't you ... can't you get out of it?'

OK, OK. I know how I'm coming across here. Pretty selfishly right? It's just, I don't know, I suppose it's my fatal flaw. I always like birthdays to be special. And I'm not just talking about my own birthday. Any birthday. I like to make them as great as possible. I suppose I'm a birthdayaholic.

But no.

Because now the one person in the world I wanted to share it with isn't going to be able to make it.

The knot of anxiety I felt when Rob showed up is turning to nausea. My emotions are all mixed up like a cheap, sickly cocktail.

'I'm sorry Ella, but this is my first flight as captain. There's no way I'll be able to get out of it. I'm sorry.'

Be reasonable, I tell myself.

If there's no way he can get out of it, there's no way he can get out of it.

'OK, OK. We've still got tomorrow.'

He shakes his head. 'No. No we haven't. I fly out tomorrow morning. I have to be at the airport at eight. I'm sorry Ella, there's just no way round it. I fly out tomorrow and I'm on the return flight the day after, with a rest day in between.'

He is not looking at me directly as he says this. He is like a guilty Year Ten pupil trying to tell me he left his homework on the school bus. Which is weird, because James – in his own mind at least – hasn't done anything wrong.

For a strange moment I think he is lying to me. 'Are you telling me the truth?'

He looks incredulous. 'Ella, what are you talking about? Of course I'm telling you the truth. Why would I lie about this?'

I look at his perfect face and wonder where my insecurity is coming from. Am I frightened that he is too good for me? Or am I frightened about something else? I think again about Rob, and whatever it was he came round to tell me.

'James,' I ask him. 'What do you see in me?'

'What do you mean?'

'I mean: what do you see in me? I'm a nightmare. I get so paranoid about things. I thought for a minute that you were lying to me ...'

'Lying to you? Why? Why did you think that?'

'I don't know.'

213

'Ella,' he says, placing his hand on top of mine. 'I'm not a liar. You didn't want a liar and you haven't got a liar.'

He's got a point.

My perfect man would not be a liar. And James is, according to the science, my perfect man.

'I know, it's just . . .

'Ella, listen to me: I won't lie to you. Do you understand? Now, if our future is going to be as long and happy as we want it to be we're going to need a little more trust.'

Trust.

Always been bad at that.

Ever since I found out about Santa being Uncle Eric. And the tooth fairy. And Milli Vanilli.

His eyes are now directly on mine. 'Do you trust me?'

'Yes,' I say, hoping it's true. 'Yes. I trust you.'

I stick out my bottom lip like a sulky child. 'It's just . . . I thought you had something big planned, that's all.'

He smiles the smile of a patient father. 'Shall I give you your present now?'

'Now? Have you . . . have you got it on you?'

He taps his pocket. 'Right here.'

Suddenly, all remaining traces of my mood evaporate into thin air and I am back to being the five-year-old on Christmas Eve after too much Sunny Delight. 'Oh . . . oh wow, am I allowed to?'

He pulls a blank white envelope out of his pocket. 'There you go. Open it.'

'Am I naughty?'

'Not at all. Go on, open it.'

I do as he says, my frenzied fingers tearing open

the envelope to reveal six tickets to see Elton John in concert. In Las Vegas. Before the wedding. At the MGM Grand.

Oh my God.

I've heard about this.

It's meant to be the best show on the planet.

'Wow ... wow ...'

'You said that when you used to play the piano you always wanted to be like Elton John. You said he was your childhood hero. And so I thought I'd get you this. It was either that or a Scissors Sisters album. But I thought you'd prefer this.'

'Six tickets?'

'For your mum and dad, Maddie and her man and us two. The wedding party, basically.'

'It must have cost a bomb.'

He smiles. 'A mid-range nuclear missile, maybe.'

I kiss him. I kiss him again. Oh hell, one more.

'I guess that means you forgive me. For not being there on your birthday.'

Something at the back of my brain tells me there is still something weird about him tonight, something Rob might have been able to explain. But as 'Goodbye Yellow Brick Road' starts to play in my mind, I am more than willing to dismiss these feelings as paranoia.

'Yes,' I tell him. 'I guess it does.'

The second something stupid

The day before my birthday, when James is flying high over the Atlantic Ocean *en route* to LA, I do something stupid. Again.

I phone Rob.

After about twenty rings he picks up.

'Hello?' he says.

'Hi Rob. It's me.'

'Ella –'

'I just wondered how you are . . . you looked terrible when you came around.'

I hear his breath down the line. He wants to say something, but doesn't.

'What were you going to tell me?' I ask him. 'Before you disappeared?'

More heavy breathing.

'Where's . . . James?' he asks me.

'He's on a flight to LA.'

'Oh.'

'Why?'

'I just . . . wondered.'

'Rob? Is there something you want to say to me?'

A pause.

Then: 'Do you love him?'

'What?'

'Do you *love* him?'

'Rob, why are you asking me that?'

'I just . . . want to know. I've just . . . got to know.'

I wonder for a second – and it's only a second –
what would happen if I answered 'No'. What would
Rob say? What would he do?

'Yes,' I tell him. 'Of course I do. I'm marrying him.'

He sighs, and in his heavy breath there is a world
of regret.

'Ella, I'm sorry.'

'Sorry?'

'I shouldn't have come round and seen you . . . it
was a mistake.'

'No, Rob it was okay, it –'

'No, listen Ella,' he says, a sudden firmness in his
voice. 'I don't think I should see you again . . . It was
nice when you came round, and good to talk . . . about
dad, but . . .' He hesitates, every word a self-inflicted
wound '. . . But you shouldn't come round again or
phone me . . .'

'Rob – '

'Please Ella. I'm sorry. Just . . . it's for the best. OK?'

'OK,' I say. 'If that's what you want then OK.'

'It is,' he says. 'It is. I've got to go.'

'Right.'

'Bye Ella.'

'Bye.'

And I am halfway to putting the phone down when
I hear his voice. 'Ella?'

'What?' I ask him, speeding the receiver back to
my ear.

'Happy birthday. For tomorrow.'

217

Birthday Girl

Maddie is either the best person or the worst person to be around when it's your birthday.

It all depends on how you feel about being woken up to Stevie Wonder singing 'Happy Birthday To Ya!' on your stereo at six-thirty in the morning.

She even mimes Stevie at his keyboard.

I have no idea where she gets the energy from. She must run on fossil fuels or something.

'What's the time,' I ask her.

'Birthday time,' she says, shoving a card in my sleepy face.

Great. It's got a badge. 30 Today!

She pins it to my shabby pyjamas, then hands me my present. *The Rough Guide To Las Vegas*.

'Thanks Mads,' I tell her.

'No probs treacle.'

The letter box goes.

'Post!' Maddie says. 'Birthday post! I'll get it.'

She comes back in with two envelopes and a parcel. The parcel turns out to be pyjamas from my mum and dad, complete with little teddy bears in dresses patterned all over them. I read their card:

To Ella,
Happy birthday!
You'll always be our little girl.
Love,
Mum and Dad
X

Then I open the other envelope.
Maddie takes a peek. 'What is it?'
I open it and I look at the card inside.

St. Anthony's Music College
Private tuition

Confirmation of Ella Holt's weekly piano
lessons under the tutelage of Mrs Eleanor
Jeffries.

Time of lessons: *Tuesday 6.30pm – 7.30pm,*
weekly
Duration: *Twelve months*

Below the print is one word scrawled in capital
letters: LOVER.

I remember what I told James.

About my biggest regret in life, that I gave up the
piano.

'It's from James,' I tell her.

'But he already got you a present,' says Maddie.
'The Elton John tickets.'

'I know. But he must have arranged this to surprise
me.'

I nearly cry. It sounds stupid, but this is the most
wonderful present anyone has ever bought me. James

must have posted it as another surprise, so I pick up my mobile and phone him.

It rings for ages and then a woman answers. 'Hello?'

For a moment I am filled with paranoia. 'Er ... hello. Is ... erm, James there please?'

James speaks. 'Hello.'

'It's me.'

'Oh Ella, hi.' It's weird hearing him. He sounds so clear, as if he's right next door. Not on the other side of the world.

I wait, expecting a 'Happy Birthday' but it doesn't arrive.

'Who was that woman?' I ask, the paranoia creeping into my voice.

'That woman? Oh ... oh that's just someone I work with. I'm with the whole crew in the hotel. I just went to the buffet and left my phone in my jacket. On the chair. She answered it.'

'Oh,' I say, feeling stupid. 'Oh. Right. Sorry.'

'Anyway,' he says. 'Are you OK? It must be early ...'

'Er yes,' I say, thinking it must be late to be eating in LA. 'It is. I was just phoning about the present.'

'The present?'

'Yes, the present. You really shouldn't have. I can't believe it. It's the most thoughtful thing ever. Honestly, it's made up for you not being here.'

He pauses for a long time. Must be the time delay. 'Right,' he says, eventually. 'Yes well, you're special Ella. I knew it's what you wanted.'

He sounds weird.

Weird, how, I'm not quite sure. But definitely weird.

The phone starts to crackle.

'It's breaking up,' he says.

'Yes. OK. Thank you. I love you.'

'I love you too. Bye.'

Later on, at school, there is another envelope waiting to surprise me.

It is on my desk, in the room where I teach the Year Elevens.

It's a light, baby-blue envelope, with 'Miss Holt' written in unjoined, trying-to-be-neat letters.

I open it and inside is a rather naff but sweet hearts-and-flowers Hallmark card. I open it up and read:

> *To Miss Holt,*
> *Roses R red*
> *Violets R blue*
> *Chocolate is sweet*
> *And so R U*
> *Happy Birthday to the most beautiful teacher in*
> *the world.*
> *Luv,*
> *?*

I laugh.

Not at the card, at the question mark.

I might not be Sherlock Holmes, but after marking about 700 of his essays I can spot Mark Dobson's fifteen-year-old handwriting a mile off.

Right at the centre

The next day James returns, shattered from LA. I go and see him at his flat and, during a post-coital chat, tell him about the card.

'So what did you do about it?' he asks me, as I feel his heartbeat quicken.

I lift my head off his chest and say, 'Nothing. I didn't want to. It was sweet, really, if you think about it. He's got a bit of a crush on me I think. It's harmless though.'

'A crush? Why didn't you tell me?'

'Because it's nothing. I mean it's par for the course isn't it? If you stand in front of a room of hormonal boys and happen to own a pair of breasts. I mean, they only need to hear the word skirt to get an erection at that age.'

To which James says nothing, but I can tell from the way his body tightens and the way he bites his lip that he's not happy about it.

'Guess who phoned me today when I got back in?' he asks me, moments later.

'I don't know. Who?'

'Lara Stein.'

'What? She phoned here?' I wondered why she always phones James before me.

'Yep. She asked how it was going. She wanted a progress report.'

'Oh,' I say. 'Right. So what did you tell her?'

'I told her about the wedding. In Las Vegas.'

I get a bad feeling. Like James has got something else to tell me.

I'm right.

He has.

'She's coming.'

I don't understand. 'What?'

'She's coming to the wedding.'

I do understand. 'What?'

'Her and that uptight skinny New Yorker. Jessica whatshername.'

'No. Why did you invite them?'

'I didn't. Lara sort of . . . invited herself.'

My heart sinks. Call me old-fashioned, but I kind of wanted my tiny friends and family wedding to be actually made up of friends and family, not some uber-rich megalomaniac who hardly knows my name and her skinny sidekick.

'What could I do?' he asks me. 'I mean, if it wasn't for her or the Perfect Agency we wouldn't have met.'

'It's not like she's paying for the wedding.'

'No . . . I know. I am. I'm paying for it.'

And I can see from his face he thinks he's paying for it in more ways than one. I am cross with him, but I let it go. The way he had let it go moments before.

'Oh,' he says stroking my hair. 'And she said there might be some media.'

'Media?'

223

'She's going to send out a press release or something. She's going to check with the hotel and see if it's okay, but she thinks it will be.'

Having decided to let it go, I am now decided to get it back. 'Check with the hotel? Check with the hotel? What about checking with me? Where do I fit in to all this?'

'Ella, come on,' he says, adding a forehead-kiss to his diplomatic hair-strokes. 'You know where you fit in. You fit right at the centre. Look at it this way: most people have to pay for a photographer. We'll have ours all for free. Come on ... it will probably make you feel more special, not less. And just because we didn't plan it doesn't mean it will be necessarily a bad thing. I thought you like surprises ... I thought that was why you ended up with me. Trust me, it will be great.'

His final forehead kiss wins me over. 'OK,' I say. 'I trust you.'

The piano lesson

St Anthony's Music College is housed in an old, red-brick Victorian building that looks like a Methodist Church.

It reminds me of the music college in Leeds I used to go to when I was twelve years old, and walking inside feels like walking back into my childhood.

'Hello,' I say to the woman behind the desk. 'I'm here for a piano lesson with Mrs Jeffries.'

The woman's ruddy-cheeked face looks at me and smiles. She has a warm, dinnerlady-type quality.

'Oh yes,' she says. 'It's just down the corridor and the second door on the left.'

I follow the instructions and knock on the door with 'Mrs Eleanor Jeffries' name written on it.

'Enter!' calls a shrill voice, from somewhere inside.

I obey the voice and find myself inside a room that is far larger than the narrow door had suggested.

In the middle of the room is a piano. It's not a grand piano or anything swanky like that. It's just an old brown upright thing that looks like it has seen better days. Just like the woman sitting on the piano

225

stool, an old lady, with a green woolly cardigan, grey hair sticking out of her head at every angle and glasses worn as a necklace.

'Ella Holt?' she says, twitching her head like a bird as she takes me in.

'Yes. That's me.'

'Splendid,' she says. 'Splendid. Now, park your bottom next to me and let's see your hands.'

I go over and sit next to her on the piano stool, and show her my hands.

'Splendid,' she says. 'A pianist's hands. Perfect long fingers ...' She notices my ring, and puts on her glasses. 'Oh, my! Now, there's a serious proposition if ever I saw one. He must really mean business with that. You must have found a good one!'

'Yes, I think I have.'

Her thin lips curl into a smile. 'They are few and far between, the good ones. I agree with Balzac. The majority of husbands remind me of an orang-utan trying to play the violin. I should know, I've had three of them. Husbands that is, not violins.'

I laugh. I've got a feeling I'm going to like her.

'I married below me,' she says, with a naughty chuckle. 'Like all women.'

She starts to play something on the piano, her fingers more nimble than their age-spotted appearance suggests.

'Playing the piano is a lot like marriage really,' she says, over the music. 'If you think of the left hand as the husband and the right hand as the wife.'

She starts playing the same notes with both hands. 'If both hands are doing exactly the same thing, then there's not really much point to it. You might play a nice tune, but it gets rather boring after a while.'

She then starts playing two tunes at once, one with each hand. 'Of course, if both hands are following completely different music, and don't know what the other hand is doing then that doesn't work too well either. That was my second marriage.'

Her fingers change position, and she starts to play the most soft and beautiful tune I've ever heard. 'The trick is to let both hands do their own thing but still to work in harmony together. Something that is so much easier on the piano then it is in life.'

She finishes the tune. 'Now,' she says, 'let's get started on you. Can you read music at all?'

'A little bit. I used to do lessons when I was younger.'

'Splendid!' says Mrs Jeffries, turning the pages in her music book that rests on the piano stand. 'Let's start you on something simple . . . Ah yes, I've got it. Perfect!'

The page opens on a piece of music that says 'Daisy Bell', by Harry Dacre.

I start to play, my left and right hands struggling to stay in time. But slowly, it comes together, and Mrs Jeffries soft, sad voice sings the tune over the top of the music.

'Daisy, Daisy, give me your answer, do!
I'm half crazy, all for the love of you!
It won't be a stylish marriage,
I can't afford a carriage,
But you'll look sweet
Upon the seat
Of a bicycle made for two!'

Mrs Jeffries claps her hands together. 'That was splendid my dear! Simply splendid!'

The monster's girlfriend

This is my worst nightmare.

This is what I have been dreading for weeks, ever since Mr Loving told me I had to do it.

I am, right at this moment, standing on the school stage in front of a sea of teenage faces. Teachers line the sides of the hall. Some parents and a local journalist are sitting on the raised, normally unused side corridor. And here I am, talking about how the only way I can meet my soon-to-be husband is through the miracle of twenty-first century scientific technology.

'A short while ago, my great friend Miss Hatfield, sitting over there, did something very naughty behind my back ... she sent off a ... off a ... questionnaire about my ... my ... my ...' Delilah? Bloody hell, what's the matter with me? My palms are sweaty. My mouth is a desert. My heart is doing an over-excited impression of a machine gun.

I know it sounds weird, with me being a teacher and everything, but I'm not good at talking in public. Talking to twenty-five Year Elevens about Shakespeare is bad enough, but standing up in front of a thousand people and talking about my love life is embarrassment squared. No, cubed.

And then I see him, behind all the parents at the back of the hall. It's James. He smiles at me, waves. He came! Last night, when I asked him, he said he wouldn't be able to make it. He said he had to go to the airport and run through the flight arrangements for tomorrow. But now he's here. I wave back. Like an idiot.

The whole school cranes their neck simultaneously to see who I am waving at.

The teenage girls in the audience 'Oooh' and 'Phwoar'.

I have totally lost it now.

'I ...er ... where was I? My good friend Mad ... Miss Hatfield ...' I'm not going to make this on my own. I look across the hall at James, my eyes screaming 'Help me'. But although he might be trained to keep his nerve during a terrorist takeover of a plane at 30,000 feet, there's no way he's got the guts to talk about his love life in front of this lot.

'... my good friend Miss Hatfield ...'

Maddie stands up.

I haven't asked her to, but she stands up and walks down the hall, up the side steps, and right onto the stage as if it was arranged. As if it was part of the assembly.

'Yes,' she says, with total confidence. 'It was all my fault ...'

She goes on to explain what happened, with me chipping in now and again. She recounts the whole story – from the questionnaire to the trip to Las Vegas – and no one seems to be any the wiser.

'Thanks,' I tell her, afterwards. 'You saved my life.'

229

'Hey, I got you into this in the first place remember.'

'I'd better go and see James before my first class,' I tell her, realising he is loitering at the back of the hall.

'Thanks for coming,' I tell him, once I get over to him. 'I made a right tit out of myself up there.'

'You were great,' he says, halfway to convincing.

'I'd better go to my lesson, but you can walk me there if you want. My classroom's right by the main entrance.'

'Sure,' he says.

So we walk out of the hall, past the school library, past teenage girls giggling into cupped hands, past Paul Loving ('Great assembly, Miss Holt,' he says), past the staff room, past the school toilets, past a group of Year Elevens who happen to include Mark Dobson.

As we pass them, one of his mates shouts, 'Dobbo's well jealous now miss!'

'Shut up!' Mark tells him, adding a dead arm to emphasise his point. Mark's embarrassment, clearly indicated by his beetroot cheeks, sends him into the male toilets.

'Who was that?' James asks sharply.

'Mark Dobson . . . you know, the boy who sent me the birthday card.'

'Oh,' he says. 'Him.' Then he looks at the door to the toilets. 'Actually, before I'd go, I'd better just nip to the loo – won't be a sec.'

'James, I've got to get to class . . .'

But he's already gone. For a moment I think he doesn't need to go to the loo and that his real reason for going into the male toilets is to confront his would-be love-rival Mark Dobson. I dismiss the thought as stupid. James isn't the type to feel threatened by a fifteen-year-old with a schoolboy crush. Is he?

Again it comes back to me. *My perfect man will want me all to himself* . . .

That's what I said to Maddie.

That's what she sent to the Perfect Agency.

No, I tell myself, shaking the thought out of my head. *I'm being stupid.*

And, as if to confirm this, the door to the gents opens and James walks out with a carefree smile. 'There,' he says. 'That's better.'

At lunch, me and Maddie have a heart-to-heart in the staffroom.

'Thanks for bailing me out,' I tell her. 'With the assembly.'

'Well, what are friends for?'

I smile. 'How's Steve?' I ask her.

'He's good. Really good. We've reached a stage, you know, where everything just seems to click.'

I tell her my theory about the Relationship Fairy.

'That's it!' she says. 'That's what it is. You wake up one morning and you just feel like everything has slipped perfectly into place, without you even realising.'

Pip comes and joins us. 'Is this a couple-only section of the staffroom?' she asks.

Maddie adopts the stern look of a teacher. 'Yes, it is. No boyfriend, no entry. That's just how it is.'

Pip sits down, half-acknowledging the joke as she munches on her carrot salad.

'They're bastards,' she says.

231

We immediately guess the 'they' refers to the half of the population sporting a penis.

'Not all of them,' Maddie assures her.

'No,' Pip says. 'All of them. They're bastards when they're fifteen and they're bastards when they're fifty. They suck you in with bullshit words and jump overboard the moment your arse gets too big.'

'Pip,' I tell her. 'You've got the smallest, pertest, hardest arse out of all three of us.'

'You could crack nuts with your arse,' adds Maddie.

'Thanks,' says Pip. 'But it doesn't alter my central thesis. Men think with their dicks and they never stop thinking with their dicks and because they think with their dicks we're the ones who have to have tit jobs and botox and pound the treadmill just because we're scared of ending up being a lonely old spinster with twenty cats. And the only reason we're scared of that is because of bullshit lovesongs and bullshit films and bullshit books that try and pretend the perfect man is out there. But it's bullshit. I'm sorry, Ella, but it is. Perfect is an abstract concept. In the real world it only exists as an illusion. What's that word? A *simulacrum*. That's it. Men pretend they're better than they are to trap us and make us fall in love with them because they know that if we realised what they were all like from the start we'd all be lesbian by now. But instead, everyone blames it on their last guy. Oh my last boyfriend was a total shit, but I'm sure they're not all total shits. Because we're all scared of believing the truth. Men are all total shits. Every lying, cheating, arse-fetishising one of them.'

She finishes her speech, along with her carrot

salad. Me and Maddie sit in stunned silence as she walks out of the room.

'Well,' says Maddie. 'If Pip ever gets tired of teaching, she could always get a job as a relationship counsellor.'

That afternoon, I am reading an extract of Mary Shelley's *Frankenstein* to the blank faces of Year Eleven.

'"The being finished speaking, and fixed his looks upon me in expectation of a reply. But I was bewildered, perplexed, and unable to arrange my ideas sufficiently to understand the full extent of his proposition. He confirmed –

"You must create a female for me, with whom I can live in the interchange of those sympathies necessary for my being. This you alone can do; and I demand it of you as a right which you must not refuse."'

I put the book down and speak directly to the class.

'Victor Frankenstein eventually agrees to create a female companion for the monster because he believes this will stop him being violent. But he changes his mind and destroys the female before she is created. Why does he change his mind?'

I look around the class and Lizzie Sprightly's hand shoots up. Thank God she's back. She's been off with laryngitis for nearly a month and she's the only one that pays any interest in class.

'Yes Lizzie?'

'He changes his mind miss because it went wrong before ... when he created the first monster ... and he thought that the monster was going to be perfect but it wasn't. So he thinks that if he creates a mate for him it could still go wrong even if he is doing it for the right reasons.'

'Very good Lizzie. Very good indeed. That's exactly right. Dr Frankenstein no longer trusts science, or himself for that matter. He knows that his good intentions have failed him so he destroys the monster's girlfriend before she is created.' I catch Mark Dobson's eye and his previously lingering eyes dart away from me. 'And after Dr Frankenstein destroys her, neither he, nor the monster he has created can have a happy life. Right, OK, whose turn is it to read the next extract from the novel? Christopher, would you like to read the next section.'

Christopher Thompson turns a whiter shade of pale. After all, this boy is to reading what the Pope is to snow-boarding.

'Page one-six-six Christopher. The second paragraph. From "The report of the pistol"'

And so he begins. '"The report ... report ... of the pistol"' – giggle – '"bought ..."'

'Brought,' I correct him.

'"... brought a cr ... a crow ... a crowd into the room ..."'

He takes twenty minutes and almost as many giggles to finish the paragraph.

As soon as he's finished the bell goes, followed by the normal stampede out of the room.

Mark Dobson, in particular, is making a very fast beeline towards the door.

And that's when I notice it.

The rip, in his shirt.

'Mark,' I say. 'Mark? Can I have a word?'

Of course, this prompts the usual noises from the

rest of the class, as if I've just asked the poor boy out on a date.

He shuffles over, his head towards the floor, looking even more awkward than usual.

'What happened to your shirt?'

'Nothing miss,' he mumbles.

'It's been ripped.'

He says nothing.

I lift up his tie and see that two of the buttons are also missing, revealing the skin underneath.

'Has someone done this to you?' I ask him.

'Please miss, it was no one.'

I sigh. 'OK. It was no one. Just try and stay out of trouble.'

'Yes miss. Can I go now?'

I find this to be a weird question. Normally Mark is looking for excuses to see me and here he is desperately trying to get away. Oh well, I suppose the crush must be over.

'Yes Mark. You can go. Have a nice half-term.'

Later on, when I'm on playground duty, I see Mark walk by with Darren Bentley.

Mark has his head down again, doing his best not to make eye contact with me. As they walk past me, and head over towards the school field, Darren looks at me with angry eyes.

'He's a psycho!' he shouts at me.

Then he runs off. They both do.

'Darren?' I call after him, wondering who exactly he meant. 'Darren, come back here!'

But they are gone, lost among all the other boys playing football on the field.

Inside the mirror

Maddie looks at me and screws up her face in disgust. 'You look like ... like a cloud.'

A cloud.

That's a new one.

The last eight dresses have been dismissed for being too 80s, too short, too long, too cream, too meringue, too lacy, too shiny and too wedding-y (a bizarre criticism of a wedding dress, but hey, it's Maddie).

Now, apparently, I look too much like a cloud. How a dress can make you look like vaporised water at high altitude I am not too sure, but it looks like I'll have to try something else.

'Have you got anything that doesn't make me look like ... a cloud?' I ask the shop assistant who has a name badge saying Wendy and who, like all the staff at Blushing Bride, is in a bubbly state of tickled-pink excitement, as if she's got an Orgasmatron wired to her knickers or something.

'Something less cloud-like?' Wendy pants. 'Let me see let me see, let me see ...'

'Something simpler,' Maddie tells her. 'More classic.'

'I'm getting married abroad,' I explain. 'It's going to be a quiet wedding. No bridesmaids or anything. So I'm looking for something a bit understated.'

'One moment, one moment,' says Wendy, apparently unable to say something just once.

She disappears out of the changing area and back into the main shop with her mad smile and her tape measure sticking out of her back trouser pocket like a tail.

Moments later, Wendy returns.

'Here we are, here we are,' she says, holding aloft a rather promising looking simple white dress with a sweetheart neck.

I take it in the cubicle and try it on. I look at myself in the mirror opposite the door and I suddenly get goosebumps.

It is beautiful.

I feel like a different person, a different me. The self I only get to see in dreams.

This is the one. This is what I will be wearing as I say my vows.

In that moment, it suddenly dawns on me. This time next week I will be married. I will be Mrs Ella Master. I will belong to James and he will belong to me.

There is a whole new life waiting for me I realise. A whole future that is now locked inside the mirror, where the woman in the white dress is still staring back at me, with fear and hope weighed equally in her eyes.

The air hostess

'This is your captain speaking,' says James, over the speaker system. 'I'd like to welcome all passengers on board the twenty-fifteen flight from London Heathrow to Las Vegas. Our expected time of arrival into McCarron International Airport will be Oh four thirty UK time, or twenty-one thirty local time. Myself and the rest of the cabin crew would like to wish everyone on board a happy and restful flight. Thank you.'

My mum, on the row in front, nudges the woman next to her. 'That's my son-in-law,' she says proudly. 'Well, he will be in a couple of days at any rate ...' And then she's off. While my dad plugs himself in to Easy Listening Classics on the in-flight headphones, my mum will spend the next eight hours giving her poor neighbour (a prim-looking elderly lady who appears to have stepped on the wrong flight) her entire autobiography.

On the lavish Club Class seats behind me, Jessica Perk is briefing Dr Lara Stein on the media arrangements for my Big Day.

'We're using a production company from LA to film it. They'll be arriving tomorrow. And we've already sent out the press release and photo call to all the relevant media . . .'

At the airport, Dr Lara told me that my wedding was going to be a media 'event', but it is only now that it starts to sink in.

'You'll be a celebrity,' she told me.

Suddenly I realise I don't want to be a celebrity. I mean, I thought the whole thing about Las Vegas weddings is that they are fast and fun and pretty private. OK, so you might expect someone to be camcording the whole thing, but you don't expect a film crew and a bunch of journalists to show up.

But then, I suppose it's a small price to pay for having the Perfect Agency's free trial. After all, without that there would be no wedding in the first place.

And yet, it feels kind of odd. As if I am an extra at my own wedding. Like I am just the snowball that started the avalanche.

I am sitting by the window.

To my left is Maddie. To her left is Boring Steve.

'Oh, this is so exciting,' Maddie says, her excitement nearly bursting her out of her seat belt. 'I can't believe it's happening. You're getting married! In Las Vegas!'

Boring Steve looks slightly less excited. He's reading the in-flight magazine as if it was the Holy Grail.

'Thank you both for coming,' I tell them.

Maddie looks at me in disbelief. 'Hey, free tickets to Las Vegas! Hardly likely to say no to that!'

I smile. 'And there was me thinking you were coming for the wedding.'

'Oh yes,' she says, teasingly. 'Of course. That.'

She holds Steve's hand as we begin to take off.

Steve puts the in-flight magazine back in his seat-pocket and he releases his hand from Maddie's grip.

My ears start popping so I open and close my mouth like a goldfish.

'Bad ears,' I explain to Steve.

'Me too,' he says.

He pulls out two small plugs from his pocket and screws them into his ears.

'Ear Planes,' he tells me, leaning forward. 'It stops the air pressure ...' He gives me an in-depth lecture on how air pressure works and how the tubes inside his ears work and how the balance of air is affected by something or other ... 'I've got a spare pair if you like.'

'No,' I say. 'I'll stick to the goldfish method.'

Steve carries on talking about the science of Ear Planes and I try, for Maddie's sake, to look interested. Maddie applauds my effort and says: 'Ignore him. He'll be on for hours.'

'*Maddie!* Don't say that.'

'Don't worry,' she says. 'He can't hear us. Not with those things in. Honestly, can't take him anywhere!'

'Well, at least he can get on a plane. Rob used to hyperventilate each time he passed a sign for the airport. I remember once he thought he could manage it so he went into Thomas Cook to book some package somewhere. As soon as the travel agent said, "Where do you want to fly from?" he had to run out ...'

My words trail off.

Why am I thinking about Rob? I shouldn't be thinking about him two days before my wedding, and I

240

sure as hell shouldn't be talking about him. But I remember his strength when I went round to see him, after his dad died, and I feel bad for laughing about his lack of strength when it comes to aeroplanes.

As we leave England beneath the clouds, I vow to leave all thoughts of Rob behind as well. Even negative thoughts.

Maddie nudges me.

'Is it just me,' Maddie asks, 'or is that air hostess staring at you?'

I look up and, sure enough, the air hostess with the drinks trolley four rows in front is staring right at me. Actually, *glaring* would be a more accurate description.

'What's her problem?' I mumble, as I put a mint in my mouth.

'I don't know. Maybe she's jealous of your sweets. She does look a bit hungry.'

Maddie's right.

The air hostes – who is still staring by the way – is a virtual skeleton. God knows what size her uniform is. It could hardly fit a Pepperami.

I mean, she's pretty, I'll give her that. Dark hair, cheekbones to die for, big lips (the only thing big about her).

'I bet she knows who you are,' says Maddie.

'So?'

'Well, I bet she's jealous.'

'Jealous? Why would a six-foot twig be jealous of me?'

'She probably fancies James.'

'What?'

'I saw this documentary on telly. About an airline. All the air-hostesses fancied the captain. Now James

241

has become a captain they'll all fancy him. It's something about the uniform I think.'

I stare back at the air-hostess, who looks away and
starts to concentrate on serving drinks.

'You're probably right.' I shrug.

The downside of falling in love with Mr Perfect is
that other people might find him equally perfect. But
I can cope with that. I mean, I suppose I should be
flattered. It's a hell of a lot better than the looks of
sympathy I used to get from other women when I was
dating Rob.

Doh!

I thought about Rob.

Right, that's it. No more Rob thoughts from now
on. Just keep thinking about how nice it is to have
someone that makes other women jealous for the first
time in your life.

The orange juice incident

'Would you like any drinks?' It's her. The skeleton with the drinks trolley, and she's doing her best not to glare.

'Erm, a vodka and coke,' says Maddie. 'No, two vodkas.'

She nudges Steve. 'Do. You. Want. A. Drink?' she asks, doing the sign language.

He points to the can of bitter. Very Vegas, I must say.

Then the air hostess looks at me, brandishing a smile as fake as her Gucci watch. 'Would you like a drink?' she asks me.

I look on the trolley for something that is sealed, so she can't slip any arsenic in it. There's a thin can of Britvic orange juice. 'I'll have an orange juice please,' I say, in my best Enid Blyton voice.

She keeps up the smile as she bends over and grabs a can of orange and a plastic cup.

'Thank you,' I say, as she hands over the drink.

'My pleasure.'

One more flash of the fake smile and then she's off down the aisle, asking Dr Lara Stein and Jessica Perk what they want to drink.

'I'll just have a water,' says Jessica.

'Oh, I'll have champagne,' says Dr Lara. 'We're celebrating.'

I pour my orange into the plastic cup and start drinking.

After a bit I get a headache so I leave the remaining orange juice in my cup and stare out of the small window at the soft clouds below. They seem unreal, the clouds. The cuddly, sheep-like type you get in children's cartoons. The kind that surround fairytale castles in Disney movies.

The clouds clear.

The Atlantic ocean glistens like a giant sheet of metal, miles below us.

I turn back into my seat.

Maddie is holding Steve's hand. Caressing it, with her thumb. Her head rests on his shoulder as she starts to drift off towards sleep.

She's been so happy recently and now I see why. Her and Steve may be incompatible on paper, but they are still a perfect fit.

Oh no. She's back.

The skinny air hostess with the laser eyes.

'Have you all finished with your drinks?' she asks us.

I look down at Maddie and Steve's empty cups and my half-cup of orange juice. My headache is still there so I tell her, 'Yes, yes we have.'

She clears Maddie and Steve's cups then reaches over for mine. She pinches the transparent plastic between her two bony fingers and –

'Oh. *Oh*. I'm *so* sorry,' she says, as she starts to mop up the orange juice that she has just spilled all over my lap. 'I'm such a clutz.'

Maddie, now fully awake says, 'How did a *clutz*

get a job serving drinks.'

I grab her arm. 'Maddie, leave it.'

Then I say to the air hostess: 'It's all right. It's all right. I'll do it.'

I take the tissue from her and start mopping my wet patch.

'I'm sorry,' she says, with fake sympathy, before walking back down the aisle.

When she's gone, mum turns around in her seat and looks at my lap. She laughs. 'Oh, what've you done, you clumsy thing!'

'It was the air hostess,' says Maddie, sending her own laser-eyed glare in the skeleton's direction.

I climb over Maddie and Steve and hunchback my way to the toilets, to wash out the orange juice. Once there, I splash my jeans, wipe them and attempt to dry them with the cloth towel. But the towel's fixed too high to the wall so I leave it and open the door. If I'm quick no one will notice the dark stain all over my jeans.

But then, over the speakers: 'This is your captain speaking, we are now travelling at an altitude of thirty thousand feet and if I could borrow your ears for just a moment I would like to share something with you . . .'

Oh no.

Oh no no no no.

He's not.

He's not going to tell the whole plane.

Not now.

Not while I've got a wet patch. Not while I'm standing up, facing the whole of club class. 'In two days time I will be marrying my fiancée Ella Holt in Las Vegas.'

Maddie starts the applause, whooping and pointing

at me. The whole plane stares at me.

'She's ever so excited,' I hear my mum tell her elderly neighbour.

'I can see that,' the old woman says, staring straight at my wet patch.

I cover my groin region and run back towards my seat, but a skeletal hand holds my arm. It's the air hostess who spilled my drink.

'No running,' she says, her false smile exchanged for an authentic scowl.

When I eventually make it back to my seat, I spend the next seven hours staring out of the window, as I wonder what, exactly, is the air hostess' problem.

Loving Las Vegas

The plane descends.

After miles and miles of black desert, I see Vegas glowing like a neon space colony on the horizon.

As we get closer we can see the giant buildings all lit up. Pyramids, skyscrapers, castles. Buildings that belong more easily in dreams than in any real location.

Which is quite appropriate really, as my body is still on British time and thinks it's four-thirty in the morning. Everyone around me is asleep, so all is quiet. Well, apart from Jessica Perk mumbling in her sleep about chocolate and cream cakes.

I think of James, wide awake in the cabin, as he touches us safely down on the airport runway.

Half an hour later, the Las Vegas dream is in close-up, as I stare with tired, stinging eyes at the Strip as we make our way to the Bellagio.

The Bellagio, according to my Las Vegas guide-book, is the largest five star hotel in the world. In fact, it's the second largest hotel in the world full stop. It says here that the top ten biggest hotels in the planet are all in Las Vegas.

And, sitting in the back of the cab with Maddie and

Steve (I'm meeting up with James later and Mum and Dad are in the cab behind), I can see that must be the case. Driving down the Strip you feel like Alice in Wonderland, as though you've taken some shrinking potion that has reduced you out of scale.

We pass a giant hotel called the Luxor which has full-scale pyramids and a sphinx outside. We pass another one with large King Arthur-style castles. Then it's New York–New York with its miniature Manhattan. The Eiffel Tower and the Arc de Triomphe are a bit further down the road and, opposite them, is our hotel. The Bellagio.

Wow.

It looks beautiful.

The taxi pulls in past an Italian-style lake and a giant fountain display. The main building, which is set back from the road, is like nothing else in Las Vegas. It doesn't look like some cast-off from Disneyland. It looks classy; a stately curved building of blue and cream pastels, overlooking the lake and the fountains.

It looks, in short, like the perfect place to get married.

All the taxis pull up.

Nice uniformed men take all our bags to the reception area.

We check in.

Maddie and Steve's room is on a different floor, but Mum and Dad's is down the corridor from mine.

'You can wait for James in our room if you like,' my Dad offers, when we reach my door.

'No, it's OK, I'll wait here for him.'

'All right,' my mum says, wide-eyed after sleeping on the plane. 'But if you need anything you know

248

where we are.' She looks around. 'Ee, isn't it posh? I feel like the Queen!'

The room is gorgeous. Not too over-the-top. A beautiful walk-in wardrobe with sliding doors. An incredible view out onto the conservatory and its network of flowerbeds.

I lie back on the bed.

My mobile goes.

'Hi, it's me.'

It's James.

'Where are you?'

'I'm still at the airport. There's been a couple of hitches –' the phone goes quiet, as if he is putting his hand over it, '– it looks like I'll be another hour.'

'Oh.'

'I'm sorry darling. There's nothing I can do.'

I hear voices. He is with people. The cabin crew, I suppose.

'Oh,' I say, trying to sound light and breezy. 'Don't worry. It can't be helped. The hotel's gorgeous by the way. I've never seen anything like it.'

There is another background voice. I try not to get paranoid. And then he says: 'Right, good. Well, I'd better go. Bye. Love you. See you in an hour.'

But it only feels like a second, as I have been napping.

'Come on,' he says, as if sleep was something for lesser mortals, 'let's hit the town.'

My perfect man will have tons of energy ...

'Aren't you tired?' I ask him. 'After the flight?'

'Tired? No way! I'm still buzzing with adrenalin. Come on ... the night is still young.'

Surreal moments

The first night in Vegas everyone does their own thing.

And our own thing happens to be a walk outside, around the lake.

'This is where we're going to get married,' he tells me, on top of the steps that are next to the raised fountains. 'Right here.'

I look at the view. The steps. The lake. The fountains. The lush trees. I get tingles down my spine.

'I can't wait.'

'Well, Mrs Master. You'll have to. But only one more day.'

After that, we take a wooden street car to the Venetian, a neighbouring hotel which includes a mini-Venice. We eat at a gorgeous Italian called Zefferino's and sit on one of the ornate balconies overlooking the Grand Canal.

'Do you fancy a go?' James asks me.

'A go on what?'

'On one of those,' he says, pointing to a gondola carrying two lovebirds and a singing gondolier past the balcony.

'Er ... I don't know.'

'Come on. Let's do it.'

So we do it.

It feels a bit cheesy, especially when the gondolier sings 'O Sole Mio' for the seventeenth time, but it's also kind of romantic. Holding hands, listening to opera, snuggling up close in the narrow boat.

'Look,' says James pointing to an oncoming gondola. 'Look who it is.'

It's Maddie and Steve.

'Whoo-hoo,' laughs Maddie.

'Arrividerci,' I laugh back, as we go past.

It's a surreal moment.

In fact, the next two days are nothing but twenty thousand surreal moments stuck next to each other.

The day before the wedding has Salvador Dali written all over it.

At the breakfast buffet, a hungover Dr Lara Stein and a perky Jessica Perk, fresh from a sleep dreaming of chocolate and cream cakes, park themselves at our table.

'This is really quite big,' Dr Lara tells me, in her screechy posh voice. 'We've got the film crew there. Some chap from the *LA Times*, a couple of British journalists, photographers, a film crew ...'

She goes on and on with a landslide of uninvited guests. I desperately want to tell her that I don't want any of them there, but I can't. I mean, I *can* but I can't. After all, I owe the Perfect Agency quite a lot. James, for a start. And that was kind of the deal.

The free membership wasn't given without a reason. It was all about the publicity, I knew that. And also, what can I do? I mean, have you seen her? Dr Lara with a hangover is not a pretty sight even with the pearls, the tan and the perfect teeth. I'd rather pick a fight with a hungry Doberman.

'Now listen,' she says, crunching down on a salami-topped cracker. 'We really appreciate you doing all this. And I just want you to know, there will be opportunities for you after the wedding. Opportunities within the Perfect Agency. After all, it's much easier to promote a dream if you've already achieved the dream. I mean, look at Jessica . . .'

I look at Jessica, who is looking less perky by the second.

'. . . When I met her she was the size of a house. And I mean a big house. With a double garage. Too many cream cakes. A year on the Slim-2-Win diet and now look at her. So what better person to be the promotions manager of Slim-2-Win than someone who slimmed and won? What better way to integrate the business side with the consumer side? And of course, it makes fantastic publicity . . .'

'Makes sense,' mutters James, munching on his toast.

'So what we were thinking of doing was taking Jessica away from the Perfect Agency and leaving her to solely concentrate on Slim-2-Win, while you could fill her shoes at the Perfect Agency.'

I look at Jessica, whose jaw is open far wider than the remaining bite of rice cake requires. Clearly, this is news to her as well as me.

'. . . Jessica's been spreading herself a bit too thin recently anyway, if you excuse the pun, haven't you Jessica?'

'Well, uh, I dunno . . . I . . .'

'Exactly,' Dr Lara says. 'So anyway, Ella. What do you think? Head of marketing and publicity for the

Perfect Agency. How does that grab you?'

By the throat, actually.

'Er ... well, I don't know. I've got no qualifications.'

'Qualifications! Hell, you don't need any of those. When I met Jessica she was utterly useless. Weren't you Jessica? You could barely tie your own shoelaces. Well, to be honest, you could barely see your own shoes. That's what I like to do. I like to take people in their raw state and shape them into something special. Train people from the ground up ...'

'Sounds good.'

That wasn't me saying that. That was James, speaking on my behalf. I nudge him, under the table and say. 'It does sound good. But I've already got a job. I'm a teacher.'

Dr Lara laughs as if I've just said a joke. And a good joke, because she's still laughing in her posh, haughty voice.

'Sorry, I don't understand. What's so funny?'

'Well, it's just I don't think you quite understand what I'm offering. Teaching is a very noble and humble profession, but let's face it there isn't much reward.'

Dr Lara keeps on talking, while Jessica studies me intensely. 'Starting salary – sixty thousand pounds. That's what? Three times what you get right now.'

'Wow,' says James.

I look at him. I remember that first date when he told me how amazing it must be to be able to teach.

'Plus hefty bonuses,' Dr Lara adds.

'It sounds great. And you're so kind to offer it ... I'll definitely think about it.'

James nearly chokes on his toast.

Jessica looks relieved, while Dr Lara looks at me like I've just landed from another planet.

'Fine,' she says, in bafflement. 'Think about it.'

Dr Lara and Jessica leave and James turns to me. 'What's to think about? It sounds amazing.'

'I thought you liked me being a teacher.'

'I do,' he says. 'I do. But come on Ella. Sixty thousand pounds. That's nearly what I earn.'

I look at James and, for a brief moment, lose sight of the man I love, the man who values me for who I am.

But I'm far too superstitious to pick a fight the day before the wedding so I say 'Yes, I know, it is good money. I'll definitely think about it.'

He's not letting go. 'But sixty thousand pounds.'

'There's more to life than money,' I say, realising as I say it that an opulent dining room in Las Vegas's most extravagant casino-hotel is not the best place in the world to prove that point.

'I mean, you don't fly planes just for money, do you? You fly them because you enjoy it.'

'I wouldn't fly them for twenty thousand pounds a year,' he says.

Deep breaths.

Count to ten.

I am not going to have an argument.

'No,' I say. 'Perhaps you wouldn't.' I watch him swallow his toast and I say it again, almost to myself: 'Perhaps you wouldn't.'

Elton John

More surreal moments follow.

There's the wedding rehearsal, for a start. The guy whose doing the wedding – the Master of Ceremonies – has the weirdest stutter ever. Just on his Ps. He must have avoided saying P words at his interview. And his name is Kirk Fangler.

Which is fine.

I'm not stutterist or weird-70s-sounding-names-ist. I'm not, it's just one more thing which wasn't in my childhood dream of the perfect wedding. Oh, and he's wearing a purple suit. Not a good sight in gleaming sunlight.

'Right, after you've read each other the vows and I've declared you man and wife you will kiss,' he explains. 'And, right at the p-p-p-p-p-p-point you kiss, that fountain in the p-p-p-p-p-p-pool behind you is timed to go off, so it kind of seals the p-p-p-p-p-p-perfect moment.'

Wah-hey!

A fountain that goes off when you kiss. How Vegas is that?

After the wedding rehearsal we meet up with every-

255

one – well, everyone except Dr Lara and Jessica – and have a drink in the hotel. Then its back to our room, get changed, and off to see Elton John in concert at the MGM Grand.

As soon as we get into the venue I realise MGM must stand for My-God-it's-Massive. Seriously, it makes the coloseum in Rome look like a public toilet.

Luckily, James got us all seats near the front.

It's a great night. The cinema screen behind Elton's piano displays rather too many naked body parts than my mum thought was 'strictly necessary' but I don't think my dad's had quite so much fun since . . . well, ever.

Maddie is the first person out of the 20,000 people in the concert hall to stand up and lead the singing, which she does with gusto. Although she slightly embarrasses herself when she keeps shouting for Elton to play 'That one from the Lion King.'

And then the most surreal moment of all happens. Elton says, 'Have we got an Ella Holt in the audience? Where is she? Where's Ella?'

I put up my hand and see my bright red face on the giant IMAX-scale screen.

Multiply leading the school assembly by having a wet patch on a plane and it's still nowhere near the embarrassment I'm feeling now.

'Oh, there she is,' says Elton. 'Hello Ella! Everyone say hello Ella.'

'Hello Ella!' says everyone.

'Well, as you know, I don't normally do dedications but Ella is a very special exception. According to my good friend Lara Stein, Ella is the first person to use the Perfect Agency to find her perfect man. Who, I believe, is sitting right next to her.' He stares at James on the big screen. 'Mmm . . . not bad. David darling, watch out! Anyway, this one's for you . . . *I know it sounds funny . . .*'

I think this happened.

I'm not even sure.

I might have blacked out for a moment during Crocodile Rock.

That's the weird thing about Las Vegas. You can never be sure where fact ends and fiction begins.

But the most surreal thing of all is that in twenty-four hours I am going to be married. Ella Holt will be Ella Master. Ella Master – it sounds so weird, it feels weird on the tongue. Like the first time you try Marmite. You either love it or you hate it, and I'm still deciding which.

The Big Day

This is it.

In ten minutes time it will be over. I will be married to the man of my dreams.

I turn around.

I see Mum and Dad smiling.

I see Maddie and Boring Steve, looking strangely glum.

I see Lara and Jessica and the photographers, journalists and the film crew.

The whole world is watching me.

I turn back.

Kirk Fangler is still talking. 'If any of these p-p-p-p-p-p-persons here p-p-p-p-p-p-present do know of any lawful impediment to this union, say it now ...'

There is a voice inside my head.

'No.'

That's all it is saying.

'No.'

It is a faint voice, but getting louder.

'No!'

I remember what James told me.

'No!'

About the elephant theory.

'No!'

About how your subconscious always tries to disobey your conscious self, like a rebellious teenager.

'No!'

So this is what's happening inside my head.

'No!'

My subconscious is staging a revolution.

'No!'

Not that it stands a chance.

'No!'

Within sixty seconds I am going to have married James and my subconscious will just have to get used to the idea. It can say 'No!' all it wants, but it doesn't change anything.

'No!'

But then I realise something. Something that everyone else seems to be realising as well.

'No!'

The voice isn't inside my head.

'No!'

The voice is rising up from the steps alongside the fountains.

James looks at me.

'What's going on?' he whispers, a glint of anger in his eyes.

'I don't know.'

James starts to panic. He looks at Kirk Fangler and says: 'Can we get on with the service now?'

Kirk Fangler sticks a finger in his ear, as if to unblock it. Perhaps he thinks the voice is in *his* head. Oh well, it certainly seems to have gone away.

The service resumes.

Kirk Fangler says 'Now we can p-p-p-p-p-p-proceed with the vows.'

He turns to James. 'If you can say after me ...'

'No! Stop! No!'

The voice is back. Louder now. And it is accompanied by the sound of heavy feet, running up the steps.

I recognise the voice. But, at the same time I recognise it, I realise it can't be true.

I turn around.

Everyone turns around.

Mum, Dad, Maddie, Pip, Lara, Jessica, the photographers, the journalists, the two cameramen, the man holding the big furry microphone thing high in the air – everyone. They all watch as a figure emerges from the side of the steps.

He is dressed in trousers and a baby blue shirt. He looks smart. This throws me for a second. But then he catches my eyes and I know for definite it is him.

It is Rob.

Rob the yob

Arriving, out of breath, at the top of the steps he suddenly doesn't know what to do. I feel his embarrassment as if it was my own.

'Rob?' I say.

'Do you know this p-p-p-person?' asks Kirk Fangler.

'I do,' I say.

'Is he a member of the wedding party? Is he a guest?'

'No,' says James. 'No, he's fucking not.'

The photographers and cameramen move in for a close-up on Rob and fail to hear Dr Lara screaming, 'Stop filming! Stop taking photos!'

Rob steps slowly forward. 'Ella,' he says. 'Ella. Can I ... can I talk to you for a second?'

James turns to Kirk Fangler. 'Where's security? Get security and get him out of here!'

Rob gets closer. 'Ella, I need to speak to you.'

I am speechless.

Literally.

I try to speak but there is nothing there. Looking for words is like looking for water in the Nevada desert.

The heat must be getting to me.

This must all just be some weird hallucination. There's no way Rob can be here now.

He can't fly.

He can't set foot on a plane without thinking he is going to die.

There is absolutely no way he could brave an eight-hour flight.

This is the man who had to rent a basement flat because when he looked around the flat on the first floor he got vertigo looking out of the bedroom window. For Rob 30,000 feet just isn't possible.

'Rob,' I say. 'It's you.'

'Where the fuck is security?' says James.

Kirk Fangler pulls out a walkie talkie from his purple suit. 'Security . . . security . . . we have a situation out on the wedding terrace . . . request back-up immediately. We have an intruder. We have a potential terrorist suspect. Repeat: request back-up *immediately.*'

Rob says, 'Ella, I have to talk to you.'

'Rob, what are you doing? I'm getting married. I'm getting married now. And how did you know I was here?'

I look over at Maddie. Her head dips towards the ground as if in answer to my question.

'Ella, I'm sorry. I'm sorry I took you for granted.'

'You travelled ten thousand miles to tell me you're sorry for taking me for granted?'

'Yes,' he says. 'I know I said we shouldn't speak to each other but that was because –'

'Rob, this is my *wedding*. I'm getting married now. Please Rob, don't do this.'

'You heard her,' says James. 'Fuck off.'

262

Rob looks at me like he has never looked at me before. Like the whole of his life is in his eyes. His whole future. 'I made a mistake Ella. A big mistake. But don't go and do the bloody same.'

James walks towards Rob, closer to the fountain. The cameras circle in. 'I should have finished you off last time,' James says.

Last time.

Last time?

I remember Rob's mysterious black eye when he turned up on my doorstep. I remember Mark Dobson's ripped shirt.

'I'm not scared of you,' Rob says. 'You might have scared me off last time, but not now.'

James, and the rest of the wedding party, turn and see three giant security guards running towards us.

'Go on then,' James says with his back now to the fountain. 'Prove it. Take a shot.'

Rob is facing the opposite direction. So he is the only one who doesn't realise three security guards the size of a 1984 Schwarzenegger are rapidly running towards him.

His arm goes back.

His fingers curl into a fist.

James is coaxing him. 'Go on. Do it. Let's see what you've got.'

I only have time to say 'Rob! No! Don't!' before his fist lands on James's jaw.

The force of the blow causes James to start falling backwards, into the fountain.

As he falls, James clutches onto Rob's shirt, and takes him with him into the water.

Right at that second, the fountain that was programmed to go off at the moment me and James kiss and seal our loving union, sprays jets of water high into the air and splashes back down on them both as they come up to breathe.

This is also the moment that the security guards reach the fountain.

Six hands land on Rob's shirt and drag him out of the pool, as he chokes on water.

'He attacked me,' James tells the Schwarzeneggers. 'I think he broke my jaw.'

This is not happening, I tell myself.

This *can't* be happening.

The security guards start dragging Rob away.

'Where are you taking him?' I ask them.

'Don't worry ma'am,' says the biggest, a man with a jaw that makes Buzz Lightyear look feeble-chinned. 'We'll take good care of him.'

Rob struggles but he's no match for the security guards. 'Ella!' he cries, dripping water as he is yanked backwards. 'Ella! I love you!'

This is incredible.

For a year of my life, I wanted nothing more than to hear him say those three words. And they never arrived. Not once. Although it was always only him and me, on our own, he was never able to summon the courage.

Oh, but now.

Now – in front of not only me but my mum and dad, my husband-to-be, my best friend, a master of ceremonies, the seventh richest woman in the world, a Slim-Win diet champion, a film crew and three security guards – he finally decides to pluck up the courage.

He *loves* me.

Well, isn't that great?

Isn't that fanvegastastic.

Rob disappears out of view, inside the hotel.

'What are they going to do to him?' I ask Kirk Fangler.

'Don't worry miss. It's under control.'

James looks at me, holding his jaw. I look at my mum who . . . oh my God, she's fainted.

I run over to her, past the film crew, past Lara Stein and Jessica Perk.

Dad is kneeling down next to her. 'Kathleen? Kathleen? Kathleen? Can you hear me?'

'Mum? Mum? Mum?'

Mum blinks back into consciousness.

She says, 'Oh, look at me.'

'Mum, are you all right.'

Kirk Fangler brings over a bottle of water as mum gets back on her feet.

James turns to me and says, 'What shall we do?'

'What shall we do about what?'

'The wedding.'

'What do you mean?' I ask him, as one of the cameramen shoves his camera right under my nose.

'I mean, we're only here for two days. And the Bellagio won't be able to fit us in for . . .?' He looks over at Kirk Fangler who says, 'The next free wedding slot we have is in a fortnight.'

I look around at all the faces.

Maddie, bless her, is reaching out to me with her eyes, feeling my pain.

Dr Lara Stein also seems to be feeling some sort of pain. The pain of having her first fairytale Perfect Agency wedding turn into an absolute farce. She is shaking her head in her hands while Jessica Perk tiptoes up and whispers in her ear.

'What do you mean?' I ask James. 'My mum's just fainted. Rob's getting God-knows-what kicked out of him by three gorillas in uniform. You've just dragged yourself out of a fountain. And you want us to carry on with the wedding?'

'Well . . . yes . . .'

I look at Mum. 'Mum, are you all right?' I whisper.

'I will be love. As soon as you've tied the knot.'

'What, you still want me to go ahead with this?'

'Yes. Of course I do.'

'Dad?'

Dad shrugs his shoulders. 'James has paid a lot of money. I offered to help him but he wouldn't let me. It would be a shame to waste it.'

Dr Lara Stein comes out from behind her hands and says, 'We need a wedding. It has to happen today.'

I look at Kirk Fangler and he says, 'What do you want to do?'

I look over at Maddie.

I want to speak to her.

I've never needed a best friend's advice more than right now. But there's no time.

'We're going to carry on with the service,' James assures Kirk Fangler.

He takes hold of my hand and we go over to where we were standing, James dripping water all the way.

The service resumes.

Kirk Fangler keeps moving his lips and making sounds, which I assume must be words, but I can't be sure. He might as well be saying 'Nanoo nanoo nanoo' because my mind is somewhere else.

I can't stop thinking the same things.

He flew in a plane.

He came to Las Vegas.

He said 'I love you.'

It echoes in my head.

'I love you.'

'I love you.'

'I love you.'

I look up at James. Ready to commit to a lifetime by my side.

He is perfect, I tell myself

He is my Mr Perfect.

'Nanoo nanoo nanoo' says Kirk Fangler.

James is my match. It's science. And you can't argue with science. Not when it's on the same side as the seventh richest woman on the planet. And a film crew. And your Mum and Dad.

No Ella.

You've got to calm down.

You're going to stay right here.

You're going to do what everyone wants. What *you* want.

You're going to marry the man of your dreams. Any second now.

You love him.

You don't love Rob.

Rob is a slob.

James is a handsome airline pilot who fills every criteria of what you are looking for.

You can't love Rob.

You can't love Rob.

It's scientifically impossible, Dr Whatshisname said so. Dr Fischer. At the love lab.

A voice breaks through my thoughts. 'Ella? Ella? Ella?'

It is James. It must be my turn to speak.

I look at Kirk Fangler and then back at James, his shirt starting to dry off in the sun.

I turn around. See the nightmare gallery of expectant faces.

Oh no.

I know what I'm going to do.

And I'm right. I do it.

Before I'm able to stop myself, I am hoisting up my dress and running back into the hotel, looking for Rob.

The free show

'Wait! Ella! Where are you going?'

It is James, running behind me into the hotel.

'I'm sorry,' I tell him. 'Tell everyone I'm sorry. I just can't do this. Not today.'

His face switches. 'It's him isn't it? You're running off to that fat pig aren't you?'

'No,' I say. 'No. No I'm not. And don't call him that.'

'Oh, he tries to break my fucking jaw and that's fine but call him a fat fucking oinky pig and I'm the bad guy.'

'Why are you swearing? You don't ever swear.'

'Don't I? Don't I? Well, I'm sorry Mary Poppins. I'm bloody fucking *sorry.*'

'It was you.'

'What?'

'You gave him the black eye.'

He laughs. *Laughs!* 'And he gave me a smack in the jaw. Now we're even. Is that what this is about? You walk out of your wedding because of that? I fly you to Las Vegas. Take you and your family to see the most expensive concert on the face of the earth.

269

Pay for the best wedding. What did he ever buy you? A pizza? A kebab? A vodka and coke? For fuck's sake, Ella!'

'It's not an auction, you know. I'm not on sale to the highest bidder.'

'No,' he says, looking across the foyer to the acres of slot machines and roulette wheels in the casino.

'With you, it's more like that place. You put everything down on the table and you walk away with nothing.'

Half the wedding are here now.

Mum. Dad. Maddie. Steve. The journalists.

A few hotel guests are watching now. Just one more Las Vegas show.

'I'm *not* leaving you. I just have to check on Rob.'

I don't wait for James's response. I turn and keep jogging through the foyer until I see one of the security guards.

'Where's Rob?'

'Excuse me, lady?'

'That man? The one you just dragged out of the fountain?'

'Don't worry, ma'am. We handed him over to the police.'

'The police? Oh no. You see, I have to find him. I have to talk to him. Where will he be?'

The security guard looks down at me with stony eyes. With stony everything, in fact. 'Las Vegas Police Station. They'll have locked him up I'd imagine.'

This is a nightmare. That's it, I'm having a nightmare. I'm not even having my own nightmare. I'm having someone else's nightmare. I'm just a figment of someone's sick imagination. Wake up! Wake up!

'Ella! Ella!' It's Maddie. She's running across the foyer towards me.

James and all the others are standing further behind, waiting for me to come back out.

'I've got to find Rob,' I tell Maddie, when she reaches me. 'He's in jail.'

'What about your mum and dad? What about everyone?'

I look at them all. Everyone furious with me. Waiting for me to come to my senses. But I'm about as tempted to cross the foyer as a Christian would be to enter a colosseum full of hungry lions.

'They can wait,' I tell her. 'I've got to find Rob.'

Maddie stares at me like I'm a crazy person. Hell, OK, I am a crazy person.

'I'll come with you,' she says. 'If you're going to jail in a wedding dress you might need a little support.'

'OK,' I say. 'Let's go.'

As soon as we head out towards the taxi rank, I hear voices behind me. My Dad, James, Dr Lara.

'Ella?'

'Come back.'

'We *need* a wedding!'

The police station and the cockroach man

Las Vegas wasn't made for daylight.

At night, when it's safely tucked away behind a world of flashing neon, it looks amazing. But under the desert sun it's like a drag queen with the make-up starting to sweat off.

The taxi drives down Las Vegas boulevard. Past all the giant hotels and casinos. Past the fake pyramids, the fake castles, the fake Manhattan skyline, the fake volcano and the fake Eiffel Tower. Past the wedding chapels and concert halls and fat tourists.

'I'm sorry,' Maddie says. 'This is all my fault.'

'No, no it's not,' I tell her. Although yes, yes it is.

'I shouldn't have ever gone behind your back. You know, telling Rob about the wedding.'

'It's OK.'

'What's going to happen?'

'I'm not leaving James,' I tell her.

She pouts her lips, disbelievingly.

'I'm *not*. I've just got to see that Rob's all right. I owe him.'

'He just punched the man you were going to marry. You don't owe him anything.'

'He flew on a plane.'

'What?'

'Rob can't fly. But he got on a plane and flew here.'

Maddie looks at me like I'm speaking Gaelic. 'Right, he flew on a plane. That explains everything.'

We arrive at the police station.

We have to sit and wait.

The man next to me, the one with the beard down to his knees, is drunk. And he smells. And he keeps talking to me.

'He's a cockroach,' he tells me. I have no idea who is a cockroach, but he is very insistent on this point. 'He's a low-down cheating cockroach. Cockroach! Cockroach! Cockroach!'

'Thanks for coming with me,' I say to Maddie. 'I don't know if I could have handled cockroach man on my own.'

'Hey,' she says. 'You know me. Anything for a bit of drama.'

'Yeah.'

Maddie looks at me seriously for a moment. 'You know what you did back there. Walking out of the wedding. Was that ... was that just about today or was it, like, bigger than that?'

'I don't know,' I tell her. 'I don't. There have been things, I suppose. Little things. Things that get in my mind.'

'What kind of things?'

'You know that Year Eleven? Mark Dobson? The shy one. Kind of cute looking, I suppose. Hangs around with Darren Bentley.'

'Yes, I know the one you mean. Looks good in shorts.'

273

'Maddie, he's *underage.*'

'I know. I was just saying. On the rugby field he looks ... nice.'

'Anyway, he's got a bit of a thing for me.'

'A thing?'

'Uh-huh. He sent me a card. With a poem. I didn't tell you at the time because I didn't want to make a big deal out of it. I felt sorry for him, really.'

'You lucky bitch! The kids never get a crush on me, not even when I wear that top. You know, that goes down to ... Anyway, sorry – you were saying ...'

'Yes,' I tell her. 'Well, I told James about him and he acted a bit weird and you know that day you bailed me out. With the assembly?'

'Yeah.'

'Well, James followed him into the toilets. And I think he ... did something.'

Maddie's eyes go wide. 'What kind of something?'

'Mark's shirt was ripped later on. On that day. And he seemed freaked out. I dismissed it at the time but I think James might have threatened him. You know ... grabbed his shirt and pinned him against the wall or something.'

'No,' says Maddie. 'I really doubt it. Mark's not as shy as he looks. He's always getting into fights. It could have been anyone.'

'Yes,' I say, hoping she is right. 'I'm sure you're –'

Before I have time to finish my sentence a police officer called Raymond comes and tells us the situation.

The situation is this: the only way I can speak to Rob – and the only way Rob can get out of his cell – is if we pay his bail.

'How much is that?' Maddie asks officer Raymond.

274

'Ten.'

'Ten dollars?'

Raymond laughs a big gummy laugh. 'That's cute.' The laugh dies.

'Ten *thousand* dollars. Cash.'

Between us, me and Maddie work out that we have immediate access to 115 dollars. 'Which only leaves us nine thousand eight hundred and eighty-five dollars short,' Maddie works out, in Maths teacher time.

'What shall I do?' I ask her.

'Ask your Mum and Dad?'

'No.'

'James?'

'Double no. No way.'

Her eyes widen and she says, 'We're in Las Vegas. What's the one way, you can make ten thousand dollars in Las Vegas?'

James's words echo in my head.

You put everything down on the table and you walk away with nothing.

I frantically try and think of another solution, but can't think of anything.

'Where's the nearest casino?' Maddie asks officer Raymond.

'The Golden Nugget. Half a mile down Fremont Street,' he says looking at us strangely.

'Right,' says Maddie, turning to me. 'Let's go.'

The Golden Nugget

The casino is a different world from that at the Bellagio.

The Bellagio is the kind of no-expense-spared casino you see in the movies. The type of place you expect to see Robert De Niro walking proudly through as Sharon Stone throws dice in a million-dollar sequin dress. At the Bellagio, even the slot machines look classy – inlaid into marble counters.

But the Golden Nugget is in downtown. And down-town Vegas is full of people who look like they should be on posters with WANTED above their heads.

Walking into the casino is like walking into a headache.

For a start, there's the noise.

Coins being vomited out of machines, roars and cheers around card tables, losers moaning into their drinks at the bar, cowboy music jangling out of the speakers.

Then there's the look of the place.

A maze of tacky slot machines and shabby roulette tables under a low fog of stale cigarette smoke.

The carpet looks like it was designed by a blind

man who was spun around really fast and then given a paintbrush. And it's covered with trampled cigarette butts and flat circles of chewing gum and spilled beer and other things that I really don't want to identify, especially while I'm wearing my wedding dress.

'Viva Las Vegas,' I mumble to Maddie, as we survey the three-dimensional headache before use.

'Well,' she says. 'The odds are just as good here as anywhere else.'

She is smiling. Actually smiling. I can't believe it – she's looking forward to this.

'Don't worry,' she says. 'My middle name's Lucky.'

'Is it?'

'Well, no. It's Lucy. But it's only missing a k.'

'Right, OK, what do we do?'

'Get some chips.'

'I'm not hungry.'

'No, *chips*. They're the plastic token things you gamble with.'

'Oh, OK'.'

We head through the cigarette smoke, place our money down at one of the kiosks and get the chips. The man doing the same next to us comes away with a sackful of red and blue tokens. We barely get enough for a decent game of Connect 4.

'Right,' Maddie says. 'Let's play roulette.'

We head over to the nearest roulette table. A crowd of men in cowboy hats and clothes in different shades of denim stare at Maddie as she puts some of the chips down on different numbers. They then start gawping at me in my wedding dress.

'Do you know what you're doing?' I ask Maddie, trying to ignore the gawps.

277

'I got drunk on a ferry to Amsterdam once and they had a casino,' Maddie says. 'I played all night.'

'Did you win anything?'

'Nope. But I ended up pulling a bloke called ... oh, I can't remember what he was called. Shagged him senseless back in my cabin. He kept on calling me Stacey for some reason.'

Much as I'd love to pursue the topic of Maddie's nautical adventures, now is not the time. The wheel has just been set in motion.

'We want red,' Maddie tells me. 'Ideally, we want the ball to land on fourteen or thirty. Well, actually ... I think it *has* to land on fourteen or thirty.'

'Right,' I say, closing my eyes.

The wheel keeps on whirring and I keep on praying' ...

14 or 30 ...

14 or 30 ...

Come on 14.

Come on 30.

The wheel starts to slow down. The numbers become visible. The silver ball teases its way around the outside of the wheel, like a ballroom dancer choosing a partner to dance with.

It slows right down.

Past 14.

Past 30.

Past 14 again.

Past 30.

Past 14.

16 ... 18 ... 20 ... 22 ... 24 ... 26 ...

It lands on 28.

No, no – I'm wrong.

It lands on 30!

30!

Maddie starts to hop up and down next to me. The cowboys stare at her like she's mad. Which, of course, she is.

'We've won! We've won!'

A handful of black chips slide towards us.

'How much is that?' I ask Maddie.

'Ten times what we had.'

'So over a thousand dollars.'

'That's right. We still need nine thousand more.'

'What?' Maddie squints under the sudden roar from the next table.

'What about the other nine thousand?'

'Eight thousand eight hundred and fifty, to be precise. Well, we'll win it.'

'What?'

'We're on a streak.'

Uh-oh.

She's making the eyes.

The same eyes she has when she made me go speed dating. The mad Maddie eyes.

'The odds are against, Mads.'

'Odds schmodds.'

'You're a Maths teachers. You're supposed to believe in odds.'

'Well what choice do you have? Either your old lover stays there or gets moved to the County Jail and eaten alive by ten-foot serial killers with handlebar moustaches . . .'

The ten-foot serial killer with a handlebar moustache that is standing next to us looks down at Maddie as if wondering whether she will fit in the trunk of his car. We smile girlishly and he turns his attention back on the roulette wheel. 'Either that or we take a

279

chance. Like when you went to the Perfect Agency.'

Take a chance.

As she says these words I realise the truth.

It doesn't matter about science.

It doesn't matter how many compatibility tests you are forced to take.

It doesn't matter how many people tell you that you are made for each other.

Love is always a gamble.

Your heart is always a ball spinning around a roulette wheel, and you never know where it is going to end up.

There is no way to predict the way you will feel.

Even when you think it is going to be the real thing, it can still end up being as fake as an Italian lake in Las Vegas.

Right now, all I want to do is see Rob. I have to know exactly why he is here.

And at the same time, I know this is wrong.

I should be going back to the hotel, trying to patch things up with James. I should be facing up to Mum and Dad, and giving the film crew what they came to see.

Maddie places all the chips down on the table.

Again, we need a 14 or a 30.

The wheel spins.

I close my eyes and pray to any God who will have me.

'Come on fourteen!' shouts Maddie. 'Come on thirty!'

I picture Rob in the police cell. I picture him surrounded by psychos and drunks and Hells Angels doing pull-ups.

I feel fear in my stomach.

His fear.

Come on 14!
Come on 30!

I open my eyes.

The wheel slows.

All the cowboys are leaning over the table, shouting orders at the ball.

The ball lands on 30.

We've won!

Oh no.

It's hopped out again. No perfect match.

It lands on 31.

And stays there.

Maddie looks at me in total despair. 'I'm sorry . . . I'm sorry . . . I'm so sorry.'

The ten-foot man with the handlebar moustache yahoos with joy as he collects his chips from the table.

'What are we going to do?' I ask her.

But even as I ask, I know there's no choice. We have to leave Rob to whatever fate awaits him behind bars. We have to go back to the hotel. Face the music.

We start to head through the cigarette smoke, out of the casino. Out into the glaring sun.

We have no money for a taxi. Or for anything.

I put my head in my hands.

I realise just how stupid I must look standing by the side of the road in my wedding dress. A runaway bride.

And then it comes to me.

I realise there is still a way to free Rob.

'Come on,' I tell Maddie, as I start to walk back towards the main road. 'Let's go.'

At the pawn shop

The old hunchbacked man at the pawn shop places the small jeweller's microscope into his eyes and stares into the emerald.

'I can't believe you're doing this,' Maddie says.

I don't say anything. I can't believe I'm doing this either.

'What are you going to tell James?'

'Erm, that it fell off? That I . . . got mugged?'

My heart sinks, knowing there will be absolutely nothing I will be able to say to him. Because that's the thing with rings. They're symbolic. When he gave it to me it was a symbol of his commitment. Of his willingness to spend the rest of his life right by side.

And so now I'm pawning it to save my ex-boyfriend, what does that symbolise? Am I getting rid of James by getting rid of the ring?

'I've got to confess,' says the old man. 'It's the genuine article.'

'What's it worth?' Maddie asks.

'I'd say seven thousand,' he says, clicking his mouth as if chewing tobacco.

'We're not going away with anything less than ten.'

The man takes the microscope out his eye and turns his attention from the ring to Maddie. Seeing that she too is the genuine article, he realises there's no point trying to push for lower.

'Wait there.'

The old man hobbles into a back room. His radio, clearly tuned to Tragic Irony FM, is playing a version of 'Can't Buy Me Love'.

'James is going to kill me.'

'He won't.'

'He might.'

'Well, don't do it. Tell the bloke you want your ring back. If that's what you want.'

She's got a point.

I mean, why am I doing this?

I didn't ask Rob to fly here. I didn't ask Rob to punch James in the jaw. It's not my fault he's locked up.

And just because he did fly here, it doesn't change anything, does it? It doesn't change the fact that I love James. Or that James loves me. It doesn't change the fact that James is the most handsome and sexy man on earth who my Mum and Dad absolutely love and who always manages to give me exactly what I've wanted all my life. He is intelligent. Sophisticated. Well travelled. Devoted solely to me. OK, so at times he's a bit *too* devoted, but that's only because he loves me.

James is full of surprises. And, aside from Rob's black eye, the right kind of surprises. Weekends in Rome sort of surprises. Emerald ring sort of surprises.

The old pawnbroker comes back out. He has ten thousand dollars fresh from his safe, right in his hands.

'So what are you going to do?' Maddie asks me.

I look at the pawnbroker's face, lined like an unreadable map. I look down at the emerald perched on the band of gold that now rests on the counter. A green eye gleaming at me, daring me to do the unthinkable.

I look at Maddie. Her fearful eyes already know what I'm about to do.

'Come on lady,' says the pawnbroker still clicking his mouth. 'I ain't getting no younger standin' here.'

'No,' I say. 'No you're not. And neither am I.'

And with that, I hold my hand out and get ready to make what may well prove to be the biggest mistake of my life.

'Actually, we need another ten dollars on top,' says Maddie, once the cash is in my hand. 'For a taxi.'

She bats her eyelids like she's a damsel in a silent movie and the old timer swallows it. 'You're killing me lady,' he says, handing over an extra ten-dollar bill from the cash register. 'You're killing me.'

Maddie's news

In the taxi Maddie is quiet.

At first, I think this is just a pass-no-judgement kind of silence, but the crease in her forehead suggests she has something to say.

'Ella,' she says, after five minutes. 'I know it's a really, *really* bad time to mention this . . .'

'Mention what?'

And then she blurts it out. 'Steve's asked me to marry him.'

She says it really fast, as if it's one word. 'Stevesaskedmetomarryhim.'

'What?'

'Steve. Last night. After the concert. We went for a meal at Picasso's. One of the restaurants in the hotel. Got down on one knee. The works.'

'Oh, my God, Mads. That's amazing! What did you say?'

I look at her ringless finger, and realise that's probably a bad question.

'I didn't say anything. I, sort of, well, *laughed*.'

'You laughed?'

I remember Steve's glum face from earlier today,

285

at the wedding.

'I couldn't help it. It just seemed so silly. We were in the middle of this restaurant and everyone was looking at us and he got down on one knee.'

I remember James on the roof of the Hotel de Russie in Rome, and then I look down at my own naked ring ringer. That proposal hadn't seemed silly at all. It had seemed like the most amazingly romantic gesture in the world. My stomach turns, as if to tell me I've just done the wrong thing.

'So what did you say when you stopped laughing?' I ask Maddie, trying to think about anything other than my anxious gut.

'Oh, well, I apologised, obviously. And Steve went red and sat back in his chair and started talking about the wine and about the abseiling waiters.'

'Abseiling waiters?'

'They came down from the roof on wires, like something out of the Cirque de Soleil, so he started talking about the pulley system, about how it must work and he just kept going on and on and on you know, the way he does, and so I had to say something in the end so I said "I'll think about it". And I said sorry for laughing and I told him it was just a bit of a shock, that's all.'

'So . . . are you?'

'Am I what?'

'Are you going to marry him?'

'Well, I was unsure,' she says with a cheeky Maddie Hatfield grin. 'You know, the whole wedding thing. But having seen what an effortless breeze your wedding turned out to be.'

'Very funny.'

She cackles. 'Sorry, couldn't resist it.'

286

'Do you love him?'

'Yes,' she says, suddenly serious. 'Yes, I do.'

'So what's stopping you?' I realise I am asking this question as much to myself as to Maddie.

'I don't *know* . . . We're so different, I suppose. He knows how to build a computer out of a box of matches and I can't even use the remote control for the telly. And look at us! It's like a giraffe and a penguin walking down the street together. I need a fork-lift truck just to kiss him. And he owns a Ronan Keating album!'

'But can you imagine growing old with him?'

'That's the weird thing.'

'What is?'

'I can. I can see us sitting side-by-side on a park bench in fifty years time, talking about all our aches and pains.'

'And? Does it scare you?'

'No,' she says. 'And that is scary. I'm scared because I'm not scared of it.

Does that make sense?'

I nod. It makes perfect sense.

Rob's cheap shot

Rob staggers out into the waiting area as if he has just served a life sentence. I think he's milking it a bit, with the whole Nelson Mandela walk to freedom thing, but I'm pleased to see him.

Maddie elbows me up onto my feet.

'Hi,' I say, straightening down my now rather grubby white dress.

'Thanks,' he says. 'There were two psychos in there. They kept calling me sweetmeat. I don't think I'd have made the night.'

'It's OK.'

What do I do?

Hug him?

Kiss him?

I do neither. I just stand there.

'How did you get the money?'

'Oh ... er ...' I hide my left hand behind my back.' Long story.'

'What about the wedding?' he says. 'Did you marry that tosser?'

Suddenly I want a refund. This isn't worth ten thousand dollars.

'Don't call him that.'

'So you did?'

My left hand stays out of view.

'Cockroach!'

I turn around to see that the cockroach man is still here, and that he is wooing Maddie with his sophisticated brand of conversation.

As romantic locations go, the waiting area of the Las Vegas police department is hardly the Eiffel tower. It's hardly even a *fake* Eiffel Tower. But I can't head back to the Bellagio.

'Why did you fly out?'

'Maddie told me you were getting married.'

'I know, but why did you come?'

'Because I love you.'

He says it again. 'I love you, Ella. I always did . . . I just never knew really what it meant . . . until I lost you. But I won't make that mistake again.'

'Cockroach!' comes the voice from behind. 'Cockroach! Cockroach! That's what he is! Cockroach!'

I stare into his eyes – Rob's eyes, not the cockroach man – and I believe him. He has changed. And with the realisation, my heart flutters as fast as a humming-bird.

But then he blows it.

Big style.

Here's how: 'He's a tosser, Ella. A total tosser.' He waits a second, deciding his next move. Then he takes the lowest and cheapest shot he can. 'He's having an affair, Ella. He's seeing someone behind your back. That's what I came to tell you. You know, that day. When I came round with a black eye. That's what I wanted to tell you. I saw him in a restaurant window in Clerkenwell. It was late . . . about nine. He was with this tall skinny girl sitting right in the window. He was holding her hands across the table. So I knocked on the window and told him to come outside. So he did, and I told him I'd tell you – and that's when he gave me the black eye. He knew you'd been round to see me and he said if I ever saw you again he'd finish off the job. Ella . . . Ella? . . . Ella? Where are you going? Ella? . . .

I am walking away from him. I don't want to believe him. If I believe him then the Relationship Fairy is an evil spirit, jinxing my one shot at happiness. Rob can't be right. He can't. I have to believe he's lying. There's no other option.

'Come on Mads, we're going,' I say, fighting back tears.

'What about Rob?'

'What about him?'

'Ella! . . . Ella . . . Wait! . . .

There's a taxi parked outside. We get in and Rob taps on the window as we drive off.

'What's going on?' Maddie asks.

'I've just made a very big mistake,' I tell her. 'Rob is a lying loser.'

And I say nothing else, just stare out of the window as Las Vegas moves by like a false promise.

Facing the music

We walk back into the foyer.

I expect to see James there, waiting for me. Or Mum or Dad or Lara or the film crew but there is no one there.

For a moment, it feels like I dreamed the whole thing. The wedding. The walk-out. It all feels too calm. Like we have arrived back into a different time. Ten years into the future or something. Or maybe I'm just delirious with heat exhaustion, or relationship exhaustion.

'So what are you going to do?' Maddie asks me. 'You know, if you want I'll help you steal a car and we could break for the border. You can be Thelma. I'll be Louise. We might bump into Brad Pitt on the way and shag him in a cheap motel room.'

She smiles at me. And I smile back.

James might be about to dump me, and never speak to me again but at least I've got Maddie to try and cheer me up.

'Sounds like a good idea. But, tempting as it is to drive over a canyon, I'd probably better face the music. What about you? What are you going to say to

Steve? I know I'm not exactly the best advert in the world for getting engaged. But don't let me put you off.'

'Well, I might just say "Yes" to get the ring. I could always pawn it.'

'Funny,' I say. 'Ha ha.'

We go over to the lifts.

I put my arm around Maddie and kiss her cheek, as a thank you.

The paunchy man next to us nudges his wife and points to my dress. 'Look Marge, it's one of those gay weddings.'

'Oh my Lord,' says Marge, before making sure they get in a separate lift from us.

Maddie gets out on the fifth floor, and heads back to her room to see Steve. 'Good luck,' she says, crossing her fingers as the doors close behind her.

My heart starts to thump against my ribcage. This is my driving test and French Oral and first day of teaching all rolled into one. I've never been so nervous in all my life.

What am I going to say?

What is James going to say when he knows about the ring?

The lift pings open.

I step out onto the corridor, my feet sinking into the plush carpet. The walls seem closer together than before. The ceiling feels lower.

I get the feeling that everything is closing in around me.

I try to deep breathe to stave off the panic, as I get closer to our room.

I keep walking. Past all the Do Not Disturb signs and food trays and newspapers on the floor.

And then I think: maybe he's not even here.

Maybe he's packed and left.

I reach the door.

Number 642.

I wait there, unable to knock. Like my fist is constipated or something. It just stays there, hanging in the air, while I try to summon up the courage.

I look down at my other hand.

My left hand.

My guilty, ringless finger.

And while I am waiting there I hear something. Something from inside the room.

A voice.

A woman's voice.

My fist is no longer constipated. I knock, three times.

'James? James? It's me.'

I hear the voice again. Or think I do. And then I hear James mumble something I can't quite catch.

There are some noises from inside the room. Like he is moving around. I wait a moment, then I try again.

'James? James? It's me.'

I try the door handle.

It's locked.

Then it starts to move from the other side.

The door opens. James is there. His trousers are on. So is his shirt. Untucked, but on.

'Ella? Where the hell have you been?'

I walk past him and inside the room, looking for the source of the female voice.

I find it straight away.

She is blonde.

She is good-looking.

And she is the newsreader on CNN, which blares from the TV in the corner of the room.

Suddenly, I feel stupid.

'I thought you were . . .'

'Were what?' he barks, angrily.

'Nothing,' I say. 'Nothing.'

'We need to talk.'

'I know. I know we do. That's why I came back.'

He looks down at my hand. 'Where's your ring?'

'What?'

'Your ring?'

I look down at my hand and fake surprise. 'Oh . . . oh my God! My ring . . . I . . . I . . . I don't know. It was on a minute ago . . .'

I expect him to explode, but he doesn't. He just slips on his shoes. 'I need a drink,' he says. 'Let's talk in the bar. Downstairs.'

This is weird.

James never *needs* a drink.

He only ever has wine, and that's always with food.

'Oh,' I say.

He does up his laces, tucks in his shirt and switches off the blonde newsreader with the remote control.

'Is it okay if I . . . er, get out of my dress first,' I ask him, as I point to the wardrobe.

'No!' he snaps. 'No, it's not.'

'It's just, I feel a bit stupid in my wedding dress.'

Immediately, I realise this is the wrong thing to say.

'What? *You* feel a bit stupid? *You* feel a bit stupid? Ha! That's rich! That's fantastic. I mean, we wouldn't want anyone to feel stupid would we? Not on their wedding day. That would be terrible, wouldn't it. Making someone feel stupid on their wedding day. I couldn't imagine how *that* would feel.'

He literally spits the words out into the room.

'Hey,' I say. 'It wasn't all my fault, you know.'

He nods to the door. 'Let's go. Now. I can't talk to you in here. I can't. Now let's just go and have a drink and talk.'

Why can't he talk in the room?

I find it very weird that a practically teetotal airline pilot who can spend twelve hours in a row cramped inside a tiny flight deck is suddenly so in need of a drink and so claustrophobic that he has to get out of the ample-sized hotel room and head for the bar.

And I really *do* want to change my dress. It's so dirty.

But then again, I'm hardly in the best position to negotiate.

'All right, all right,' I say, treating James like he's got 'Handle with Care' tattooed on his forehead. 'Let's go.'

He nods, and opens the door, holding it for me to walk through. Under normal circumstances, this would strike me as a gentlemanly gesture. But these are not normal circumstances, and it strikes me as a desperate attempt to get me out of the room as soon as possible.

And just as I am halfway out of the door I hear it.

Hear what, I'm not quite sure, but it was definitely something.

'Come on,' James says, ushering me forward out onto the corridor. 'Let's go.'

And I'm about to do it. I'm about to put my other foot out of the door, shaking the mystery noise out of my head as if I'm hearing things. But then I hear it again, coming from inside the room.

The mystery noise

'What was that?' I ask James.

'What was what?'

'That noise.'

'What noise? There was no noise. Now come on, let's go.'

I look behind me, trying to identify what made the sound.

The bed?

The switched-off TV?

The trouser press?

'You know what? I really want to change my dress.'

I start to walk back into the room. James grabs my arm. Hard. The threat of violence lights his eyes. 'No,' he says. 'We're going. *Now.*'

A flashback from the questionnaire.

My perfect man will be assertive, and know how to get his own way.

I look down at his hand pressing into my arm. The same hand that was responsible for Rob's black eye.

'I want to change my dress.'

'No.'

'I. Want. To. Change. My. Dress.'

A man walks by wearing a T-shirt that says '*Elvis '68*' and wheeling a suitcase behind him. He looks at James's grip on my arm, then up at me. 'Are you all right ma'am? Do you want any help?'

'No, she doesn't want any help,' James says. 'Not unless you're a psychiatrist.'

'I'm all right,' I tell the man, worried that James might be about to start another fight.

The man and his suitcase walk off down the corridor.

James lets go of me and tries to shut the door, but I slip back inside the room just in time.

'Ella! Get out of the room now!'

James comes back inside.

I take off my shoes, and walk over to the wardrobe.

James lunges for me, but I resist his grip. I place my fingers inside the scooped-out wardrobe handle and slide it open, looking for something more comfortable to wear.

And that's when I see it.

Her.

Standing, completely naked, where my clothes should be.

The skeleton in the wardrobe

'Aaagh,' I scream, like when Drew Barrymore finds ET in the toy cupboard.

It takes a second – the second while I am screaming my tonsils out – for me to recognise the naked woman in the wardrobe.

But then I realise.

The air-hostess-cum-pipe-cleaner. The one who spilled orange juice over my lap.

After the scream there is a weird moment when no one knows what to do. We just stand there in our separate points in the room, a literal love triangle, each of us as still as a photo.

During the weird moment I notice the woman's body. A skin-wrapped skeleton. She must be like a minus eight or something. Her rib-cage is a xylophone – you could play a tune on it. She's so sharp and pointy I don't know how James managed to fuck her without cutting himself.

The weird moment ends when she giggles.

That's right, *giggles*.

If you find a naked woman in your fiancé's wardrobe you'd at least expect her to have the decency to keep a straight face.

'Oops,' she says, covering her hand over her mouth.

I turn to James.

I look around for a weapon that will be able to cause instant death. The trouser press? The remote control? The room service menu?

'Look, Ella. It's not what it looks like. It's not ... what you're thinking.'

Panic presses down on his face like G-force. The fear and shame in his eyes telling me far more than the words that manure out of his mouth.

My perfect man will have a healthy appetite for sex ...

But there's healthy, and there's downright greedy.

'How long?' I ask him.

'What?'

'How long have you been fucking that skeleton in the wardrobe?'

'Hey!' says the skeleton. 'You fat jealous bitch!'

I place my hands back in the scooped out handle and slide the wardrobe shut.

'If you open this door in the next five minutes I'll kill you, I fucking swear,' I inform her, through the wood.

She stays quiet, so I turn my attention to James. Mr Perfect.

Hah!

'Now Ella,' he says, his palms facing me, 'just calm down.'

'How long have you been fucking her?'

'You're the one who ran off to your ex-boyfriend in the middle of our wedding.'

'I'm not *sleeping* with him.'

'No? Well, how do I know that?'

'Well, until you open the wardrobe and find him stark-bollock naked inside, you can fucking well assume it. You fucking pig cunt bastard!'

'Ella, please. It didn't mean anything.'

'Thanks a lot,' says the wardrobe.

'She was nothing. It was ... nothing. It's just, when I'm away from you ... on long flights ...'

'How *long?*'

'It was just like porn ...' he says, sounding less like Mr Perfect every second. Or masturbation, but with a real woman. That's all. I was thinking about you, I promise.'

'Two years,' says the wardrobe.

'Two years? Two *years?* You've been fucking her for two years?'

'Ella, listen, she's just some tart from the airline.'

'That was before you met *me.*'

'It was nothing. She's engaged too. To someone else. It was just sex, that's all. Just sex.'

'You small-dicked son of a bitch,' says the wardrobe. 'I faked all my orgasms!'

'Ella, come on,' he says, with pleading eyes. We're perfect together. We're scientifically matched. You know that. We've both been stupid. *Equally* stupid. Now I'm willing to not talk about whatever you've done with your ring and forget about you walking off at the wedding if you can just forgive this stupid mistake.' He points to the wardrobe.

This stupid mistake.

It is in that second that I realise he is right. We *have* both been stupid. But my stupid mistake wasn't pawning the ring or walking away before I said my vows.

The mistake was believing that love and romance are the same thing. The realisation is like a punch in the stomach: I don't love James. And I didn't even love him before I found a naked anorexic in my wardrobe. I always thought that I must have loved him because he ticked all the right boxes.

He is gorgeous. Tick.

He is rich. Tick.

He says the right things. Tick.

Shared interests. Tick.

Well travelled. Tick.

Good sex. Tick – although the skeleton in the wardrobe begs to differ.

Full of surprises. Double tick with cherries on top.

If I loved James, if I really loved him, I would have stayed by his side and married him.

'Come on Ella,' he says. 'I love you.'

'No,' I correct him. 'No, you don't. If you love someone you don't need to do this, behind their back.'

'We're great together ... come on, Ella ... if I didn't love you I wouldn't have flown you and your Mum and Dad to Las Vegas would I? Would I? I wouldn't have flown you to Rome and taken you to the most expensive hotel in the world would I? Would I? I wouldn't have paid for your piano lessons. I wouldn't have done all these things if I didn't care about you. Would I? Would I? Would I?'

The piano lessons.

They meant more than everything else.

And for a second, the memory of the gift jars me, knocks me off course. But then I look at the wardrobe and I am back on track.

It wasn't real. Everything about what we had

looked perfect, but it wasn't. It was as fake as this whole city.

I look at his jaw. The purple bruise starting to appear. I am tempted to plant a punch on the other side, just for the sake of symmetry. But I don't. I don't want to touch him. And I certainly don't want him to touch me.

That's why, when he reaches for me, when he grabs my shoulder, my whole body jerks away from him.

'Get. Off. Me.'

I push his arm away and that's it. That's when his face switches to that of a monster. I feel like Dr Frankenstein, scared of the thing I had once wanted so much. I storm out of the room and start walking down the corridor.

'Ella! Ella! Ella!' he roars, after me, but then he stops. 'Ell –'

He quickly shuts the door and leaves me out in the corridor.

I wonder why and then I see the reason walking towards me.

It's Mum and Dad.

A very public drama

I turn, thinking they might not have realised.

But I'm wrong.

'Ella?'

'Ella?'

I freeze. A rabbit caught in the headlights.

'Ella Holt, what on earth are you doing?' asks my Mum.

On earth I am trying to make myself invisible so my parents can't pour a whole ocean's worth of salt into an already gaping wound.

'Ella?' It's my Dad's voice now. Less brittle than Mum's. Softer, genuinely confused.

I turn around. I am shaking. Visibly shaking.

Mum is walking fast towards me down the corridor, past all the closed doors and the secret dramas they contain.

Dad is behind her, less eager to reach the very public drama that awaits him.

'Where are your shoes?' Mum asks me.

'What?' I am dazed, still seeing James's monstrous face in my mind.

'Your shoes Ella. You are standing out here in the

303

corridor with no shoes on. Anyone could see you.'

I look down at my shoeless feet.

'They're ... they're in the room.'

'Why aren't they on your feet?'

'I had a row with James. I walked out.'

'We heard!' she says. 'What on earth has got into you? Why did you do it Ella? Why didn't you finish the wedding? Why did you do that stupid thing? Why? Why did you do it? Why? It makes no sense. Why? Why?'

Oh God. She's crying. She's bloody crying.

Dad's hand rests over her shoulder, and he looks like he's at a funeral. His eyes are telling me, as clearly as only my Dad's eyes can, 'I am so disappointed with you.'

And still my Mum's watery whys keep coming.

'Why? Ella? Why? He's so perfect for you ... Why? I don't understand it. We were so happy for you ... so happy ... after all the mistakes you've made in the past we finally thought you were going to settle down ... your Dad was so happy ... so proud ... Ella ... have we done something wrong Ella ... is that why you did it, to punish us?'

I look at her in disbelief. 'No, Mum. Of course it's not.'

A happy, possibly honeymooning couple with golden tans and golden smiles walk past, trying to ignore the shoeless woman in a wedding dress and her mother's nervous breakdown.

Dad stares at the couple and then stares back at me. His mind is an open book. The book is called, 'Why Can't My Daughter Do The Right Thing?'

'Then why, Ella?' cries my Mum. 'Why?'

I am tempted to tell her.

I am tempted to reveal all the skeletons – or skeleton – in James's closet. But that is not the truth. I didn't walk out of the wedding because of some air hostess. I didn't even *know* about the air hostess.

So I tell her the fact of the matter.

'We weren't in love.'

'What?'

'Me and James didn't love each other. We thought we did, but we didn't. It was a mirage. There was nothing there.'

She is not listening to me. She is looking at my hand. 'Where's your ring?'

'Mum, I don't love James. That's why we're not getting married. And there's no point wearing a ring if I'm not getting married.'

I conveniently forgot to tell them about the pawnshop, or the Golden Nugget, or Rob's bail.

'Love?' Mum says. 'Love?'

It's like I'm speaking a different language.

Mum is no longer crying.

She has gone beyond tears now into a level of total bewilderment.

I look at Dad for support, but he is a wall of silence.

'Oh get in the real world, Ella, for once in your life,' my Mum says. 'You've got your head full of all those romantic books you read. All those silly pop songs clogging up your brain. That's the trouble with everyone nowadays. That's why you get all these divorces and single mothers. People go round with their head full of romance and get themselves into all sorts of trouble. Love doesn't happen by magic. You have to work at it.'

I don't believe what I'm hearing.

'So you think I should have married him even though I don't love him?' I ask.

Dad tuts.

His one contribution to the debate is a tut.

Typical.

Then Mum says: 'I think you should think very hard about your options. Men like that don't grow on trees. He can give you security Ella. *Security*. Don't you know how important that is?'

I look at Dad's hand on Mum's shoulder.

'What about you two?' I say. 'You wouldn't have married Dad if you didn't feel one hundred per cent.'

'Ella, nothing's one hundred per cent. And anyway, we're not talking about us. We're talking about you.'

Her words prod my anger button. 'We're *always* talking about me!' I yell, forgetting where I am for a second. 'About how hopeless I am, about how I never manage to do anything right, about how my head is always full of the wrong ideas, about what a total failure I am ... well, I'm sorry. I'm *sorry*. I'm sorry I'm such a disappointment for you. I'm sorry I'm not married and I haven't got kids for you to play with. I'm sorry I want to be with someone who makes *me* happy and not just you.' And then I really lose it. 'I'm sorry I wasn't a boy. I'm sorry I was the only big disappointment you could have. Because that's what it's about, isn't it? That's what it's about. I've never been good enough have I? Just because I wasn't born with a willy between my legs. Just because I was your last chance. Well, it's a lot to live up to, you know. It's a lot of pressure being the only child. It's a lot of pressure with you two breathing down my neck all the time. And it's never been good enough has it? Never! I get eight As and a B in my exams and what do you concentrate on? The B. Always the B! I move to London and you act like I've gone to the bloody moon! I rent a flat with my friends and you act like I've set up my own hippy commune! I mean, what do you want? Do you want a remote control for me? Is that what you want? You press the Marry button and I marry. Press the Mortgage button and I buy a house. Press the Kids button and I have kids. Well, I'm sorry. I don't come with batteries. I don't do exactly what you say exactly when you say it. If that makes me evil then I'm evil. Throw me in a dungeon with all the other silly women who believe in love and who want to be happy in life. I mean, is that such a crime? To want to be happy? Is it? Is it? Is it?'

I half expect my head to start spinning around. But it doesn't.

All that happens is that my mum and dad look at me for a very long time as if they are debating whether or not to call an exorcist for their clearly possessed demonic daughter.

I look at the doors to all the rooms along the corridor and wonder how many eyes are currently at the peep-holes, watching the show. One more over-the-top display in a city of over-the-top displays.

I tell you, there's something about Las Vegas.

It makes you act different. More intense. Like an exaggerated version of yourself. It shines a glaring spotlight on who you really are, and you have to face the uncomfortable truth.

I think my mum is about to faint again.

Her mouth is open, but no words arrive.

'Mum,' I say, softer now. 'Mum, I'm sorry. I

didn't mean to say all that. I'm sorry. It's just, you know, it's been a weird and horrible day and I'm all over the place. I'm sorry. I didn't mean to shout at you.'

My Dad offers a second tut.

A disappointed tut.

A tut that contains a lifetime of mistakes and self-pity.

He shakes his head at me. And then he speaks. He *speaks*!

'I suppose you're going to run off with that loser then. That fat psychopath.'

'I'm not running off with anyone,' I tell him.

'Oh,' says my mum, deciding not to faint. 'You're going to wait for the right man! She's thirty and she thinks she's got all the time in the world! Never mind getting old! Never mind the biological clock! You'll end up on your own if you carry on like that. And we won't be here for ever. So who's going to look after you? Tell us that. Who's going to be here for you? That stupid Maddie girl or whatever she's called? She barely seems capable of looking after herself.'

'Mum, she's my *friend*. Don't talk about her like that.'

'Oh grow up, Ella Holt, for God's sake girl,' my Mum says, through a scowl.

'Grow up? If you want me to grow up why do you always talk to me as if I'm thirteen? Why do you buy me a doll for my birthday?'

Uh-oh.

Shouldn't have said that.

Her face crumples and she starts to cry again. She must have an entire sea inside her.

'Mum, I'm sorry ...'

Dad says to me, 'We can't carry on out here. We're making a right show of ourselves. Let's go back to your room.'

'But –'

It's weird.

Although I hate them going on about how perfect James is, I still want to shield them from the truth.

Somewhere, deep inside me, I still want them to think he's great.

I don't want them to get hurt by the truth, even if it will make everything easier to understand.

'But –'

They are walking past me, down the corridor towards the room.

'Mum ... Dad ... wait ...

I follow them.

'Why don't we go downstairs?' I ask them, remembering what James said to me. 'Why don't we go to one of the bars and have a drink?'

'You've got no shoes on,' my dad reminds me.

'Come on,' Mum says, when we reach the door. 'We're here now. Where's your card? For the door?'

'Oh ... er ... er ... er ... I haven't got it. I forgot to take it. I've locked myself out.'

'Well, James is in.'

She is about to knock.

'No, Mum, please. Don't.'

She looks at me. Eyes so sharp they hurt.

She doesn't knock.

She doesn't have to.

Because at that moment, at that exact moment, the door opens wide in front of her.

Cool Hand Luke

The skeleton is standing there in the doorway. She's dressed this time. Well, if a boob tube and a skirt the width of a rubber band can qualify as 'dressed'.

'Who on earth are you?' Mum asks her.

The skeleton giggles.

My Dad quickly puts two and two together and makes seventeen. 'It's a call-girl, Kathleen.'

The skeleton stops giggling and starts to look affronted. 'In your dreams granddad,' she says and storms off.

I tug my Dad's sleeve. 'She's an air hostess. She was ... seeing him.'

James is there, he looks up, sees me. Sees my Mum and Dad.

'Ella,' he says. 'You've come back. You've seen sense.'

He smiles at my Mum and Dad as if nothing has happened.

'I knew they'd talk you round,' he says winking at my mum.

My Mum stares up at him, as angry as I have ever seen her. The guarded expression she normally has on display for anyone who is not a blood relative stops.

'You smarmy little sod,' she says, before delivering a slap on his jaw. She goes for the same side Rob went for earlier.

Thwack!

James stands there, holding his jaw. Stunned.

'Mrs Holt ... don't know what Ella told you ...'

'She didn't tell me anything. I can see for myself the stamp of you. Now, come on Ella ... let's go.'

And we are about to leave, when my dad leans in towards James. Conjuring up all his favourite Clint Eastwood and Paul Newman movies in a single breath he says, 'We're not going anywhere. He is.'

James is amazed, and looks desperately into my father's eyes for some sign of the soft-touch who formerly possessed his body.

'Mr Holt ... I'm sorry ... but this is my room ... I paid for it ...'

I tug my Dad's sleeve. 'Dad, it's OK. Come on, please. Let's just leave it.'

Dad ignores me. Keeps his eyes locked on James.

'My daughter has all her clothes in the room. She has no shoes on her feet.'

'I'll get her shoes ...'

'You'll do more than that,' says Dad. 'You'll pack your bags and you'll leave.'

'Mr Holt, I'm sorry, but I paid for the room.'

'With your wages?'

'Yes. With my wages. And?'

'The wages you get from the airline?'

James has no idea where my dad is going with this. He just nods and says, 'Uh-huh?'

'The same airline that I'd imagine takes a very strong view on inter-staff relationships?'

Now James gets it.

'Yes,' he says, reluctantly.

'And the same airline that doesn't like its pilots fiddling for free tickets?'

James says nothing at first but his eyes speak volumes. 'You wouldn't,' he manages eventually.

'Oh,' my Dad says, a resolute smile widening his lips. 'This may be Las Vegas lad, but I wouldn't bet on it.'

James closes his eyes. Nods.

'Give me five minutes,' he says, through gritted teeth. 'I'll pack my stuff and go. Just give me five minutes.'

'Five minutes,' Dad says. 'And we'll take the card. For the door. And Ella's shoes.'

James hands over the card and then my shoes. No Prince Charming and no glass slipper. He looks at me one last time before closing the door.

Dad whistles the theme tune to *The Good, The Bad and the Ugly* in quiet triumph.

I want to cry.

I want to cry more than I've ever wanted to cry in my life.

But I have already given myself enough humiliation to last a whole year so I keep the tears under lock and key, as I put on my shoes.

'Let's go downstairs and wait in the foyer or one of the cafés,' suggests my Mum. 'There's no point in waiting here.'

My Dad touches her shoulder, 'Your mother's right. Come on, Ella love. Let's buy you a drink.'

312

My Mum squeezes my hand as we walk down the corridor towards the lifts.

'It will turn out all right love,' she says. 'It'll all turn out all right.'

The runaway bride

My Dad walks over from the bar, precariously carrying three drinks over to our table.

'Right, there we go. Glasses of white wine for the girls. Beer for me.'

I sip my wine.

My Mum is still holding my hand, rubbing her thumb over the skin as if trying to massage away the pain.

'I'm sorry love,' she says. 'We're both sorry.'

In thirty years I honestly don't think I've heard my mother apologise. Not to me, at any rate.

I don't think it's because she always believes she's right. I think her aversion to the s word is more to do with control. She has spent her entire life trying to steer me through life's giant obstacle course, telling me which path to choose and which short-cuts are best avoided. To admit to being wrong would be to admit a fault in her navigation system. And I suppose she thought that if I knew she was wrong about something, I wouldn't listen to her advice any more.

Of course, the opposite is true.

Now she is here, stroking my hand, apologising for

her wrong opinion of James – and me – I want to listen to her more than ever.

'Don't worry Ella,' my Dad says after sipping his beer. 'You'll be back on your feet in no time. Won't she, Mum?'

'Of course she will.'

My Mum and Dad smile at each other. Their smiles, despite my Mum's earlier objections to the word, are filled with love.

'You're just . . . a lot to live up to,' I tell them. 'You're so right for each other. You're so strong.' The tears I locked up five minutes ago are now escaping as fast as runaway prisoners.

My Mum's thumb goes into overdrive. 'Now, come on love. Don't cry. Don't cry. Here, I've got a tissue. There you go. There you are.'

For about the next two minutes I am lost in the crumpled Kleenex my Mum has just handed me.

Then I hear a voice above my Mum and Dad's words of warm sympathy.

'Look what we have here! The runaway bride!'

I look up and see a stern-faced Dr Lara Stein standing, arms folded, by our table. Behind her is a dark-suited Jessica Perk, who is smiling smugly, safe in the knowledge that she has no new contender for Lara's professional affections.

My Mum turns round. 'Could you leave us alone? My daughter is visibly upset. She's had a horrendous day and the last thing she needs is some posh cow – some jumped-up millionaire – rubbing her nose in it.'

Dr Lara Stein's jaw drops.

A snake could have come out of my Mum's mouth and bitten Lara Stein on her silk-covered arse and I doubt she would look more surprised.

315

The woman who spends her time surrounded by Yes men and Yes women like Jessica Perk doesn't know what to do when faced with the biggest No person she has ever come across.

'Oh,' she says, finding some sort of composure. *'She* has had a horrendous day. Oh, poor little Helen –'

'Ella,' my mum corrects.

'What?'

'Ella. My daughter's name is Ella, not Helen.'

Dr Lara flaps her jewellery-heavy hand. 'Whatever she's called I'm sure she's the one who has had to deal with her three biggest shareholders pull out. I'm sure she's the one who has just had to watch her business evaporate before her eyes because the show wedding became the no-show wedding.'

She turns directly to me as Jessica Perk's smile climbs up the smug-scale.

'Mr Perfect not good enough for you is he?' Dr Lara says, with the kind of condescension that comes naturally to a privately-educated Oxbridge graduate with a billion pounds in the bank. 'Your perfect match wasn't up to scratch? A decade of scientific research got it wrong, did it? The schoolteacher can do better than an airline pilot can she? Can she?'

My Dad turns around in his chair. 'Now, listen here. You can stop talking to my daughter like that. It wasn't Ella's fault that you matched her up with a two-timing sleazebag. Mr Perfect! You're having a laugh!'

'What are you talking about?' Dr Lara looks even more gob-smacked than before.

'I'm sorry I let you down . . .' I tell Dr Lara, as I dry my eyes.

'You don't have to be sorry about anything,' says Mum.

316

'... it's just, I don't think love is something you can work out on computers or in science labs.'

Dr Lara turns an angry shade of tomato.

'You ungrateful little –' She storms off. Leaving her sentence unfinished. Jessica Perk lingers a second longer, making sure we all see her entry for the Smuggest Smile of the Year Competition. Then she too walks out of the bar, exhibiting about as much independence of mind as Long John Silver's parrot.

'I guess there goes my career at the Perfect Agency,' I say.

'You're better off without them,' my Dad says.

'All that glitters isn't gold,' adds my Mum.

'No,' I say, realising the full truth of those words. 'I suppose it isn't.'

The balcony scene – part two

Back in the room.

The same room I arrived in forty-eight hours ago, giving James the benefit of the doubt when he was late back from the airport.

Back facing the bed. The wardrobe. The lies, still fresh in the air.

'I might lie down for a bit,' I tell my Mum and Dad, once I've got out of my wedding dress and into my jeans and T-shirts. 'I'm tired out.'

My Mum nods. 'All right love. We'll leave you. For a bit. We'll pop back in half an hour.'

They go. I lie down, but my mind is still running a marathon.

Thoughts of James fast-forward through my brain. No, not thoughts. Feelings.

All those feelings that I've built up since I met him. All that emotion that I poured into him. All those plans. Where can they go now?

I feel like I've failed. Like all that energy has been a total waste of time. I am thirty years old and what do I have to show for it? What, exactly, was the point of my twenties? I gained nothing apart from

318

two dress sizes and premature crow's feet.

All those lies he told me. All those mysterious phonecalls he never answered. They will have been from her, the skeleton.

I close my eyes, but it's no good. I can't sleep. I go over and open the window onto the balcony to let some air in, then collapse back on the bed.

I think of Rob.

Oh God, Rob!

I left him at the police station. I should try and find him, but he could be anywhere now.

I remember the day he turned up at my door with a black eye.

He was trying to tell me then what he told me in the police station. That he had seen James with someone else. That James was having an affair behind my back. And would I have believed him then any more than I believed him two hours ago? Probably not. I'd have probably given him another black eye to match the one James gave him.

And then I hear something.

My name.

'Ella!'

It's Rob's voice.

'Ella!'

I shoot off the bed.

'Ella!'

I head for the window and go out on the balcony.

'Ella!'

I look but I can't see him.

'Ella!'

There are people everywhere. Couples walking around the flower beds, holding hands.

'Ella!'

And then I see him, waving his arms.

'Rob!'

'Ella!'

'What are you doing?' I ask him.

He says something but his words don't make it up to the window.

'What?'

'I'M SORRY ABOUT WHAT I SAID.'

'It's OK,' I call back, realising half the hotel is looking up at me. 'You were right.'

Rob shouts something else, but again I don't hear. And, much as I want this Romeo and Juliet scene to go on for ever, if the Bellagio security Schwarzeneggers catch Rob screaming at the top of his lungs they'll probably get him locked up again.

'Rob. Wait there! I'll come down!'

So I put on my shoes and head through the giant maze of the hotel until I am outside in the gardens.

'Hi,' I say, breathless.

'Hi.'

'I'm sorry about leaving you at the police station.'

'Don't worry,' he says, with a deadpan expression. 'It was a nice walk. I could do with the exercise.'

I see one of the security men who kicked Rob out before, patrolling the flower gardens.

'We'd better go and talk somewhere else. Out of the hotel.'

So we sneak through the foyer, but we see one of the Schwarzeneggers behind us, in one of the giant mirrors.

We start quick-walking and hope he doesn't notice Rob. Oh no. He just has.

He's talking into his radio and running this way.

'Run!' I say to Rob.

We both sprint out of the hotel, down the steps, past the fountains and the lake and jump onto the monorail that stops outside the hotel. It starts moving just in time.

On the monorail

'Phew,' I say, as we sit down on one of the seats. 'That was close. And you're not even out of breath.'

'I've been trying to get fit. Going to the gym and stuff. Working out.'

'Wow, you really have changed! Flying on a plane. Working out.'

We pause, look out of the window as we pass giant billboards for Siegfried and Roy and Elton John.

The invisible wall that was there between us when I went round to his flat has been razed to the ground.

'I caught him, you know,' I tell him. 'With her. The woman. Two hours after the wedding and he was with someone else.'

'I'm sorry,' he says, and his face tells me he genuinely means it.

'Better to find out now than five years down the line.'

He nods. 'Some people just don't know what they've got. Not till it's too late.'

Something about the way he says this makes me realise that we are no longer just talking about James. I wonder if he's thinking about his dad.

'I can't believe you got on a plane,' I say, trying to lift his mood.

'Well, it wasn't easy. As soon as they shut those doors I thought I was going to die. I spent about six hours in the bathroom trying to control my breathing. Before they started the take off I thought I was going to have to run up and beg the air hostess to let me out of the plane.'

'So what stopped you?'

He looks at me as if it is the most stupid question in the world.

'You,' he says. 'You stopped me. I started to realise, since you left, and since . . . my dad died, that the easy option isn't always worth taking. That's why I quit my job.'

'You quit your job? Why?' I remember all the business books he took out at the library.

'I hated it. I didn't want to be a recruitment consultant all my life.'

'I know you hated it,' I say. 'You always hated it. But I never thought you'd actually leave. I mean, you *talked* about leaving, but there's talking and there's doing . . . wow, I can't believe it. So, what are you doing now? I mean, work-wise?

'What I always wanted to do but could never be bothered. Photography. I've set up my own business. Got the right camera. I hire a small studio in Clerkenwell with it's own dark room and everything.'

Clerkenwell. So that's why he saw James there, with the skeleton. 'How did you afford all that?'

'Got a business loan from the bank. Put a business plan together. And I saved up, stopped going to the pub every night. Sold stuff on eBay. The PlayStation. All the games.'

For a second I think I am hearing things.

Did he just say he stopped going to the pub every night?

Did he just say he sold his PlayStation?

It makes no sense.

I always thought the pub and the PlayStation were inscribed in his DNA.

'You were right,' he goes on. 'I was wasting my life.'

'No . . . I never said *that* . . . did I ever say that?'

'It doesn't matter,' Rob says, turning to look at the artificial pyramids of the Luxor hotel in the distance. 'It was true. I was wasting my life. When I lost you and then my dad I realised I had to sort myself out. And I also realised it wasn't so hard. Don't get me wrong, it's tough setting up a business. But it's going well. I mean, it's mainly cheesy stuff. Family portraits, weddings . . . but it sure beats recruitment.'

I look at him and smile. I feel proud of him, I really do. 'But what about right now? Aren't you losing business being over here?'

'Yes,' he says, as we pass a giant sign saying MIRAGE. I've lost a bit of business. I've tried to rearrange appointments as much as possible. But I went round to see you, the other day, to try and talk to you again. To try and tell you everything. But I saw Maddie instead, and she told me about Las Vegas. About the wedding. And then I knew I had to do more than just tell you – I had to show you. I had to prove to you I'm a different person. And okay, I might have lost a few clients, but there's more to life than money, isn't there?'

I remember James's bafflement when I said 'I'll

think about it' to Dr Lara's job offer.

'Yes, there is,' I say. 'A lot more.'

He puts his hand on mine. I pull away.

'Sorry,' he says.

'It's all right,' I tell him. 'It's all right. It's just ... I'm in kind of a weird place right now.'

'I see what you mean,' Rob says, as we pass a crowd of tourists applauding a fake volcano, mideruption.

'I mean after James. My head doesn't know where it's at.'

The words slap him in the face. I guess he thought he could show up in Las Vegas and show how much he's changed then win me over.

He does his best to disguise his hurt and says, 'It's OK. I'm not expecting you to come back to me or anything. I just ... wanted ...' Words fail him. He gives up, as the monorail reaches its next stop.

'We could get off,' he says.

'We could. Or we could just stay on. It goes round in a loop.'

'We could stay here all day. Seeing the same things over and over again.'

'We'll spot something new each time,' I say, realising I could be talking about more than just the monorail. 'Sometimes you see something that you missed the first time round.'

LOVER

We stay on the monorail and talk, as the same Las Vegas sights slide by.

Then Rob asks me a question that knocks me side-ways.

'How are the lessons going?'

'The lessons?'

'Yeah.'

'What, at school?'

'No. The piano lessons.'

I stare at him for a second and wonder how he knows about them. Maddie must have told him. It certainly can't have been James. It seems strange that he's bringing up the subject at all, really. I mean, that was probably the most thoughtful thing James ever did for me.

'Oh,' I say. 'They're going great. I've only had one. But it went well.'

'Good, I'm glad you liked it.'

'Er . . . why?'

He looks at me like I've asked another weird ques-tion. 'Because I didn't know which teacher or music college to go for. So I went to the Yellow Pages and went through them all until I found Mrs Jeffries. She seemed really sweet ... a bit eccentric ... but I thought that would be down your street.'

'How do you know that Mrs Jeffries is my piano teacher?'

He's still looking at me weird, like a doctor searching for symptoms. 'Because she's the one I chose.'

'What do you mean *you* chose? You're not making any sense.'

He laughs. '*I'm* not making any sense?'

'I don't understand.'

'Mrs Jeffries, from the music college,' he says. 'She's the one I chose. I phoned her up, then bought you the lessons. I always knew that was your biggest regret in life, so I thought you'd –'

'You? It was James.'

'James? What are you talking about?'

I try and remember the card inside the envelope. I picture it in my head.

There was the printed out sheet from the music college and then there was the capital letters at the bottom, LOVER.

'You never called me your lover. I thought it must be James.'

'Lover? What do you mean?'

So I explain. 'On the card. It said LOVER and a kiss. That was hardly your style.'

He closes his eyes, and a penny drops. He smiles an ironic smile. 'I didn't write LOVER I wrote LOVE R. As in Love Rob. You know, Love from Rob.'

LOVER.

LOVE R.

Oh my God.

I don't know what to say.

My mouth is in goldfish mode, opening and closing with nothing coming out.

I remember the sex I had with James after that. I-can't-believe-you-were-so-thoughtful-sex. I can't believe you were such a lying bastard, more like.

'Mr Perfect strikes again,' I mumble.

'What?'

'Rob, I'm sorry. I was stupid. I thought they were from James. I'm such an idiot. If I'd have known they were from you I would have thanked you. I'm sorry.'

Rob smiles. 'Don't worry. Hey, after last year I was the last person on earth you expected to remember your birthday. Anyway, I'm just glad you liked the present.'

'I did, I did, it was the best gift ever.'

I hug him.

It's an awkward hug, not least because of the claustrophobic dynamics of the seat we're on. But as I hold him close I realise I don't want to let him go.

I close my eyes, feel his heart, feel the rise and fall of his chest. His rough, sandpaper cheek prickling mine. It feels familiar and different all at once, and it's a nice feeling.

No.

I can't.

I can't be falling for Rob.

It must just be a rebound thing.

Yes, that's all it is. A rebound thing.

It used to be nice when things were definite.

When Mr Perfect was Mr Perfect.

When Rob the Slob was Rob the Slob.

But as I close my eyes and keep him close, I realise nothing is definite. Finding Mr Perfect isn't about filling in questionnaires or undergoing scientific tests.

It isn't always about looking for someone new, someone better, someone just over the horizon, someone who fills every single criteria. Or who ticks every box.

Sometimes, Mr Perfect is a hell of a lot closer than you think. It's just sometimes he's in a very good disguise.

The happy beginning

Two months later ...

It's a perfect English country wedding.

Everyone is there, in the church.

All the family, all the friends.

The organ starts. The wedding march begins. The whole church turns around to face the bride.

And she looks beautiful, she really does, as she enjoys the last few precious moments of being Miss Maddie Hatfield.

She turns and sees me, beams like a lighthouse. I can't believe it. Only a few months ago, the idea of Maddie forming a monogamous relationship with any man seemed ridiculous. Let alone a giant systems analyst who can happily talk for seven hours about the inside of a microchip. But there's no denying it, he's her right guy.

I follow behind, with Pip next to me.

For the last six weeks Pip's been mine and Maddie's own personal trainer, kickboxing us all into wedding day shape. Between us, we lost a stone and a half, and a couple of plant pots, but that's a small sacrifice when you've got a hundred people staring at your rear view for three quarters of an hour.

In fact, it turns out to be even longer than that. The

vicar is one of those who likes the sound of his own voice and so he goes on about the significance of marriage as the bedrock of a healthy society for about twenty minutes.

Maddie nearly cracks up during the vows.

'I, Madeleine Lucy Hatfield do take Steven ... giggle ... Roberts to be my lawful wedded husband.'

Pip looks at me and winks, both of us sharing in Maddie's day.

By the time Steve squats down to kiss the bride my legs feel like they are going to buckle from the 7000 sidekicks Pip made us do yesterday, but somehow I manage to hold out.

After the service, we go outside for the photos. The photographer came on my recommendation, so I can't blame anyone but myself that he wants so many shots with the bridesmaids in.

'OK, that's it ... in a bit closer ... that's lovely ... right ... now, one with both sets of parents,' says Rob, like a true professional.

This is his seventh wedding in the last two months, and so he's having to get used to working six-day weeks. Not that he seems to mind – I've never seen him so focused. It's kind of sexy, actually.

'You needed to lose me to find you,' I told him the other day to cool him off.

You see, I gave him two months. I said to him, in Las Vegas, 'Let's try being friends first. Before anything else.'

'Two months?'

'Yes,' I told him. 'Two months.'

He comes over to me at the reception, between snapping.

'There you are,' he says. 'I've found you. They're not cutting the cake for another few minutes.'

'Hi handsome,' I say, and I mean it. Now he's lost those pizza pounds on the treadmill he looks great in a shirt.

'How are the piano lessons going?'

'Good,' I say. 'I'm going to do my Grade Three next week.'

He whistles. 'Grade Three.'

Then he pauses, building up courage. 'You know ... I was thinking ...' He couldn't look any more sheepish if you covered him with wool. 'You know, about what you said ... you know, about being friends for a couple of months ... seeing how it goes ... and I know that was two months ago and I just wanted to say ... I don't want it to be, you know, awkward between us ... I mean, I'd rather have you as a friend than not have you at all ... because I've enjoyed it ... being friends ... so if you want it to stay like this then that's great ... really, really great ... that's fine ... I just ... you know ... wanted to let you know that friends is good ... if that's what ...'

I stand there, and watch him drown in his half-sentences. I should help him, really. I mean, it's a pretty cruel spectator sport. Oh, what the hell, this is fun.

'You see ... I won't mind ... because it's been nice ... I don't want you to feel ... obliged ... I just want you to be happy ... I won't ... maybe we shouldn't gamble ... I won't hold it against you ...'

'Just kiss me,' I tell him.

'What?'

'Just kiss me ... before I change my mind.'

332

He looks confused. 'What . . . a . . . *friendly* kiss on the cheek?'

I point to my lips. 'I was thinking right about here.'

'Oh,' he says. 'Right.'

I close my eyes and feel something hard press against my stomach.

'Rob?'

'Yes?'

'Your camera. The lens. It's . . . er, sticking into me.'

'Sorry,' he says, and swings the camera around on his back. 'I'll try again.'

He leans in, his lips touch mine. Then a voice. One of Maddie's mad uncles talking to Rob. 'They're cutting the cake.'

I giggle as we break the kiss.

Rob goes over and starts snapping away while Maddie and Steve hold the knife and grin like maniacs. I watch him, preserving memories of other people's happiness, and think about what he said.

Maybe we shouldn't gamble . . .

He was right. It will be a gamble. But if you don't take a chance, you're never going to win big are you?

The cake is cut.

The photos are taken.

Rob returns to my side.

'Right,' I say, as I tug him close. 'Where were we?'

We kiss and I hold his warm body as I hear Maddie cheer somewhere behind me. It feels great, being so close to him; like coming home.

'That felt perfect,' he tells me, when the kiss ends.

'No,' I say. 'It felt better than that. It felt . . . perfectly imperfect.'

333

He looks confused. 'Perfectly imperfect? That doesn't make sense.'

'Trust me,' I say. 'It does.'

'OK,' he says, a soft smile spreading across his face. 'I trust you.'

He hugs me as I close my eyes, and in the darkness I pray for a lifetime of this perfect imperfection.

Turn the page to read more from
the painfully funny and
deliciously sexy Andrea Semple . . .

THE EX-FACTOR
Meet Martha Seymore: relationship doctor

She's the girl who gets paid to sympathise with the cheated and jilted, the under-sexed and over-attached at *Gloss* magazine, but when she finds out about her boyfriend's one-night-stand, she starts to doubt whether she really has any of the answers.

Not only does she have to admit a failed relationship to her colleagues, but also to her old frenemy, Desdemona, blond, perfectly evil and newly engaged to Martha's very first boyfriend. Realising she's just as clueless as her hapless readers and tired of always doing the right thing, Martha decides it's time to ignore her own advice. She's going to go for what – and who – she wants, even if it's wrong . . .

THE MAKE-UP GIRL
Hi. My name's Faith and I'm living the London dream!

I work in a fabulous PR company, have loads of thin, glamorous friends but most of all, I have a perfect, handsome boyfriend. He never wants to watch the football and he always thinks I am the most beautiful girl in the world.

The only problem is that he doesn't exist.

I made him up, just like I made up my perfect life and my perfect job. It's what I do. I'm a single, lonely, low-paid, make-up girl and it's far too late to tell my family the depressing truth. Except that my sister's just got engaged, which means I've finally run out of reasons why my family can't meet my man . . .

I have less than two months to turn my perfect fictional boyfriend into reality.

Wish me luck?